OTHER
PEOPLE'S
MONEY

OTHER PEOPLE'S MONEY

JUSTIN CARTWRIGHT

BLOOMSBURY

LONDON · BERLIN · NEW YORK · SYDNEY

First published in Great Britain 2011

Copyright © by Justin Cartwright 2011

The moral right of the author has been asserted

Extracts from *At Swim-Two-Birds* © Flann O'Brien, 1968,
reproduced by permission of A. M. Heath & Co. Ltd

Bloomsbury Publishing Plc
36 Soho Square
London W1D 3QY

www.bloomsbury.com

Bloomsbury Publishing, London, Berlin, New York and Sydney
A CIP catalogue record for this book is available from the British Library

ISBN 978 1 4088 0388 2 (hardback)
ISBN 978 1 4088 1413 0 (trade paperback)

10 9 8 7 6 5 4 3 2

Typeset by Hewer Text UK Ltd, Edinburgh
Printed in Great Britain by Clays Limited, St Ives plc

For Nigel and Maria,
dear friends

When the capital development of a country becomes a by-product of the activities of a casino, the job is likely to be ill done.
— John Maynard Keynes, *General Theory of Employment, Interest and Money*, 1936

Matisse's studio was a world within the world: a place of equilibrium that, for sixty continuous years, produced images of comfort, refuge, and balanced satisfaction. Nowhere in Matisse's work does one feel a trace of the alienation and conflict which modernism, the mirror of our century, has so often reflected. His paintings are the equivalent to that ideal place, sealed away from the assaults and erosions of history, that Baudelaire imagined in his poem 'L'Invitation au Voyage':

Furniture gleaming with the sheen of years
would grace our bedroom;
the rarest flowers, mingling their aromas with faint gusts of amber,
the painted ceilings, the fathomless mirrors, Eastern splendour.
... all would speak, in secret, to our souls, in its native language ...

There, everything is order and beauty, luxury, calm and pleasure ...*

Robert Hughes, *The Shock of the New*

---

* Translation author's own.

Service of Thanksgiving for the Life of
Sir Harry Trevelyan-Tubal, cbe, bt.
at St Paul's Cathedral, in the City of London

The Queen and the Duke of Edinburgh were represented by Sir Thomas Carew Knollys, the Prince of Wales was represented by Colonel Lord Maltravers of Deeside, and the Duke of Kent was represented by the Hon. Jonathan Bowes-Griffon at a service of thanksgiving for the life of Sir Harry Trevelyan-Tubal, CBE, Bt.

The Bishop of London, the Right Reverend Crispin Smythe, read the prayers, assisted by the Reverend Kevin Pegley, Vicar of All Hallows in the City of London. The Ambassador of the United States of America, the Hon. Mr S. Fielding Klipspringer, the Ambassador of France, Comte Henri de Mossigny-Mumm, the Lord Mayor of London, Alderman Sir Tristram Tarkington, the Lord Lieutenant of Middlesex, Lieutenant General (Rtd.) Sir Augustus (Bobby) Popham, MC also attended.

Among others, members of the family present were Lady Trevelyan-Tubal (widow), Sir Simon Trevelyan-Tubal (son), Mr Julian Trevelyan-Tubal (son) and Mrs Kimberly Trevelyan-Tubal (daughter-in-law), Lord Andrew Finch-Tubal (cousin), Mr Thierry Lane (cousin), Miss Daisy Trevelyan-Tubal (great-niece), Master Sam and Miss Alice Trevelyan-Tubal (grandchildren), Mrs Simon Cassirer (stepdaughter), Frieda, Grafin von Westerhagen (sister) and Freiherr Fritz-Dietlof, Graf von Westerhagen, the Hon. Charlotte Stammers (niece), Miss Poppy Trevelyan-Tubal (niece), Monsieur Jean-Pierre Loup, with other members of the family.

The Duke and Duchess of Albemarle, the Duke of Chelsea, the Earl and Countess of Mayo, the Earl and Countess of Wendover, the

Macallan of that Ilk and Lady Macallan, the Malcolm, Lord of the Western Isles, Sir Frederick Blackwater (representing the Performing Arts Benevolent Fund), the Secretary of State for Business, Innovation and Skills, the Rt. Hon. Oliver Goldstone, QC, MP, Lieutenant General Sir Archibald FitzHealde, KBE (representing the Honourable Company of Pikemen and Musketeers), Mr Adrian Porch, MBE (representing the Fishmongers' Guild), Sir Dominick Westwood (representing the Royal Opera Company), Mr Ruud Kronwinkel (representing the Koopman Charitable Foundation), Ms Alice Freemantle (representing the Association of Private Bankers) attended.

Among others attending were Mr Nigel Stafford, Mr Bryce Boyd, Ms Estelle Welz, Mr Morné Nagel (on behalf of the Disabled Rugby Footballers' Trust), Mr Artair MacCleod, Ms Amanda Stapleton, Mrs Arthur Green, Professor Sir Simon Greene (on behalf of the Judaeo-Christian Foundation), Monsieur Paul-Henri Colle (representing the Community of Cap d'Antibes), Ms Shirley Simms, Mr Len Snibble (representing the staff of Tubal and Co.), Ms Tineke Pachod, Mrs Alicia Bruce-Caldesi, Monsieur Franck Dangereux, Ms Inez Duegenheim-Arndt, Ms Lulu Whitbread, Signor Giovanni Paschetto, the Dowager Lady Huntingtower, Comte Hervé de la Marinière.

The Trumpeters of the Household Cavalry performed an arrangement from Purcell's Trumpet Voluntary, accompanied by the organist Dr Claude Brown, FRCO. Sir Simon Trevelyan-Tubal (son) read extracts from his own work, Mr Julian Trevelyan-Tubal (son) delivered an address and read a poem by W.H. Auden, Miss Poppy Trevelyan-Tubal (niece) read from the work of Hugh Plunkett-Greene, the Bishop of London gave the eulogy. Sir Alfred Brendel played three pieces by Chopin and Anne Sofie von Otter (mezzo-soprano) sang a lied from her songs of Terezin. The Honourable Company of Pikemen and Musketeers mounted guard outside the Cathedral of St Paul's.

1

AT THIS TIME of year, Antibes is at its best. The almond blossom is out, the sea loses its darkness, the cold rains have mostly been swept mysteriously away, the mistral has cleared the skies and the geraniums are being planted out. There is a sense that the warm earth-life of Provence is beginning again after the longueurs of the winter.

Behind the tastefully crumbling and slowly fading wall that protects the Villa Tubal from the eyes of idle passers-by and garish tourists, the three gardeners are busy. They are Algerian, with sad, stubbled faces. Sir Harry Trevelyan-Tubal likes to sit in the garden. He particularly likes the scent of the umbrella pines and the mimosa, and the wafts of thyme, which come on the mistral off the hillside behind the house. Good health is often attributed in these parts to the mistral.

Since his stroke, three years ago, he has difficulty writing, but every morning he dictates letters to his son, who is standing in for him at the bank, giving him his instructions and his advice. He also writes to old friends and to important financial and political figures. His secretary, Estelle, types these letters and they are FedExed to their destination. Now, slightly dragging his left leg – some days it is better than others – he walks for the first time this year along the gravelled path between the low box hedges to his spot on the terrace, where his breakfast is laid out on the blue Provençal pottery he favours for informal occasions. On this terrace overlooking the cove and the boathouse beneath, Churchill once painted, watched by the young Harry. Despite the tardiness of his leg, he doesn't at a distance present a figure of pity. He is elegantly dressed in a light-brown jacket, which has threads of a gold colour woven into it, so that it looks almost vibrant in this clear light; the jacket is paired confidently with plum-coloured trousers and two-tone deck shoes. On his head, partly hiding the thick grey hair, is a panama hat, just sufficiently irregular to indicate to those who care about these things that it is a Montecristi from Lock & Co., who have supplied him with hats for sixty years and more. Nothing in his wardrobe or indeed in the whole villa is vulgar or mass-produced or discordant. In some magical fashion, which doesn't involve interior designers, the villa has reached this state of grace by increments. The Trevelyan-Tubals are not so much at home with their surroundings as the masters of their surroundings. It's as if inanimate objects, even landscape, are subject to their will and taste. And in a sense they are: the landscape, which now looks so natural, was created eighty years ago by Sir Harry's father on a rocky and scrubby peninsula.

Sir Harry's breakfast has been laid on the table and the sunshade has been perfectly positioned so that the plates are in deep shade. Because Lady Trevelyan-Tubal is at Mulgrave House in Chelsea Square – she's been in London all winter – Estelle, seventy-one, sits with him. She does not eat, but sips a *café au lait* cautiously, and keeps her notebook at the ready for his dictation. Once, many years ago, he told her that the way she drank annoyed him, and so she still sips with determined restraint. But she adores him, and has done for more than thirty years. The bank pays her salary and she has her own small house out of sight, behind the clay tennis court and its pavilion. This little house is itself built in the style of a Provençal *mas*.

Sir Harry allows her to dab his mouth when crumbs from his almond croissant stick to the foam that eating inexplicably causes to gather in the corners of his half-frozen lips. She has also become his interpreter, because not even his wife can really understand him when he speaks. Estelle doesn't fuss or hurry him.

'Did Julian reply?'

'Not yet, Sir Harry. He is still in Paris at a meeting of the trust, and won't be back until later today. Early evening, probably.'

'Well, look, Estelle, I think we should get on with it, don't you?'

He puts his coffee cup down abruptly and it lands on the terrace, smashing, but he appears not to notice. She summons a maid, who is standing some way off, to clear the table.

He begins. She believes she is able to understand every word, although his voice is strangely distant – she used to think of a bird trapped in a chimney – as if the words are reaching his mouth by a back route. Sometimes she is reminded of her brother Lionel's telephone, made with a length of hosepipe and two baked-bean cans: she had to wait upstairs while he spoke to her from the back garden, his voice faint. He would break off to shout instructions. There are strangled yodelling notes in Sir Harry's vowels, and a wind-instrument harshness in his consonants, so that the rhythms of speech have been scrambled en route from wherever speech originates. But she is used to it.

'My dear Julian, the almond blossom is out and the . . .'

He points to the Mediterranean.

'Shall I put "the sea", Sir Harry?'

'Yes, yes of course "the sea".'

' "The sea is . . ."?'

'The sea is calm and as blue as a . . .'

' "A duck's egg"?'

'Duck egg. Julian, may I remind you that it has always been the policy of Tubal and Co. to look after our animals' (she changes this to 'customers') 'with the greatest possible care, because our livelihood depends upon the silken thread of connection which runs between us and them, and which continues over many lifetimes so that the bank, as I like to say, is in a sense a . . . ?'

' "A living organism", Sir Harry?'

'A living organism, which depends for its very survival on keeping the lifeblood flowing. Our business . . .'

Estelle is happy to see him warming to his theme.

'Our business is based on the confidence . . .'

'Of our customers?'

'Our customers, as my father . . .'

He falters.

'Sir Ephraim?'

'As my father, Sir Ephraim, was fond of saying. Too fond.'

He stops now and gazes out to sea where the first yachts of the new season have appeared, looking crisp and clean and hopeful.

'Too fond. The shit. We are not running a casino.'

Estelle feels deep sadness. He has dried up. The old phrases have escaped in staccato fashion from inside his head and the supply is diminishing. She will tidy them up before sending them. Her sadness is not without an element of self-interest, because for the last thirty-two years she has been the pilot fish to his whale, swimming in his bow-wave, deeply but discreetly in love, and now she can see that the magnificent whale is beached. She doesn't say it to anyone, but he has more or less been abandoned by the family. Young Simon is in the African jungle and Julian hardly ever visits and Fleur hasn't been since Christmas. She seems to spend her days in the gym. She obviously finds her husband's condition difficult to live with.

His eyes are still turned towards the Mediterranean. He sees, she thinks, only blobs of colour, like the Matisse of a view through a window to the port of Collioure, his first purchase in 1952, which hangs in the front hall and which these days he often looks at for hours on end. She knows it cost him £4,900 and is worth some millions now. Twenty million at least. But he has absolutely no interest in the value of his paintings and only sells if he tires of a painter. Nonetheless she is logging them all in her spare time. The world for him has lost its infinite subtlety. His speech suggests that his understanding is not what it was, but she hopes that, in his brain, somewhere behind the portal where the words appear, he is still able to understand and appreciate these subtleties. He once delighted in surprisingly small natural things and events – seasonal changes and moss on the path and birdsong and the bindings of books – as well as the opera, the ballet and a day or two fishing for salmon on the Tay or for trout on his stretch of the upper reaches of the River Test, where the waters are clear and the trout wary. Many of the bank's clients have enjoyed the box at the opera and the openings of the exhibitions that Sir Harry sponsored. Julian doesn't like the opera. He thinks it diverts attention from the real aims of the bank, which are the creation of value, and sends out the wrong message, in ways that his father doesn't begin to understand. Before his stroke, his father had railed against hedge funds, apparently unaware that hedge funds were, for a while, responsible for a sixty per cent growth in their clients' portfolios. That had made them a whole lot happier than a few nights watching men in tights leaping about at Covent Garden. Under Julian's regime – until recently – the bank sponsored golf and a whole day at Ascot. Horse racing, of course, appeals to the Gulf States, but now, she has learned, all sponsorships are under review.

Estelle hasn't told Sir Harry that the box has been sold. He still speaks of going to the opera and of taking a party to Glyndebourne. Estelle has the impression that Fleur is embarrassed to be seen with him, now that he stumbles and sometimes dribbles, and speaks in this strange, trapped-avian voice. She is much younger than Sir Harry, but then she knew that when she left the playwright to marry him.

Estelle looks at him as he stares out to sea. She wonders what he is truly thinking. Somehow, despite the tragedy that has taken him, he seems to retain his ability to be cheerful and also to choose unerringly what to wear. At a distance there is nothing of the invalid about him although close up the skin of his face has a sort of white, fungal bloom. Like an apple stored in a shed. He is too thin, so that as he sits his thighs barely disturb the plum trousers. They look like the trousers on a marionette, lacking substance. Yet he seems serene. Occasionally, as he is dictating his letters to Julian, he becomes agitated. Now he watches a yacht tacking on the bay with approval.

'We must get the . . .'

He points at the yacht.

'The boat out?'

'Yes. Tell . . .'

'Bryce?'

'Tell Bryce that I want it out before Christmas.'

'Easter, I think. I will make a note.'

'Julian and the children want sail.'

He never forgets Julian's name and Estelle finds this touching. At that moment one of the house servants, Antoine, walks over. He speaks to Estelle in English, because she has never learned much French.

'Madame, there is a gentleman at the gate. He wishes to speak with Monsieur Julian.'

'Who is he?'

'He is the Russian gentleman who has bought Villa Floriana.'

'I will speak to him.'

Estelle goes to the front gate. It is their new neighbour, Boris Vladykin, standing there in very large shorts. He is sweating and his breath smells of alcohol.

'Good morning, Mr Vladykin.'

'I want speak to Mr Julian.'

His face is broad and sweaty; the spring sunshine is hot.

'He is not here, but he is coming soon. What do you wish to discuss?'

His English is poor.

'I want to talk to Mr Julian about boat.'

'*Niobe* is in the boatyard at the port for repairs. I don't know anything more. Goodbye, Mr Vladykin. Mr Julian is coming down next week. He will know.'

She shuts the gate and walks back through the house and out on to the terrace. Vladykin rings the bell again, but she ignores him.

Harry makes a noise, which Estelle interprets.

'It was Mr Vladykin. I don't know what he wants. He was wearing those ghastly shorts.'

Harry is disturbed. His face is flushed and his eyes are pained and restless. She wonders what Vladykin wants. She feels a spreading unease. The barbarians are at the gate.

2

JULIAN TREVELYAN-TUBAL sits in the back of his car as the driver takes him to Luton Airport. He's thought about getting rid of the Bentley, but he doesn't want to cause alarm: the family have always been driven in Bentleys. When people still cared about such things, a Bentley spoke of restraint, where a Rolls-Royce suggested something flashy and unreliable. The argument for selling the Bentley is that the top man should demonstrate that he is in touch with the new financial realities. Also, footballers and hedge-fund managers and property developers now drive sporty little Bentley Coupés and convertibles, and Bentley long ago decided to drop their steady-Eddy image. In a way, he thinks, they are doing just what the banks have been doing. He sits inside the car, an eight-year-old Arnage, feeling as though he is being transported – silently – to his own funeral. He sees Len glancing anxiously at him in the rear-view mirror but he ignores him. Len likes a chat. His opening gambit is usually about the traffic. He has views on most things, deluded but harmless. His father sent him for driver-training at Crewe about twenty years ago and he behaves as though they embalmed him at the same time.

Perhaps the way round this dilemma is to go green: all directors of the bank, including the boss, will drive one of those hybrid cars that run on gas and batteries, demonstrating their commitment to a greener, less wasteful future, and so by proxy to more ethical business practices. Or is the word responsible, rather than ethical? Nobody in the City really gives a monkey's about green politics, but they know better than to say so publicly. He makes a note to tell his assistant to look into it and to bear in mind the PR benefits; also, they still have one almost viable hedge fund, which has a huge investment in sustainable batteries, and possibly the whole story could be tied in to that. At least it might attract some more investment into the fund. While he worked under his father, he was known for original thinking. His father was far too fastidious to use terms like 'thinking out of the box' or 'pushing the envelope' – he thinks language should remain in a state of paralysis – but that is what Julian was doing; that was in his carefree role until a few years ago. His father never fully understood the detail of banking: not many important bankers do. *You don't ask the captain of the vessel to stoke the engines, after all.* (His imagery, as well as his understanding of banking, was outmoded.) He was close to the top people at Barings when they went down in 1995, but he never learned the lessons: he had no idea what was happening in the engine room.

As Len pilots the Bentley free of the City, Julian imagines that anyone looking in at him, a forty-one-year-old man, expensively tailored, peering at some papers on a walnut fold-out shelf, would see someone who was living in another – and not even parallel – universe, with his £200,000 car, his old retainer Len at the wheel, his Lobb shoes (invisible but easily imagined) shining like billy-o, a man who was born to wealth. And they would probably believe – not so far wide of the mark – that he had done nothing to deserve it. But they wouldn't understand – why would they? – that it is not so easy to be born rich in a world where everything that surrounds you from birth is old and beautiful and patinated, a world where you are steered, like it or not, towards the family business, where all around you people are deferential but behind your back dismissive. This world presents you with a choice: either you have nothing to do with it and open yourself to gibes and sneers by becoming a remittance man like his brother, who the newspapers once liked to call *the hippy Tubal* or *the hairy heir*, or you try to make a success of it. His father liked to bang on about the customers and the sacred trust – Estelle still sends his rambling letters, freely translated by her from the gibberish – that links banks and their clients with a silken thread. Sadly his theory, that keeping his Eton chums happy at the opera is the essence of banking, proved inadequate. Things moved on long before he retired, although he inhabited a large and moribund office at 11 Bread Street right up until the day of his stroke. He never understood that to produce a decent return you need financial instruments that banks of deposit never dreamed of. The cosy world, in which, for example, undisclosed assets could be left undeclared and untaxed, had changed for ever. Still clad in his plum trousers and rakish hat, his father is now more or less trapped inside the resounding empty tomb that is the extent of his life.

He reads a letter from Estelle. It is one of her updates on his father's – imagined – progress. She tells him that his father is looking forward to the sailing; the boat has been painted and will be back on its mooring soon, and that the gardeners are doing a fine job in the spring weather. She knows Sir Harry is looking forward to his visit.

At Luton the Citation is standing by, making low noises and trembling, like a fridge. Private jets have come down in price and the board has decreed that they may still be used where discretion is needed. Len assures him that he will be here on Wednesday to pick him up; his face is rumpled with honest concern, like Sid James's in the *Carry On* films his father loved. Len calls him 'Mr Julian'. Soon the plane is surging into the darkening sky and he accepts a drink from Kevin, co-pilot and steward. These executive-jet companies have some quaint ideas: there's always champagne and *pâté de foie gras* and Stilton and smoked salmon and malt whisky as though they imagine that's all their clients will eat. In his experience the old rich, at least, like fish cakes and jam roly-poly. His father loved cottage pie. Julian accepts a slender smoked-salmon sandwich. The pilots are joshing, chubby young men from the deep, rugby-playing suburbs.

Usually he finds flights relaxing. Once you are up there in the nothingness you can plunge deep into your own thoughts. But tonight he is troubled. The family trust is lodged in Liechtenstein and with the help of his lawyers, his brother and compliant auditors, he has unlocked it to provide £250m. to the bank. It's a loan with a limited life, but still he is glad his father won't know anything about it. In fact he's dreading signing the deeds. The cabin lights are dimmed and he's now sitting all alone in a bright cone directed from the overhead lamp towards his table. The light seems to suggest that he is under interrogation. It's at these moments he knows that he is not really cut out to be a financial mogul. Up front the chubby but sensible Kevin and James are steering the plane blithely towards Zurich where a car will be waiting to take him to Liechtenstein. Years of family discretion dictates that they never, apparently, set foot in Liechtenstein, where wealth tax is 0.16 per cent per annum. In fact this will be only the second time he has visited, but the deeds need signing urgently and quietly, and out of sight of the ratings agencies, regulators and financial journalists. Every board-room and every lawyer's office in London leaks like a sieve. The ABA rating has been a prized asset for twenty-five years. He tries to take comfort from the fact that the bank has been in trouble more than once in the years since Moses Tubal first hung out his shingle in 1671. In 1847 the bank underwrote the Argentine River Plate Company, which failed. Only a loan from the Rothschilds kept them afloat then.

He dozes uneasily, in the shallows of sleep. When he is disturbed, he dreams of riding his pony. At prep school he wrote anguished, weekly letters to his mother, asking about the pony's welfare. The pony's happiness, he now understands, was the only way he could express his emotional despair. Mummy was far too brusque to notice. Perhaps she was already suffering at his father's wandering hands. The pony's name was Coppélia, the result of his parents' love of the ballet. His friends' ponies were called Nobby and Flash and Blaze and Socks. In his mind as he sleeps he is still drawing pictures of ponies in the margins of his exercise books. He believes he can speak to horses. Horse conversation is not profound or commercially-minded, but calmly and reassuringly banal. The only thing that gets ponies going is the rumour that French people eat horses. His pony friends tell him that it is a disgrace. Even now in his sleep he feels outraged. He wrote a school essay called 'The Disgraceful Practice of Eating Horse Meat in France', which earned him a gold star from Miss Robinson, his English teacher, and the eternal enmity of Madame Le Nôtre, his French teacher. Madame Le Nôtre was an enthusiastic carnivore and also – she said – the direct descendant of the gardener. He wondered why you would be proud to be descended from a gardener. At Haylings they had seven, men whose skin was permanently weathered. It was much like the colour of his father's military-tan shoes. Estelle has a source of supply for Kiwi Military Tan Polish, still popular down under.

When he was at prep school the boys had to demonstrate that they could swim by making a crossing of the Cherwell in their pyjamas and dressing gowns after weeks of practice in the swimming pool. Health and Safety have stopped that. In his dream he remembers R.O. Venables sinking and being pulled out by Mr Applethwaite, housemaster of Jellicoe, who dived in wearing his baggy tracksuit and old cricket sweater. In his dream he is now riding his pony across the school meadows and into the river to save Venables. The pony tells him, gravely, to sit back in case she stumbles.

He wakes as the plane shudders briefly before landing smoothly in Altenrhein. The car is pulled up on the tarmac to the side of the runway. He thanks Kevin and James, who have put on caps and jackets to see him off. They will stay overnight near Flughafen Altenrhein.

While he is scuttling across Austria in the dead of night, his mouth furred, a migraine developing ominously, the bones in his neck grinding on each other, he hopes his children are safely asleep; Sam is at primary school, and Alice has one more year at nursery school. As soon as things have settled down and the asset ratio is back where it belongs, he will give Cy Mannheim a call in New York to say that he is ready and that will be the end. Although Tubal's is small compared with commercial banks, Cy believes it has something First Federal wants, class. Julian feels clammy now. He swallows two Migraleves. The lights in the customs cabin at the border crossing

– barely a formality – are swirling and he knows it's going to be the worst sort of migraine. Across the border he steps out of the people carrier and into a Mercedes where Gilles Dax of Arendt and Oppenheim is waiting. Dax makes very stiff and formal conversation. He mentions the weather. He doesn't mention the plane or the transaction. They drive towards Vaduz across a huge arched bridge which spans the Rhine. Arendt and Oppenheim have their offices behind the National Bank. They drive straight into an underground car park and are shown into a lift that takes them up a few floors to the boardroom, which is all reassuring wood and gilt with the sort of Empire furniture that looks as though it has been retrieved from Napoleon's private office – winged ormolu lions, Egyptian motifs of falcons and sphinxes, and plenty of that ornate Napoleonic N which also adorns chocolates in France. The air itself is heavy with discretion. A young woman in a business suit is standing by. She is introduced by Dax as Marie Delder, chief legal officer. Nothing in her demeanour suggests that she finds it unusual to be presiding over the withdrawal of £250m.

'Everything is ready for signature, sir,' she says in that reassuring Swiss way, as if life is essentially about being prepared and methodical and sensible. He sits at a vast desk like a president at a peace conference, and she stands, sliding the documents towards him in leather folders. As she leans over him for a moment, he detects a scented warmth which touches him – his mind is jumpily susceptible to such thoughts – with its suggestion that she is nervous. As nervous, perhaps, as he is.

'OK,' he says. 'Let's do it.'

He signs in six places. Dax countersigns, as CEO of Arendt and Oppenheim, and Marie Delder witnesses the authenticity of the documents as legal officer. He wonders how long they will take to file with the Liechtenstein authorities once he has sent back the documents after his father has signed. Some time, he would guess. The money will now be directed to two bank accounts in the Turks and Caicos and two in Switzerland and one in the Isle of Man before lodging itself, under various guises, in the bank's retained-earnings account, where it will not be subject to scrutiny until the accounts are published in eleven months' time; in the meanwhile the auditors can be relied upon to take these assets at face value in their interim report. The ratings agencies will receive some inside information by the usual channels as soon as possible about the healthy inflow of deposits. Dax, of course, knows that the money is to prop up the bank and he probably knows the disastrous hit they have taken on the sub primes and collateralised debt instruments they bought and the hedge funds they financed. The bank still owns – among many other useless CDOs – chunks of mortgages on an alligator farm in a swamp, two thousand worthless homes in Mississippi, a shopping mall in a town which has been flattened by a hurricane and a lake-side clapboard holiday development in Antigua which is currently underwater, so that, when the waters recede, the holiday homes will be pulp. He could let the last hedge fund go, but the bank would lose close to $500m. and the rating could slip to a point at which deposi-tors could cause a run. The thing about banks – his father used to say – is that they should stick to what they know. He cited the scan-dals of Enron and WorldCom, and how the banks and the auditors were dazzled by the apparent success, even as the insiders were steal-ing $33bn. And now Tubal and Co. is stuck with $800m. of utterly useless and finely diced mortgages in territories they have never even visited. Not only that, but no one in the bank knew what the traders and hedgies were buying; they went along with them because they too were dazzled by the profits others had apparently made. Just before his stroke, his father heard about the mortgages, and tried to unwind the position, but it was too late. In a way his stroke came just in time.

Julian's head is now throbbing unbearably. He thinks its origin is in the occipital lobes. His migraine often comes on in times of tension. At its worst he has a kind of stomach upset and his vision becomes blurred, and then there is the almost unbearable pain. His father was made of sterner stuff. Actually, his father lacked imagination, and this probably protected him. He didn't believe in risk and because of that the bank was slipping behind when Julian took over. But maybe a certain narrow vision is what is required to be a success in any field, a set of clearly defined and unalterable views on everything and a bland insensitivity to the opinions of others. Autistic people are usually obsessed with ritualistic behaviour and he has often wondered if his father, with his obsessively polished shoes and his hatred of small changes, isn't more than a little autistic. Now his little rituals probably sustain him; he looks at his pictures, he takes breakfast either in the *orangerie* or on the terrace, he chooses for himself a buttonhole, which Estelle snips and carries like an eager bridesmaid, he eats the same two or three dishes day by day and he dictates his incoherent letters, which he believes are sustaining his son.

Julian is driven to an apartment in the old town, somewhere under the ducal castle, and Gilles Dax delivers him to a waiting housekeeper who offers to make him tea or coffee or to produce a light meal. It's 2 a.m. and he longs to go to bed.

'No,' he says in French, 'if I need anything in the night I can help myself. Just some still water by the bed, please.'

She has turned down his bed, she shows him the neat sandwiches in the fridge, and indicates the drinks cabinet and wishes him a good night. She has deep furrows between her eyes and heavy eyebrows which almost meet, so that her eyes appear to be in permanent shade, but her smile somehow contains real kindness – he is on the lookout – and a motherly concern for his welfare. For the second time in an hour or so, he finds himself touched by human kindness and weakness. Before her death his own mother's concern was directed towards dogs. While he was swimming the Cherwell, a heroic pyjama-clad little Leander, like an escapee from a domestic farce – she was involved in dog rescue, as a patron and benefactor of Wandsworth Dogs' Home. Her car was infiltrated with dog hair and it usually smelled of dogs – wet, scabrous or in season – and always it retained the scent of dried Fray Bentos, the scent of the canine diet that once clung to the rear ends of the dogs and was now embedded in the seats. As a boy he hated travelling in her car. He didn't know then, but his father's interests extended beyond the patronage of the ballet and theatre into a lively concern for the careers of young actresses and ballerinas. Fleur was an actress. She hasn't visited his father all winter, but then perhaps he hasn't noticed. Estelle, of course, will be thrilled to have him to herself.

He swallows another pill. As he waits for it to take effect, he drinks a long glass of water and tries to read a magazine article about financial services in Liechtenstein. His eyes lose focus and begin to film over. He feels desperate, utterly rudderless, as though his eyes are merely responding to the turmoil inside his head. He puts the magazine down. Who reads this stuff? Actually, Tubal's puts out similarly meaningless guff, which pretends that their analysts and fund managers – including the disastrous Fortress Lion hedge fund – understand the markets and – worse still – that the markets are inherently rational. Before he walked into investment banking he should have noted what Keynes apparently said: 'You might just as well read a sheep's entrails as the Romans did as make predictions about the markets.'

Fortress Lion once appropriated the bell curve and its original, the Gaussian curve, in a prospectus. To lend credibility to their claim that, with the curve, the markets were knowable, they printed the formula for standard normal distribution; he can even see it now, lodged in his troubled mind:

$$f(x) = \frac{1}{\sqrt{2\pi\sigma^2}}\, e^{-\frac{(x-\mu)^2}{2\sigma^2}}$$

How impressed the clients were to find that algebra (if it was algebra) had removed the uncertainty from markets. The prospectus did not mention that Carl Friedrich Gauss devised his equation in order to analyse astronomical data in 1794 and that later it was used to predict population growth. Professor Kuhn, Nobel Laureate, didn't mention it either.

He tries to call Kimberly. He can imagine her warmly asleep in Ladbroke Square. Her phone goes straight to answer. He takes comfort from her breathy, upbeat message, which always sounds as though she is trying out for the Radcliffe cheerleading squad. He whispers, 'Love you, will call from the villa.'

In the Liechtenstein morning, which arrives surprisingly soon, he finds that in the night his migraine has retreated, like a bear to its winter cave, where it is growling only indistinctly. The housekeeper has prepared him a breakfast of ham and cheese and fruit, with fresh croissants, rye bread and a pot of coffee. All his life he has been cosseted and it seems particularly shameful to him this morning after what he has done. He gives the housekeeper a huge tip, as though he is propitiating the Madonna and asking her to intercede for him. She tries to refuse, but he insists.

He adds, '*C'est parce que vous êtes une ange.*'

She probably thinks he is crazy, and in a sense he is. Dax arrives in another car, and assures him as they drive that all has gone smoothly. Dax smells of cologne, like an old-fashioned boulevardier. He remembers one of his father's chums, Leo Mountjoy, saying it was important always to have your own cologne to hand to douse yourself, so that you never aroused suspicion by coming home differently scented. Women, he said, are very sensitive to scents. Very sensitive, like forest creatures; they can catch a scent at fifty yards. Leo Mountjoy kept chorus girls. Julian tells Dax that he will send him his father's endorsement of the deeds by special courier.

At the border another car is waiting to take them to Altenrhein where the plane is straining at the leash.

'Ready to lift off, sir?' James asks.

'Yes.'

'Are we going home, sir?'

'My family home. Nice Airport. Staying for one night.'

'Right, let's just get your bags on board. We have some nice fresh croissants and the morning newspapers, and Kevin has printed out the online *FT*, sir.'

'Lovely. Thank you.'

A few minutes later James reports that they have a slot in five minutes.

When the plane lands in Nice one and a quarter hours later and the door opens, Julian gets the warm and welcome scent of his boyhood holidays, of baking hillsides and wild thyme and some of that clinging saltiness of the Mediterranean. When he's sold to Mannheim, he and the family will move here.

A car is waiting. Standing beside it like an undertaker is Jean-Marc, driver and handyman.

'*Bonjour, Jean-Marc. Tout va bien?*'

'*Oui, merci, Monsieur Julian, tout va bien.*'

3

FOR THE PAST three years, Artair MacCleod has been living in an old lifeboat station, overlooking the estuary of the Camel River. At low tide he looks out on the river's deep channel to broad mudflats. He has gradually moved towards the edges of the country as if centrifugal forces are pulling him there: in fact the force is the availability of grants in the regions, places that are thought to need help with the arts, because life there is culturally thin and can only be sustained by subsidy. The fiction endures because the people in these regions have votes, even if they have little spontaneously produced culture. So Artair, himself a playwright and actor manager, has gradually migrated from the metropolis to various provincial cities and finally – there is nowhere further he can go without a boat – to this estuary.

His grand project is to produce a five-hour play based on the life and novels of Flann O'Brien. But today he has taken a break to start hand-writing his manuscript, because he has heard that a university in Texas will pay good money for original manuscripts; his is, in fact, mostly a cut-and-paste job from the work of O'Brien, with stage directions added in marker pen. He has laboriously written out six pages of the first part of his play. The whole project has taken him three years so far and he still has to write episodes three to five, inclusive. He has written to the trust, which pays him a stipend, asking for a special grant to allow him to suspend his other activities – now largely children's plays, done with a nod towards Gaelic or Cornish – so that he can devote himself to finishing this major project, which, he wrote, is soon to enter pre-production. He anticipates negotiations for a suitably grand Celtic location to stage this epic work, which will be a landmark production for the minority cultures, but pre-production and development come at a cost. He has had no reply in the three months since he first wrote but he has also been busy approaching various arts organisations and the Arts Council itself.

In order to make the original manuscript authentic, he is using an old Waterman's fountain pen and some woven paper, which laps up the ink. He believes this will add to the verisimilitude. He is writing out what will be the play's manifesto and opening scene: the narrator, Flann O'Brien, is addressing his friend Brinsley over a few pints. Brinsley, to be honest, doesn't have much of a part. He's more the straight man. They are sitting in the snug of the Red Swan in Dublin.

It was stated that, while the novel and the play were both pleasing intellectual exercises, the novel was inferior to the play inasmuch as it lacked the outward accidents of illusion, frequently inducing the reader to be outwitted in a shabby fashion and caused to experience a real concern for the fortunes of illusory characters. The play was consumed in a wholesome fashion by large masses in places of public resort; the novel was self-administered in private. The novel, in the hands of an unscrupulous writer, could be despotic. In reply to an enquiry, it was explained that a satisfactory novel should be a self-evident sham, which the reader could regulate at will the degree of credulity. It was undemocratic to compel characters to be uniformly good or bad or poor or rich. Each should be allowed a private life, self-determination and a decent standard of living. This would be for self-respect, contentment and better service. It would be incorrect to say that it would lead to chaos. Characters should be interchangeable as between one book and another. The entire corpus of existing literature should be regarded as a limbo from which discerning authors could draw their characters as required, creating only when they failed to find a suitable existing puppet. The modern novel should be largely a work of reference. Most authors spend their time saying what has been said before – usually said much better. A wealth of references to existing works would acquaint the reader instantaneously with the nature of each character, would obviate tiresome explanations and would effectively preclude mountebanks, upstarts, thimble riggers and persons of inferior education from an understanding of contemporary literature.

BRINSLEY: This is all my bum.

Artair does not think this is all my bum at all. He believes that theatre and novels are too often constrained by reality. He loves the idea that characters in a novel or a play have a life of their own and don't have to submit to the author's will. He believes that each life is several lives, and that the distinctions between myth and reality are too sharply drawn. The old Celtic myths – so called – contain deeper truths. One or two of the reviews of his work have suggested that he has lost control of his characters, but none of them has said that he did it deliberately. Actually in regional children's theatre, you seldom get reviews, and those you do get are more guides to where to park the children on a rainy day than critical exercises.

Artair believes that this play will be his masterwork, combining the appeal of a great – and to some extent – forgotten Irish novelist with the nostalgic appeal to the Gaelic/Celtic past. He can see it attracting interest (and grants) in Galway and Dumfries, in North Wales and down here in Cornwall – Kernow in the old tongue – and even in Brittany where they are keen to keep alive the Brezhoneg language. His readings have always gone down well there.

As he is carefully blotting Brinsley's last sentence – *This is all my bum* – he suddenly sees Daniel Day-Lewis as Flann O'Brien. Not only would Daniel Day-Lewis make a wonderful, tortured, poetic and glamorous Flann O'Brien, he would also lift the whole enterprise out of the mire of dutiful regional theatre into a cosmos of serious, deeply committed acting. It could easily lead to a movie, in fact it would certainly lead to a movie if Daniel agreed to do it. Daniel is English, but he lives in Ireland and feels a deep kinship – Artair is sure – with the Irish prehistory that Flann O'Brien both loved and parodied. He wonders where Daniel stands on Celtic myth. He seems to be a very serious sort of feller.

Out of the broad but salt-stained windows, through which the lifeboat men used to keep watch, he sees the mud emerging as the tide recedes. Out to one side is the open sea, and Smugglers' Doom, a sandbar that only shows at very low tide. Directly across the estuary is the wreck of a small fishing boat, scuppered, the locals say, and now he sees the wheelhouse appearing, draped in seaweed bunting.

Like all creative people, he feels refreshed and vigorous after his thunderclap of an idea. The ideas are all out there, he knows, and we – he extends his largesse to all genuinely creative people – are the lightning rods. We bring the ideas down to earth. Now the remains of the winch on the fishing boat that pulled in the nets appear. The winch is mottled and rusted. He never tires of the action of the tides. Long-legged birds with probing beaks – he's not good on the names of birds, but he believes they are either sandpipers or curlews – are already arriving to prospect in the mud. Oddly enough, they keep their underbellies snowy white, even though they spend so much of their lives in this mud: nature – an infinite resource for the fertile mind.

Dear Daniel Day-Lewis
   I know this comes rather out of the blue, but I want to tell you that I have laboured in the theatrical vineyard for some years.

(Does this sound a little stilted? Yes it does.)

Dear Daniel Day-Lewis
   Now that my life's work, a five-hour, three-part play based on the life and works of Flann O'Brien is nearing completion, I wanted to make contact with you. I have spent a lifetime working in Celtic and Gaelic theatre, and as you know Flann O'Brien was a Gaelic speaker and very well versed in the old myths and history. It has taken me three years to complete the play, and all that time I have had it in mind as a suitable vehicle for your immense talent. In fact

my admiration for you goes right back to the film about a crippled Dublin lad, Christy, I think his name was. In your more recent film, There Will Be Blood, *oil spouting everywhere, you were positively elemental. In a long career I don't believe I have ever encountered an actor with such emotional intensity. What you have done, which so few actors have achieved, is to harness a huge inner power, while doing very little to attract attention. (As my colleague Kenneth Tynan once said of the young Richard Burton.)*

Now, to the project I mentioned – nearing completion – a life of Flann O'Brien using his own novels as the starting point. Two versions are proposed, a five-hour three-part play – to run on consecutive nights – partly in Erse with rolling subtitles (a trick I have learned from Jonathan Kent's Japanese Hamlet*) and a feature film with yourself playing the part of Flann.*

As you know, he was a wonderful, protean character, brought up speaking the Gaelic as I said, and steeped in the romance of ancient legend, but keenly aware, from his seat in the snug of the Red Swan, of the parodic possibilities of the Gaelic nostalgia. He was also one of the few great Irish writers of his time who never left Ireland, at that time a repressed and dreary place. Now of course people are making the reverse journey. You, I believe, are one of those who were nurtured by the Home Counties of England, like me. I was born in Blackheath, London SE3.

Perhaps he is being a little too chatty here. Perhaps he should be more businesslike. He has seen a picture of Daniel's lovely wife and it reminded him that he and Fleur were once a similarly golden couple. Fleur had just starred in his production of a banned Czech play in Twickenham – her Czech accent was good, although one critic wondered why a translation should be played with accents. She was a spy, sent in by the Communists to report on Václav Havel; instead she changed sides and fed her bosses disinformation. It didn't end well for her character. Harry Trevelyan-Tubal backed the production. Later he offered to back a production of the play in the West End with Fleur in the lead, with what he called a more commercial director. The transfer to the West End lasted just seven weeks, but it achieved

Sir Harry's aim: Fleur became the third Lady Trevelyan-Tubal and gave up the theatre.

> *Anyway, dear Daniel, I am living in hope that you will take an interest in this project, and read the script. (Which, by the way, the university at Austin, Texas, famous for its collection of original manuscripts, has entered into negotiations to buy.) Please reply to me at the Lifeboat Theatre Company at the address above . . .*

He seals the letter with some of the sealing wax he has bought to use on the Texas-bound manuscript. For Daniel he lights the candle and drops a splodge of boiling wax on to the envelope – some falls, inevitably, on to the remains of an Asda quiche – and presses the molten wax with his signet ring. Too late he realises that it would have been better to have taken the ring off first, because Daniel is now to receive a couple of hairs from his scalded knuckle along with the wax, which has extirpated them. The signet ring was a gift to him from Fleur when they were married. It has engraved on it the outline of a griffin. He gave her a curtain ring, in those days a recognised, and economical, sign of bohemian tendencies.

Buoyed by his plan to enlist Daniel Day-Lewis, he walks up the road from the boathouse to the village. From there he takes the bus to Pentire where the library offers free computer and internet usage. Although you have to pay for printing. He finds that Daniel Day-Lewis's agent is William Morris, located on El Camino Drive, Beverly Hills. He looks around the library, and imagines that El Camino Drive is very different from this rather gloomy, enervated room. He sees palms and David Hockney swimming pools. So this letter will be going on a long and circuitous journey to California and back to Ireland. In the meanwhile he will have time to finish the first draft and also, of course, send his manuscript off to Texas. He wonders how long the professors and other expert littérateurs will need to assess the value. They already have some of Flann O'Brien's work, and a few boxes of Joyce's leftovers and some stuff that once belonged to Yeats, so they will welcome this manuscript.

Now that the tide is more or less out, he gets what Flann O'Brien described as the ancient smell of putridity, although O'Brien was talking about the history of Ireland rather than the mud, but everything – past, present, character, myth, mud – is interconnected.

After he has posted the letter he wonders whether he should have explained in more detail what he has in mind: a play and a film which explore O'Brien's idea that fictional characters do exist and can resist the author who tries to make use of them in his fiction. He recalls a film about John Malkovich, and perhaps he should have mentioned that to Daniel, to demonstrate that he is not just talking about hoary old myth and creaking theatre, but postmodernism. If anybody can give Flann O'Brien flesh and blood, and box-office appeal, it's Daniel. Daniel has that magical, alchemical power given to very few actors.

Then he pops into his bank to see if his quarterly grant has finally arrived. He's asked the bank to phone him when it comes, but as he's right outside, he thinks he might as well drop in and save the postman's shoe-leather. The cashier on duty is new. She has a full, seamless face; it has, he thinks, the appearance of a sea creature, a seal or a dolphin, the eyes almost flat on the surface, so that she has something of the charming innocence of those creatures.

'Hello,' he says, 'I don't think I've had the pleasure of seeing you before.'

'I've only been here for a few weeks. I used to be in Truro.'

'Magnificent city, lovely cathedral. I am Artair MacCleod,' he says, and pauses, but she shows no surprise. Truro is some way off.

'What can I do for you today, sir?'

'Ah, what a question. I think I'm obliged to give you the shorter and less interesting answer. My quarterly grant from Tubal and Co. should be in by now, and I would like you to check. It's already two months overdue.'

'Certainly, sir. Do you have any ID?'

'ID? ID? What's that?'

'Proof of identity. A credit card, perhaps.'

'No, I have no credit cards.'

'Or your driving licence?'

'No, I don't drive. I have never taken to it.'

'Unfortunately, sir, I am not allowed to give details of anyone's account without ID.'

'Look, my dear, I have been banking here for ten years. I am the director of the Lifeboat Theatre Company and – dare I say it – a well-known figure in the community. A public figure. So ID is not necessary.'

'I'll have to call Mr Trefelix, sir.'

'Call him. I have nothing to do at all. Oh yes, I forgot, nothing apart from speaking to Daniel Day-Lewis about a production of mine and negotiating with the university at Austin, Texas. But please, go ahead, summon Mr Trefelix. And while you're at it, why don't you assemble an identity parade of local deadbeats and line us all up for mugshots and injections of sodium pentothal?'

He's warming to his speech, but before he can get fully into the part of innocent accused, a victim of Senator McCarthy or a Tom Robinson, young Mr Trefelix appears.

'Oh hello, Mr MacCleod. Thanks, Mandy, I will take over. Could you come with me, Mr MacCleod, if you have a moment?'

'Certainly.'

He has an image of entering the manager's office, for tea and biscuits under a railway clock, but Trefelix leads him into a small, windowless meeting room.

'Sorry about that, sir,' he says. 'I was going to write to you – you don't have email at home yet, do you? No? No problem. I was going to write to you to say that Tubal and Co. have refused payment.'

'What? What's the reason? What did they say?'

'They simply refused.'

'Didn't you ask them?'

'We can't do that, sir. Apart from anything else there are data-protection issues around this which mean that we are not allowed to ask questions like that. You will have to take it up with them.'

'I will, you can rely on that. Oh yes. I'll get on to them right away.'

He stands up.

'There's one more thing, sir. We won't be able to pay the quarterly rent on your property, which fell due last Monday, until we receive funds.'

Artair is standing in a crouch, with his hands on the flimsy blond-wood desk.

'Don't be fucking ridiculous. This is Tubal's bank we are talking about, not a warehouse scam with call centres in Kazakhstan. Tubal and Company. The oldest private bank in the land.'

'Sir, it's out of my hands. The payment, I think, is from a private individual, not the bank itself.'

'Can I tell you something, you fucking intellectual and artistic pygmy, this money is a lifetime grant made to me by the private family trust of Tubal's. My ex-wife is now Lady Trevelyan-Tubal and this is a legally enforceable contract, if you like, a sort of alimony, and it cannot be cut off. Are you sure it isn't just a malfunction of your notoriously useless systems?'

He says the word 'systems' with fastidiousness and drawn-out emphasis.

'Mr MacCleod, I understand your concerns. I really do, and by the way my children are looking forward as usual to the Easter production *The Wind in the Willows* at the primary school, but the rules have been tightened up.'

'I am in mid-negotiation with Daniel Day-Lewis, about a major collaboration. My collection of manuscripts is being priced even now by a leading American university. I have a full touring programme this spring.'

He's sounding, he thinks, not like a stage victim, but a real victim. There's a slight, weak whine in his voice.

'Sir, I am sure it's just a slip-up on their part. Like most banks, they may have laid off staff. Look, I shouldn't be saying this, but most banks, including ours, are making cuts.'

'When I have spoken to my man at Tubal's, I may decide to move my account elsewhere.'

He straightens himself up, with difficulty: Lear leaving the hovel on the heath.

'If it was our fault, I would understand. But anyway, when you've got to the bottom of it – and I am sure it's just a glitch – please call me.'

'I reserve my judgement.'

But when he tries to speak to someone at Tubal's, using a number he has had for years, he is redirected to a call centre, where they disclaim any responsibility for any family trust and suggest he write or email head office for the appropriate address and to explain the nature of his problem.

'I don't have a problem. You're the one with the fucking problem.'

'I am sorry, sir, it is our policy that staff must terminate abusive calls.'

The line goes dead.

The tide has turned again and he can see the green-blue seawater beginning to jostle the darker, mud-laden river water, creating a series of small, turbulent rapids in the channel. Once he had a boat, but he was not good with boats.

He tries to imagine what could have happened at Tubal's. Trefelix is probably right, a glitch in the system. Funny word, 'glitch'. He thinks it must be Yiddish. The man who took his wife, Sir Harry Trevelyan-Tubal, comes from a family which once spoke Yiddish, although insulated from the shtetl by generations of Eton and Oxford and foxhounds – there's a Sassoon somewhere in the line – and villas and Bentleys and ski chalets and discreet servants and post-Impressionist and fauvist paintings, while he – Artair MacCleod, playwright, actor, Gaelic scholar – lives in a draughty and crudely converted boathouse overlooking expanses of mud. Fleur, he has heard, doesn't get on with Julian, the son who took over as chairman, just two years before Sir Harry had his stroke. Since Harry and Fleur were married – nearly twenty years ago, he thinks it was – he has not exchanged a word with her. He's not allowed to: as part of the settlement that included his grant, he had to agree never to talk to the press about their life together and never to contact her under any circumstances, except through her solicitors. All he knows of her is what he reads in the papers and what little gossip reaches him. He tries now to find the address of the solicitors. He realises, as he sifts through randomly stacked papers, dating back ten, fifteen years, that he has no idea where he has filed – or deposited – the solicitors' telephone number and address, although he thinks they are called Fetlock's, certainly something to do with horses. He feels confident that his brain is circling its prey: all he has to do is wait. But the phone rings and it is the bookkeeper from the Royal National Lifeboat Institution in Newquay, so she says.

'I'm a bit busy, what can I do for you?'

'Ah, Mr MacCleod, I just wanted to say that your standing order for the rent has not been paid.'

'No, no, absolutely right. I was in the bank earlier today and the manager's assurance was that it was the result of – these are his exact words by the way – a glitch. It should be with you very soon. I've asked them to give it the old hurry-up.'

'Oh good. By the way, I'm taking the children to *Thomas the Tank Engine* when you come to Newquay. And we loved last year's *Wind in the Willows* in the community centre. You were wonderful as Mr Toad. Poop, poop.'

'Thank you. And thanks for bearing with me. My assistant is on leave, so it may not be straightforward, but you have my assurance that it is in hand with Tubal and Co., the private bank.'

'By next week, do you think?'

'Inshallah. The moving finger writes.'

'My son wants to be an actor, thanks to seeing you in *The Wind in the Willows*.'

'Put him off. Tell him to get a job playing a piano in a brothel.'

'He wants to eat potted meat and go sculling. In fact, he thinks he's a vole.'

'Good career choice, vole. Far better than being an actor. Got to go, sadly – Daniel Day-Lewis is waiting for my call.'

'Is he in *Thomas the Tank Engine*?'

'No, this is not part of my touring and community work, more a Hollywood production. Thanks so much for calling. I will leave some free tickets for you at the box office. How many do you need? Six? Oh, well four is all I can manage.'

A madwoman.

Like Oblomov, like Flann O'Brien, he feels a terrible urge to go to bed and stay there.

4

ESTELLE WAKES EARLY. Too early to be able to get going: there are certain proprieties. All her life she's lived within hushed, unspoken proprieties. How did she become their servant? When she wakes at this time, before she can go and make sure Sir Harry has had a good night and she can release the night carer – there are three, all fully trained, on shifts – she sees herself far too clearly. She lies in her bed with a cup of tea. Her little house, Provençal from the outside, is wholly English inside with a flowery rug relieving the cold gloom of the terracotta tiles and some nice, homely needlepoint cushions on the sofa. Her bed is covered in an old rose chintz bedspread. She tries in her own way to replicate the effortless good taste of the family, but the fact is that, although she has some nice things, including a Regency card table and a one-hundred-and-fifty-piece canteen of silver – never used – she knows the place is a mishmash. Taste seems to be a barrier you can't scale in one or even two generations. She wonders if her house has the scent of spinsterhood. The scent of disappointment, compounded by the solitary person's self-regard, the close scrutiny of the self, which leads to patent medicines and corn plasters and mouthwash and many creams.

She should have left the bank when he married Fleur. She was still young enough then. But when Harry's first wife, Eleanor, killed herself she had foolishly hoped that he might turn to her, Estelle. It was like something from Jane Austen: the plain governess who hopes her good qualities will win through with the master in the end. But he was arranging for Fleur, the twenty-five-year-old actress, to be cast in a play he was financing. How quickly she went from occasional actor in commercials and corporate videos, with one or two walk-on parts in proper theatre, to ornament of the social pages, photographed with Harry at Ascot, with Harry on his yacht, *Niobe*, with Harry at Covent Garden, with Harry – pleased as Punch – at the first-night party for *They Came from Xanadu*. It was a turkey. She wanted to leave Bread Street, but she couldn't for the very simple reason that she loved him. Now she has him more or less to herself, but he shows no signs of gratitude for her devotion. In the bank he told people that he couldn't live without her, that she was a force of nature. A wonder.

Now he seems barely to notice her; she is, as they say, part of the furniture. She lives in hope that his old self will return. She sees signs of it. But the truth is that the only things that engage him deeply are the twenty-two pictures in the house and of these he is particularly entranced by one of the Matisses. What does he see when he looks at the Matisse? She thinks that he is gazing through a window, perhaps deep into his past, as if the painting of Collioure draws him away from his restricted world into something more vibrant. She's not sure how this could work, but she is glad that he is happy looking at his pictures. In the old days, before they closed the asylums and homes, they allowed the inmates to stare endlessly at walls or television sets that were never turned off on the grounds that nothing was going on in the inmates' minds anyway. Who knows what goes through Harry's mind? She sometimes imagines that it is paging endlessly through half-submerged experiences and ideas. She hopes that this compulsive rifling is pleasurable; what hell it would be if every memory was painful. Only sensations – music, pictures, aromas and sunshine – seem to work directly on him. She understands him and helps him with his letters to Julian, but he doesn't acknowledge – he's not capable of acknowledging – that she is writing them, interpreting his thoughts. In fact he still appears to suggest in little ways that he is doing her a favour. And in a way he is, because he is all she has now. They are locked together.

*   *   *

It's time to get up. Julian's plane will be in Nice by noon and she must help Harry choose a jacket and she must cut some flowers for his buttonhole. She likes Julian, but she knows that his father was very harsh and dismissive with him. Julian is only a year or two younger than Fleur. Estelle dresses in a simple cream silken dress, quite businesslike. She doesn't want Julian to think that she sees herself as a proxy wife. She's become tubular in shape over the years: she feels the dress snagging as she uses the flat of her hands to smooth it.

She calls through to the nurse who says that Sir Harry has had a quiet night. The nurse is called Virginie and her husband is out of work: as a consequence she has a pared-down look. Unemployment seems to be high in this part of France. Estelle doesn't allow the nurses to choose Harry's clothes: she's not territorial – it's just that she knows what he likes. Her life is finely attuned to his, so that in some ways they are one entity. She's never told anybody about her sense that they have merged in this way.

Sir Harry is excited, also a little confused, by the prospect of Julian's visit. He seems to think Julian is coming sailing, but in fact Julian needs some documents signed. She helps him to choose his clothes by laying out three of his favourite jackets and trousers. He decides by his own mysterious lights to wear the pale moleskins and the very light cashmere jacket which has a series of faint blue rectangles, the veinous blue colour of a tattoo, just visible in its Golden Virginia richness. He has difficulty pulling on his trousers and she has to help him as he sits on the bed. His legs are painfully thin, the thighs bowed from the pelvis; the skin on his thighs, like his jacket, is tattooed, hieroglyphs rising to the surface in response to some deeper agony. When he's dressed he pomades his hair vigorously and looks at himself in the mirror with satisfaction. He smells of citrus. Jamaican Limes. She leaves him shaving with explosions of foam, and goes to see if his breakfast is ready. He has elected to have it on the terrace overlooking the sea. She waits for him. In the umbrella pines the turtle doves are calling. She loves their liquid, innocent calls. When they gather to migrate, the French slaughter them in their tens of thousands. At this time of year the doves have already mated and seem to have taken on

34

a domestic frame of mind. She has some seed which she scatters on the grass just beyond the terrace and they land softly and diffidently to feed. Sparrows appear, chipper little Edith Piafs, and dart about to pick up the smaller seeds.

In the distance she sees Harry approaching, hat jauntily in place, with Antoine some way behind carrying the tray. Out on the bay, just past the Eden Roc, a slim speedboat, which the French call a *cigare*, slices up the blue-white surface of the sea, leaving a record of its passing, a cicatrice on the water for many minutes. It's a mystery. Some moments after the boat has disappeared around the rocky point which marks the end of the villa's five acres of garden, the horrible clattering roar of the overpowered engine makes land.

Harry sits down and hands her his stick. He looks out to sea happily as Antoine lays out some fruit, expertly sliced, a pot of coffee and some pastries.

'Pwidge,' says Harry.

'Porridge,' Estelle explains.

Antoine goes off to prepare the large oats they order specially for him from Nice.

'Julian's on his way, Sir Harry.'

'Julian?'

'Yes, he's coming.'

'Julian?'

'Yes, Julian. He has some business to discuss with you.'

'Sailing?'

'No, I don't think he's got time. He wants your advice. He relies on you.'

'Nice boy. Jolly nice boy.'

It comes out as, 'Nighboyjuhuhuhullynighboy.'

But she knows.

He doesn't ask after Fleur. He hasn't spoken her name for weeks. She has phoned to postpone her visit again and now hopes to come at Easter with a few friends who will stay in the guest cottage down by the boathouse. Harry watches the doves, moving about in a stately pigeon gavotte. Gradually they return to the trees and resume their gentle but insistent love songs. Estelle brushes crumbs from Harry's mouth, which she thinks is unusually pink. She isn't sure if this is a good sign. His consultant is coming down from Queen's Square in just over a week to carry out some tests.

Antoine arrives with the porridge. Harry likes warm milk with porridge and she feels the jug to be sure. She pours the milk on to the jumbo oats. Harry shows no interest. He's gazing, rapt, out to sea. She looks to see if anyone is watching and then she feeds him. Without taking his eyes off the sea he eats the porridge, opening his mouth like a fledgling when he's ready for more. From the direction of Port de la Salis a flotilla of small dinghies appears. It's the first time this season that she has seen the sailing school out. Harry points. It's as if he was expecting them.

'Dinghies,' she says.

'Ding-hees,' he repeats, his voice very thin and distorted, like a wartime radio broadcast.

She has to accept that his speech is becoming harder for others to understand, despite the therapy. But as he becomes more isolated, he also becomes more cheerful. Now he's waving happily in the direction of the dinghies, which are moving quite quickly on a flat sea. Here on the headland, sheltered by the garden, they feel no wind. She has cut a few oleander flowers and three small roses and she holds them up for his approval. He chooses a pale, faintly green rose, which she sticks through his buttonhole and fastens with a pin. It looks just right with the jacket. He is unerring in his taste.

He doesn't want to write letters today. She goes into the house to make sure the driver knows what he is supposed to be doing and to be sure that the lunch menu is working as planned. Once she wrote acerbic memos to bank CEOs and dealt with begging letters from cabinet ministers; now she is a housekeeper. A carer. She hates the word. She stations the day nurse, Sylvie, in the garden, not too near to annoy but close enough to keep an eye out, and returns to her little house and her catalogue of paintings. Picasso once lived in Antibes and left the commune many paintings and drawings, but Harry has never been to the museum. He detests Picasso; daubs compared with

Matisse and Cézanne. Some of his pictures are on loan and she has made it her business to remind the museums that they must all be returned. Her database of his pictures and their locations, as well as their provenance, place of purchase, and the cost price, is almost complete. The collection, before the slump, was worth $150m. on paper and probably a lot more in reality. He hasn't mentioned them in his will and she guesses that this is one of the things Julian wants to discuss. Of course both the boys and Fleur will want to know where the pictures are going. The problem is that Harry left it too late to decide, but Estelle will interpret. Estelle is willing. She replies to an email from the head of the Kunstmuseum, Köln, refusing permission to extend a loan.

Later after she has spoken to Chef – he is preparing Charenton melon, a salad of crayfish, noisettes of Provençal lamb, followed by a sorbet or clafoutis – and she is reassured that everything is on schedule, she walks out to the garden. Out to sea, *Niobe* is anchored now. She is a wonderful boat, white-hulled, and a hundred and five feet long, three-masted with two immense Rolls-Royce engines fitted in 1929. Harry has sent for binoculars and is examining her. Estelle hasn't told him that Julian has a Russian buyer for the boat. This may be its last outing. She was commissioned by the second Baronet, Sir Isaiah Tubal, in 1899. Julian wants to make sure that the boatyard has done the work as ordered. The agreed price is $8m., down from $10m. She discovered this from Bryce, the skipper. She tells Harry that Julian is on his way from the airport and that lunch will be ready at one o'clock. Harry has always liked lunch at one, precisely, served in the summer dining room, which was originally the *orangerie*. Once it was full of grapefruit, satsumas, navel oranges, La Valette limes, mandarins and clementines, but now a few glossy lemon trees in elaborate pots do little more than nod to the past. It's a lovely room, which looks down over three terraces to the sea. She tells the day nurse to take Sir Harry to his room for a short nap, and reminds her to make sure that he is dry before he comes to lunch.

The chauffeur phones to say they are a few minutes away and she goes to the flagged hallway at the front of the villa, and stands in the little loggia after telling security to open the front gates. The car arrives, scrunching the freshly raked gravel.

Julian is wearing jeans and a linen jacket. In his hand he has a gift for her. It's wrapped with that incredible care – almost art – with that skill the Continentals bring to small everyday tasks. He's a very good-looking boy, but not by his mere presence as assertive as Harry. He kisses her on both cheeks.

'Estelle, wonderful, wonderful to see you. How's Dad?'

'He's happy, I think, although his speech is still not good.'

'But you understand him?'

His boyish, although drained, face is cocked slightly, as if eagerly awaiting good news.

'I like to think so. How are the children and Mrs Trevelyan-Tubal?'

'The kids are fine. But for some reason I worry about them all the time. Anyway, Kim is fine too. She's got a new project.'

Estelle doesn't ask what this is because he makes it sound like a stay of execution. A lot of busy men want their wives to keep themselves amused, she's observed. It's as if wives are by their very nature inclined to be a negative force, a dead weight.

'Lunch will be ready when you want it, Julian. Do you need me there?'

'Of course. What a silly question. I also want to run out to the boat quickly before lunch to see if the work's been done properly. Can you ask someone to get a dinghy ready?'

'It's ready. Bryce is standing by.'

'You never miss a trick: the queen of Bread Street. Will you come back? I need you.'

'You don't need an old bat like me hanging about. You are in your own bedroom and the luggage has gone up. And thanks so much for the present.'

'You are an angel. My God, I love it here; every time I come, I am reminded of just how much I love it. The moment I step off the plane I get that scent immediately. It's astonishingly powerful. Irrational. I think of it as the scent of childhood. OK, I'll go down to the boat and be back in forty-five minutes. Stel, I always look forward to seeing you, it's always a huge joy. Where's Dad by the way?'

'He's just getting ready for lunch.'

'OK. Stel, I know what you have done for him and I appreciate it from the bottom of my heart. We could never have coped without you. But then you know that.'

He is becoming just a little grey at the sides. And he also seems to be assuming his father's immense charm now, as if the supply has been bequeathed to him and he's come into the legacy early. He was a shy boy. When he took over, the financial papers talked of the baton passing. One commentator spoke of the poisoned chalice; the bank was not so much a family bank as a fading bank, he wrote. Julian saw that standing still – his father's preference – was eventually going to lead to disaster. She opens the present, a lovely Mont Blanc fountain pen, bought in Liechtenstein.

Julian rows, although there's a twenty-h.p. outboard. He needs the exercise. Every rock in the cove, every little stretch of coarse sand, every precariously perched pine tree is known to him. As a child you explore topography at a very basic and personal level, and the places where you have been happy become embedded for ever in your consciousness. Near the water there's a faux-rustic summer house with a tiled roof; when his mother was still alive it was used for teas and sometimes suppers as the sun was setting. He still thinks of it as the building in Valéry's poem: '*Ce toit tranquille, où marchent des colombes/entre les pins . . .*' absurdly translated by C. Day-Lewis, father of Daniel, as 'This quiet roof, where dove-sails saunter by, between the pines'. Pigeons don't saunter, for starters.

This happiness recollected is my true inheritance.

As he reaches the boat, Bryce calls down to him, 'Welcome aboard, Boss.'

'She looks wonderful. Great job, Bryce.'

He climbs up the steps, his nose practically pressed to the newly gleaming hull. A sail has been rigged over the wheel deck and a table laid with drinks.

'Wanna go for a ride, Boss?'

'Yup. Once round the bay. How are the engines?'

'Bonzer. And as quiet as a vibrator in a nunnery.'

Being Australian licenses Bryce to make these remarks. He starts the engines. There's a deep, brief shudder as they come to life and settle into a contented and powerful throbbing.

'Beautiful, beautiful,' says Julian, and he is genuinely moved.

'Cast off,' Bryce calls, and they leave the mooring slowly.

These engines don't roar so much as sing – a deep, male-voice chorale.

'You wanna see what the old girl can do, don't you, Boss?'

'I do, Bryce.'

Julian takes the wheel.

'Let's give it some welly.'

He envies Bryce; it's not just that his life is uncomplicated, but that he seems perfectly happy at all times: he loves boats, he loves barbies, he loves drinking, he loves wearing shorts, he loves girls and he loves sport. He's even the *pétanque* champion down at the port. It doesn't cause him any anxiety that he knows nothing about art and books and finance. If he has a philosophy, it is that we live for the day. *Vivre pour vivre*. And me, what am I doing? I'm living for an ideal of what this family apparently stands for. But I don't actually know what that ideal is.

The boat cuts through the water effortlessly. *Like shit off a shovel*, as Bryce so elegantly phrases it. Julian wonders when he should tell Bryce that the boat is almost definitely sold to the Russian oligarch, the same one who has just upset the locals by buying the Villa Floriana for €120m.

Estelle senses as she fusses around the villa in the welcome bustle that she has become a little depressed here alone with Harry. There's something vindictive about a stroke; it robs the victim of humanity, but it also takes it out on those closest to him. She wants to believe that deep down Harry is the same person, but when she wakes in the middle of the night she wonders, despite herself, if he hasn't turned into someone entirely different, a form of life that looks more or less like its former self, but in fact has the instincts and the coldness and the mean horizons of something very primitive. *Fleur, of course, is delighted that I have taken on the burden of looking after her husband.*

When the boat comes back, there's a bit of a stir as if a barque had made land on the coast of Illyria. The servants are animated, there are flowers in all the rooms, the air itself is lively; the song of the turtle doves enters the house modestly through the open French windows. As she walks along the corridor to the library, where Harry now sleeps, she sees out of the tall windows Julian and Bryce walking through the pines towards the house. Two boys happy together. Harry is sitting on his bed as if waiting for a train.

'Lunch is ready, Sir Harry, and Julian is back.'

'Where he been?'

'He's been in the boat, testing the engines, I think.'

'Sailing?'

He struggles with the word.

'No, I don't think so. Just a spin around the bay, Bryce said.'

He needs a little help standing up, but once he's up he starts to walk purposefully, although insecurely, like a man on an icy road. She has a feeling that he is going to crash down at any minute. His legs are so thin, she sees, her heart breaking, as if she's only just noticed.

Julian is waiting for his father. He looks a little tousled, reddened and boyishly happy.

'Hello, Dad. You look great.'

'Hello, my boy.'

The sound must be shocking to Julian. He looks at Estelle for a moment, then takes his father by the lower arm to steady him and leads him to a banquette where they sit, side by side. Bryce is now ferrying the drinks over. It's part of his good-bloke persona: affable, helpful and deeply competent.

'Jeez, Estelle, I'm as dry as a nun's nasty. What can I get you?'

'Bryce, what kind of language is that?'

'Strine. We're total barbarians. Now this one is for Sir Harry. What would you like?'

But before she can decide, she sees Julian beckoning to her.

'I need you. I really can't understand what he's saying. Is he getting worse?'

'I think maybe he is.'

'Look, I have to get him to sign a power of attorney. A Lasting Power of Attorney, as it's called. There are all sorts of things that for some reason need his say-so. The papers are ready. Will you witness after lunch? I am afraid you have to testify that he has signed of his own free will. If he's gone past that point, we have to get a doctor to sign. But you do understand him, don't you?'

'Yes. I do. Yes.'

'Good. Somebody, not family, has to witness, somebody who has known him for at least two years.'

'Of course. I understand.'

'We can't really wait. There's turmoil and madness out there.'

She wonders exactly what he means. Now Harry is speaking; he looks agitated and defenceless. Estelle feels the deadening sadness seeping into her, like damp on a wall. His mouth is forming words, but they come out as though he were speaking to parrots in their own language – harsh, peremptory little screeches, which have become separated from their parent consonants.

'He is upset. He says you haven't answered his letters.'

When she and Harry are alone together his decline is not so obvious.

'OK, Dad, don't fret. We'll have lunch and talk later.'

He puts his hand on his father's shoulder. His father's lips are speaking silently, but not even Estelle can interpret.

'Dad, thank you so much for your letters. Particularly about caring for our customers. I have sent a memo out to all the staff, quoting you.'

He has, but it's part of a hasty restatement of so-called core values.

Harry utters some words.

'He says you don't read his letters.'

'I value his letters enormously. Dad, I really do.'

He and Estelle help his father up and he totters to his usual place at the head of the table. The seaward side of his face has a deep colour, flaring alarmingly.

'Estelle,' Julian says when his father is safely seated. 'I know you love him and I also know that you are freely interpreting his ramblings for me, and oddly enough I appreciate it. But I can't write back every day, or even read them all. It's hopeless. Will you just email me a few notes telling me how he is and so on? You know, what's on his mind? Give me a digest.'

Even as he says this he wonders if there is anything on his father's mind; perhaps his mind is just sifting aimlessly through the remaining, dwindling stocks of memory. Mostly he looks cheerful but now Julian thinks he detects a deep fear of what's to come. But then who knows if futurity is a concept he can understand?

'I will send you a few notes,' says Estelle. 'He is deteriorating. It's only when I see him with you that I see it clearly. It's not good. I wanted to ask you, can we get the consultant down here more quickly?'

'Absolutely. Email my office and tell them I want Mr Abbott down here as soon as possible, if you think it's necessary.'

They sit around the old patriarch, drawn and repulsed in equal measure. Bryce talks about the boat, in the hopes of interesting him, but his eyes are fixed on the windows. His face has a kind of haughtiness which Julian recognises, the higher boredom of the rich and privileged.

After lunch with a little help from Estelle, Sir Harry Trevelyan-Tubal, Bt. signs the trust deeds and the Lasting Power of Attorney. Julian asks Estelle to put them somewhere safe until he leaves.

In his room that afternoon Julian – short on sleep – lies down and he dreams he is riding his pony. The pony is speaking to him, but he can't make out what she is saying. Maybe the pony has taken her cue from his father.

5

WHEN SHE WAS very young, Fleur believed that she liked older men. She liked the fact that they were besotted with her youth – her girlishness – and she knew that as a result there was very little risk of being deserted. Both her husbands offered something she needed at the time, although she rejects the demeaning idea that women are pathologically needy. Nor was it, as some have suggested, because her father left them when she was twelve. She wanted to break out of suburbia and the stifling intensity of her mother's ambition for her. It was, of course, wholly vicarious. With Artair she was attracted by his access to the theatre and with Harry it was the prospect of a more civilised and elegant world. The money was not the thing itself. She long ago realised that everyone has in the mind an ideal world which they think is their due. At the Shirley Simms Stage School there was a lot of talk about living the dream.

At first she was drawn to theatre with its fading rehearsal rooms and chummy dilapidation and she loved actors. They were heroic, an alien tribe, *i zingari*, living among the host nation. What they were doing was alchemy, able to create with a few tattered curtains and poorly painted flats a world which was more real and maybe more significant than the one surrounding them. Actors could be drinking cheap whisky or warm beer in the dingiest theatre bar in Manchester, but they hoarded the knowledge that for a few hours each day they were absolute masters of a universe they had created. Sadly, the truth emerged that she wasn't much of an actress. She could be earnest, dance competently, sing a little, and she could be tragic; above all she could be passionate, but somehow she couldn't connect with the audience. They just didn't believe her, however hard she tried. In fact the harder she tried, the less believable she became. When Harry came along he was certain that money and promotion could turn her into a star, but he was wrong. When she married him and gave up acting she felt a great relief.

She is waiting at the gym in Kensington for a South African called Morné. He was until recently a professional rugby player with Saracens, but a serious skull fracture means that he is now a personal trainer, at least until he passes his coaching exams. She is in love with his body, although his mind is a mystery. It may be a mystery in the sense that there are depths she hasn't yet plumbed, but she is not sure. He has theories, about motivation and the techniques required to succeed in life, involving focus, but she doesn't understand them. He seems to like her but she can't be sure of that either. He may be earth-bound, but his body is sublime. She's devoted to it, an acolyte. Morné is tall and muscular and planed. His arms and legs seem to be made up of bundles of fibres. She wonders now why she favoured older men with their dewlaps and saggy scrotums and heavy eyelids and the hairs sprouting from their ears and nose. She understands that she is now receiving what her husbands had received when she was young: a transfusion of youth, a recognised therapy like sheep-foetus and human-placenta injections, something that old, rich people have always been able to buy in discreet clinics. She is only forty-three and she knows that Morné thinks she is well preserved – *in great shape* – but well preserved is not the same as young. When they make love in the small room where the yoga mats and the ladies' hand weights and the boxing gloves are stored, she finds herself in a delirium under-mined by anxiety because Morné is almost sixteen years younger than she is and almost certainly has other women closer to his own age. He understands the proprieties and never asks questions and never volunteers personal information although he is quite big on popular psychology. His voice is deep and measured – a lot older than his body – and he sounds as if he is talking in a cave. He goes about sex in a maddeningly efficient way, as if it's an extension of the workout and he is on a schedule. They are able to embrace afterwards on a mat for a few sweaty minutes before he looks at his cheap watch. She bought him a present, an antique Rolex Prince from Burlington Arcade.

'Thanks, Fleur. It's beautiful, but I don't want you to think we are having sex for some purpose. Ja, no, that would be wrong, and I don't think you could handle it. I promise you I am not looking for anything. If you accept that, I will keep the watch, otherwise I must give it back now.'

'No, please, I want you to have it.'

Somehow he put her in the position of the grateful one, grateful that he should have accepted a £10,000 watch. Now he's a little late and, like a schoolgirl on a date, she fears he may not be coming. She does some stretching; Morné is a great believer in stretching.

'Howzit, Fleur. Sorry I'm late. The bus ran over an old doll and we all had to get off. I ran from Elephant and Castle. OK, today I think we should work a little on your butt. In a nice way.'

'Yes please. In a very nice way.'

God, she sounds pathetic.

He puts on some music and shows her what he wants her to do.

'This is the number one exercise for firming the glutes.'

'Do I need it?'

'Everyone needs it.'

His glutes are like iron.

'You don't.'

'Ja, maybe, but I am in the gym all day. No problem. OK, let's go. Take this barbell and squat, thighs parallel to the ground. That's it. Now hold that, lift one leg in front of you, ja, just like that, back straight. Feel those glutes.'

She's keen to please. In this world all muscles have a distinct personality and they are all diminutives: abs, pecs, glutes, but she's moved some way beyond irony. She wishes she could talk to a friend about Morné.

'You live in South London?'

'Ja, in Brixton. It makes me feel at home. OK, now work it – one, two, three, four and five. Now the other leg.'

How little she knows about him and how she longs to know more. Also he shows no interest in her life outside the gym. It's perfectly acceptable to be seen with her in the Starbucks in Kensington High Street, but that's the limit of their joint range. She wants to take him away somewhere, but she sees that there is no hope of that. Rugby has given him an elemental, old-fashioned philosophy, a sort of sporting Ten Commandments. He's planning to go back to South Africa and buy a place in the country and coach African children. Coaching sounds like secular missionary work: whitey still in charge. She doesn't say this, because he is holding all the cards in this game. If it is a game. So many of her girlfriends have said that they entered affairs knowing from the start they were doomed. Avril left her husband for a drunken painter. She said she knew it was a train crash waiting to happen. In the family court the judge handed her husband custody of the children. He accepted that they wanted to stay with their father.

Back home, glowing, she is standing in Harry's library. He collected books avidly, through a network of agents. He specialised in rare travel and exploration books and maps, with a sideline in natural history. His last great purchase before the stroke was a first edition of Darwin's *On the Origin of Species*, still in its original green cover. He had always wanted one. (Bibliophiles have little fetishes.) She had come to see that books for Harry were not so much for reading as to compliment him. These rare and beautiful books were artefacts which demonstrated his taste. Easy to do if you've got millions, of course, but still he had a kind of unerring judgement so that he was equally at one with the Sotheran catalogue and his tailor's swatches. He lived – she's already using the past tense – fully in this world. Julian has never been completely at ease in it. And his brother, Simon, turned his back on it completely although he is really just a dropout with a trust fund and a network of contacts around the world to smooth his way as he seeks his true self in constant travel, usually to places which eccentric gentleman travellers have endowed with a kind of cachet by passing through. Simon was once stuck in a hole in a tomb made by grave robbers in the Kidron Valley near Jerusalem. He shouldn't have been climbing over the tomb in the first place, and the Israeli police were harsh with him after they had pulled him out, until a second secretary from the embassy was able to spring him by telling the police that his family owned a bank and one of his predecessors had endowed a settlement just outside the Old City. It became Simon's favourite anecdote, frequently repeated. These privileged boys are never quite able to escape the ties of silk that bind them.

Harry. Poor Harry. Estelle emails her with accounts of his progress. She loves him. *She loves him more than I do. So much so that she imagines he can speak.* After the stroke Fleur tried to look after him, but she found it very difficult. The essence of Harry had gone. Harry looked like his old self, but he had become another person. Angry, supercilious and impatient. He seemed to hate her and she couldn't bear that. His voice, insofar as she could understand it at all, belonged to someone else who was inhabiting his body. She finds it deeply disturbing and frightening even now. She hated trying to feed him. Estelle doesn't mind feeding him. She seems to think it is her job rather than the nurses' to wipe his face, as if he notices or appreciates this intimacy. Maybe Estelle has always longed to touch him, and now she is licensed to handle him the way a French housewife handles fruits in the market. After Easter she will go to see him. He's deteriorating. She wonders what life without him will be. She walks down the length of the library, built on the other side of the garden in what was the stable block. She hasn't been in here for months. All these books, all these unread books, full of useless knowledge, written by know-alls, busybodies, self-important pedants.

At stage school the official philosophy, the mission statement, was *Live the dream*, which was believed to take care of the whole range of human aspiration. *Live the dream.* She's not equipped for life as a forty-three-year-old widow who is having sex with her personal trainer. She runs her hand over the skin of the books. The covers are dimpled or as smooth as marble or as textured as cowhide or as soft as chamois leather. Harry said he liked the smell and feel and the bindings of books. She picks one out and opens it – it's a series of botanical plates, the flowering trees of Australasia. She puts her face in it and inhales, hoping to capture some lost essence of Harry. What she smells is a deep, endless and impenetrable tedium. She scents the grave. And in this way, she is truly capturing the essence of Harry: nullity.

Panicky, she rings Kimberly.

'Hiya.'

'Hi, Kim, can we have supper? I know Jules is away somewhere?'

'Antibes. Seeing the old guy. Sure, I would love to do supper. You want to come to our place and we go out after?'

'That would be good. Can you book somewhere?'

'Sure. How areya, honey? It will be great to seeya.'

Kimberly speaks in that way young American women have, perky and direct, as though the world is new and exciting. London hasn't got her down one bit in eight years.

'I'm fine, Kim. I worry a lot, but who doesn't?'

'Any sign of improvement in Harry?'

She says *improve-mint*.

'Who knows? I haven't seen him for six weeks. I can't bear to see him suffer.'

'Jules will let us know. He usually calls about six. Come over and let's hang out.'

'I'll be round, what, 7.30?'

'Whatever. It will just be so fun to see you.'

It is true that she can't bear to see Harry. She finds that there is something creepy about him now; that voice which comes from within his head rather than from his mouth seems to her threatening, as though an impostor, a fraud, has stolen his identity. When she's with him he looks confused, as though he doesn't really know who she is. Once in his bedroom downstairs, equipped with frames and a commode and gloomily scented by his many medicines, she came to see him and he was sitting with his pyjamas open. His penis was semi-erect. What memories had reached him when he saw her? Maybe he exposes himself to Estelle.

I want to lose this awful fear. I'm longing for him to die.

Estelle says that Harry is quite happy. Estelle alone has cracked the code and understands his every encrypted word. To Fleur his words sound as if they have made a few detours and bounced off the inside of his skull before shambling out of his mouth. She thinks of Quasimodo in the Disney version of *The Hunchback of Notre-Dame*. Was Quasimodo living the dream? Did he dare to dream? She remembers the songs, especially 'Heaven's Light'. In musicals everyone is living the dream like mad.

She calls to speak to Amanda Stapleton, but she gets the organ grinder's monkey. He says that Amanda could make time to see her tomorrow after three.

'Fine. I get back from the gym about three on a Thursday, could she come at four?'

'Just let me look at her diary. Yes, that will be fine, Lady Trevelyan-Tubal.'

Of course it will. The conversation will earn them £650 an hour, plus disbursements. She's amused by the way that, in the higher reaches of the law, the business of money is swaddled to keep out the light. Actually hourly rates have dropped recently in City law firms. She sometimes wonders, although she never says it, what powers this whole merry-go-round. Who is actually creating the money? You don't see many horny-handed sons of the soil around Chelsea. The bank itself sits in the middle of its own magic circle of money – staid, reassuring, and very, very rich. It pulses benignly, broadcasting goodwill outwards to its clients. On the family it seems to exercise a soothing effect. She thinks of the Hindu temple she visited in Mumbai with its scented inner sanctum, the *garbhagriha*, where the deities are housed and the priests – surprisingly chubby – flap gently about like diligent housewives, giving off a kind of age-old assurance. She toyed with the idea of taking up Hinduism, just because of this serenity. The bank has the same narcotic-spiritual effect.

She gives up on the books. The scent of books, certainly of old books, is a myth, a self-serving myth, a kind of conceit, if that is the word: *I love the smell of books; they are so evocative of childhood,* they say. She remembers most vividly not the smell of books but of ballet shoes and chalk and the aroma of the dressing-up cupboard and stage make-up and the distant piano notes of 'Für Elise'. These things all have a direct contact with flesh-and-blood human beings. But she has seen that Harry's generation, from the very rarefied altitudes, are afraid of real human contact. For them it is all form and style and front. How did this happen?

It's odd this friendship with Kimberly. Fleur is married to Kimberly's father-in-law, and she is Kimberly's stepmother-in-law. And yet they are less than six years apart. Kimberly has hinted to her that Julian is not as 'attentive' to her as he was before he took over as chairman, and of course she takes this to mean that she is not getting as much sex as she would like. Funny word, 'attentive'. Americans, counter-intuitive as this may be, are often more decorous than most English people. The English have lost faith in the idea of absolute standards.

As she is getting ready to go round to Kimberly's, Morné texts her. *wld u like to come rugby satday?*

Rugby? Why would he ask her to rugby? She tries to deconstruct his text. Rugby is what he loves most in the whole world. And he is asking her to share it with him. She feels that it must mean that in his eyes she is attractive or he wouldn't be taking her to meet his friends. His rugger chums. She has moved beyond well preserved. She feels wildly happy.

luv 2. see u @ gym.lol

Kimberly likes a dry Martini and she prepares one for each of them. Compared with Mulgrave House, Kimberly's house in Notting Hill is modest, even spare. Mulgrave, impeccable in every way, is huge, and, with amounts of pictures, classical artefacts, tapestries and books, looks less like a house than a museum. Here, backing on to Ladbroke Square, all is light and airy and contemporary. Kimberly and Julian collect modern pictures and modern furniture. Kimberly has two huge canvases by Andrew Wyeth in the living room. One is of a lighthouse and one of a barn in the snow. She sips her Martini, which has an extraterrestrial glow.

'God, Kim, that's strong.'

'You know what Homer Simpson said about the barman: "He knows just how I like my Martinis, full of alcohol." By the way you look great and so-oh happy.'

'It's the alcohol. In a few moments I'll be singing.'

'Oh hell, no, we better go. One for the road?'

'Why not?'

A little drunk they enter the restaurant conspiratorially as if they know something amusing not revealed to anyone else. They sit down at a low black table. Kimberly's skirt is halfway up her thighs. She has great thighs because she comes from the sporting New England clan of the Fitzhughs, related in some way to the Kennedys. They all look fantastically, aggressively healthy, until they die young. Her face is not exactly beautiful, but it is engaging, with memorable, strong tomboy features, and an Irish broadness between the eyes and the cheeks, which must have been a Darwinian thing, an adaptation to the coastal winds off the Irish Sea. At the same time, Kim is unmistakably American. How is it that from a huge, polyglot nation you can almost always pick out an American face in Europe? Kim makes her feel a little limp and flabby, but then Morné is working on that problem. Her glutes, apparently located right in the middle of each lobe of the bottom, are hurting. Fusion food, ordered by Kim, arrives on black plates – little parcels of this and that accompanied by very thin slivers of Oriental vegetables or perhaps fruit, and emblematic parts of tasty creatures – a crab, a sea urchin, a lobster, a pigeon – decorate each plate. It looks like an elegant cemetery of tiny animals.

Kimberly is talking to some young man she knows, who has sidled up in that tousled, oh-gosh-what-a-surprise-to-see-you way, Chelsea boots (back in fashion), jeans turned up, striped shirt and a jacket. These chaps always wear a shirt and a jacket in restaurants. T-shirts are for the underclass or for children.

'Fleur, meet Sebastian, a friend of Julian's – and mine, of course. Sebastian, meet Fleur, my mother-in-law.'

'Mother-in-law? I wish I had a mother-in-law like you.'

'I think it's kinda cool to have such a lovely mother-in-law,' says Kim.

'I'll just have a drink until my date arrives,' says Sebastian, sitting hunched on a small round stool with no back. He looks like the sort of chap who would prefer to drape himself on a chair.

'What do you do, Sebastian?'

'I'm unemployed. I was working for a hedge fund, but sadly it was heavily invested with Madoff's Ascot.'

'Oh dear. Was that your idea?'

'Luckily, no. Can we talk about something else? So you must be married to Sir H.? How is he?'

'He is recuperating at the villa in Antibes. He's making slow but steady progress.'

'Old school. Of the best sort, of course. Pity we weren't listening. The markets have no fucking logic.'

More drinks arrive. Sebastian, she sees, is a drinker. He has that slightly bemused-spaniel look around the eyes. But then, who's throwing stones? She and Kimberly are now both pretty much smashed. The evening is beginning to collapse into a sociable sink and she feels that anything is possible. When she goes out with Harry there is a bubble of artificiality around them, a brittleness. People treat them with too much respect. In his charming way, Harry likes deference: it means that only he can dominate a conversation. Kimberly is talking to Sebastian now, who is, after all, eating the small, exquisite but alien offerings. She guesses he would rather be chowing down on spaghetti Bolognese, certainly something less stylishly pointless. The restaurant is now packed; people are even waiting outside. They are briefly revealed in the blue silken Notting Hill evening as the door opens. She hasn't stood in line for anything for years.

'His wife left him. Kinda sad,' says Kimberly as Sebastian gets up to pilot his date from the door through the throng. 'Julian says he's a loser. Can't close a deal. Still, good-looking loser, don't you think?'

'Yeah, I suppose so. I'm not really in the market.'

'Come on. Of course you are. Life's one big market. This, coming towards us with Sebastian, is an old girlfriend called Samantha. Her husband went off with a Thai ladyboy just after Christmas.'

'You're joking, I hope.'

'No, I'm not. These Englishmen are as weird as snakes. So, so weird. They have a whole lot going on we will never understand, believe me.'

'OK, I'll take your word for it.'

'Samantha, hi, this is my mother-in-law, Fleur.'

'Oh Jesus, Kim, I wish you would stop saying that. Hello, Samantha.'

Samantha looks puzzled and muted. Perhaps she is depressed by her husband's defection with a ladyboy, as she has every reason to be.

They all squeeze up together. They order more delicate parcels and neatly dissected crustaceans. Fleur is warmly happy: she has a secret that she can't share; it gives the evening a special subtext. She can feel it in her body, even in her glutes: sensuality – sexuality – has taken possession of her.

Later she thinks of Harry lying in that hangar of a bedroom, fluting and groaning and back-diving into his past, in a welter of misdirected and aimless thoughts. She feels ashamed. Tomorrow she will ask Amanda where she stands if Harry dies.

What Kimberly says is true: English men are very weird. In Fleur's experience, starting with the teachers at the Shirley Simms Stage School (same initials as the SS, only longer), all men have a sexual hinterland that is more real to them than the place they are living. Her own father had lived fairly placidly amongst them for fourteen years, before it turned out he was gay and a vigorous cottager. His night shifts at the *Mirror*, subbing away on the sports pages for Mr Maxwell, had merely been a part of his nocturnal activities. When somebody felt obliged to tell Fleur's mother, she was relieved; much later when Fleur was at drama school and as a result was presumably in close contact with homosexuals, her mother told her the whole story: she knew something was wrong. *This isn't a judgement on gay people*, she said, *just an observation. He was always kind, but I felt I never knew him, as if I was living with a member of another species. Don't get me wrong, I am not saying I have any prejudice against them, just that it seemed to me he had other priorities, so it was a huge burden from my shoulders to discover that it wasn't because of me. And only then – silly me – I understood why he chose to be on nights four times a week.*

Fleur hasn't seen him for ten years and the last time was by chance in Bond Street, where he was arm in arm with a younger man in an Adidas tracksuit. Her father was in a large overcoat, with broad lapels of some cheap pale fur. The companion, who looked as if he might have been a Palestinian, was quite possibly the only person to have been seen wearing a tracksuit in Bond Street for decades. For a moment they nearly spoke; but they passed silently, both accepting that, apart from some genes, they were now totally unrelated. She had been reinvented as a society wife, and he as an old queen in a panto-mime coat.

For some reason Sebastian's hand is resting on her thigh. She looks at him briefly. He seems to need reassurance; Samantha is staring fixedly at someone on a nearby table. Fleur squeezes his hand and places it gently on his own thigh. Perhaps he's too drunk to realise where it came to rest.

6

AT EXETER UNIVERSITY Melissa Tregarthen studied philosophy and sociology. When she signed up she thought that it would be an intellectual walking tour of the human psyche. The prospectus promised Hobbes to Wollstonecraft. Mary Wollstonecraft was something of a hero for her at Queen Eleanor's School in Truro, but it seemed that none of the philosophy tutors, apart from Amethyst Dane, had ever read her or even thought of her as a philosopher. Amethyst Dane was a feminist and she loved Dorothy Wordsworth, who was the true genius in the brother–sister relationship and had sacrificed herself because of her love for her less talented brother. The other tutors mainly liked people who were interested in the dialectic or Greek and Roman ethics or the social contract. Mary Wollstonecraft, said Lancelot Pease, Roman philosophy, was only in the prospectus to snare the credulous; all young women, he said, pass through a stage when they imagine they could be heroic feminists. Melissa read the *Grasmere Journals* closely, under Ms Dane's direction.

Now Melissa's editor at the *Cornish Globe and Mail* has asked her in to see him. She's only been working here six months and has graduated from court reporting (*Two Truro youths guilty of joyriding in Newquay*) to arts and leisure (*Lifesaver Festival launches all-new surf boat*). The editor likes her. He's a rumpled fellow, who once worked – it is rumoured – in Fleet Street but suffered a breakdown. He couldn't wait to come back to Cornwall, where you could take a lungful of air which had travelled undisturbed from Nova Scotia, rather than one which had passed through the lungs of twenty wheezing cockneys on its way to yours. The newspaper is housed in a seedy but grand Edwardian building on four floors at the end of the High Street, just before the junction where the street loses heart and gives way to the mean suburbs of bungalows with slate roofs. She was brought up in one of these. The old printing presses, long silent, are still there in the basement of Twelvetrees House. Melissa's family home has a sloping fireplace of slate, with a hole next to the fireplace for stacking wood. Her parents think it is the last word in modernity.

The editor's name is Edward Tredizzick, a proper Cornish name, like hers. The editorial floor is crudely divided into small open-plan work-stations, although the editor has a frosted-glass partition around his corner office; he doesn't like to see what's going on. Particularly now that the daily circulation has fallen to thirteen thousand. She knocks and he lets out a sort of exasperated moo on a falling note, which she knows means 'Come'.

He's smoking as usual, another reason for having himself boxed in.

'Melissa, come in.'

He doesn't look at her for a moment but continues to read the early edition of the *New York Times*. He has a very sixties hairstyle, with a low, solid grey fringe. Oddly it doesn't make him look young. His skin is deeply folded, probably the effect of smoking for fifty years. He has a growth on his top lip, which could have been prospering there undisturbed in the shadow of his nostrils for a very long time. It could be removed in about thirty seconds, she thinks, as her verrucas were in the Royal Infirmary. But Mr Tredizzick doesn't seem to care. Perhaps it's a point of honour with him to leave his face in the order which nature has decreed. Above his desk he has a sign which reads, *To search for an ultimate reason is emotionally understandable, but not intellectually coherent.* As a graduate of sociology and philosophy, the first time she saw it she felt duty bound to ask him where the quote had come from.

'I found it in a Christmas cracker,' he said.

He looks up.

'Now, Melissa, you have probably noticed that I think you have the makings of a very good journalist. The problem is that journalism, yes, even the *Cornish Globe and Mail*, founded 1862 by Sir Josaiah Twelvetrees, a great man who believed – wrongly, as we now know – that newspapers could hasten the spread of understanding, even the *Globe and Mail* is in steep decline. Revenues have fallen twelve per cent over the last year, thanks to our capitalist geniuses in the City of London. 'I have here a letter' – he moves the printout and scrabbles around – 'I have here a letter, a real letter, not an email, from the managing editor who has in turn received a letter from head office, declaring that we have to cut staff costs by fifteen per cent.'

'Oh no. You're going to sack me. I love it here, Mr Tredizzick.'

'I'm not going to sack you as such, Melissa, but you are going to have to go freelance, although I would be very disappointed if you were to work for anybody else. You won't be paid a salary, but you will be paid the top freelance rate for any piece we use. You may also want to blog. We have a plan to use blogs more and more and we will pay £60 for each one we use. I don't know how blogs work, but you can ask Gavin in IT.'

Melissa wonders how Mary Wollstonecraft would have taken this and what she would have said about the rights of women. But she sits silent, her eyes welling.

'Melissa, please. Don't cry. Newspapers have to discover how to make money again. You're young enough to blog and so on. You also have energy and curiosity. Unfortunately, as you get older, you tend to lose those. You're only twenty-two, aren't you? If anybody's equipped to survive this, it's you. What is happening to newspapers, particularly newspapers like this one that hope to be bought by somebody with deep pockets, is that they are cutting fixed costs. So we are going through the motions, but I am not intending to cut down the editorial content at all. In fact, I want you to go and see Cornwall's second greatest theatrical producer, Mr Artair MacCleod, about his thrilling new spring programme. I want a sparkling piece, informative but not PR, and I want to know why he's rolling out bloody *Thomas the bloody Tank Engine* for the third year in a row. He's supposed to feed the Cornish mind. If there is one. Don't cry. You can make it work. Ask him about the Arts Council, but not too much. Unbelievable though it may be, our readers don't give a monkey's about the Arts Council.'

Back at her desk she wonders how she is going to live. Sixty pounds a blog, if they buy it, and the miserable freelance payment, subject to approval, will never add up even to her modest salary. She's about to call Artair MacCleod, but then she wonders if this is a freelance job or if she is still on salary, at least to the end of the month. She emails the editor, and he assures her that she is on salary for a full four weeks.

'Think about your blog,' he writes, 'a young Cornish girl's take on our duchy. That sort of thing. You'll be brilliant.'

That sort of thing. She rings Artair MacCleod.

'Mr MacCleod, Melissa Tregarthen here from the *Globe*.'

'Ah, the old *Gobble a Male*. Your name sounds familiar.'

'Yes, we've met once. We talked about your *Wind in the Willows*. The editor would like me to interview you. Could we do that tomorrow?'

'What do you want to talk to me about?' he says, rather guardedly.

'Oh, your spring programme. Spring and summer, in fact.'

'I'm very busy at the moment on a major project involving Daniel Day-Lewis. How long will you need me?'

'About an hour. And then at some stage a photographer will need to take your picture. Can I give him your number?'

'Absolutely fine, as long as he isn't a budding Irving Penn.'

'No, I don't think he is. No surprise. But I would like to know about your Daniel Day-Lewis project.'

'It's hush-hush at the moment, my love. Anything I tell you will be off the record. Understood?'

'Oh, absolutely.'

'There's no reason why you should know, but the agents are always the problem. They are absolute bastards who love to throw their weight around. The reason is that so often in their miserable lives people have failed to return their calls. And so when they have a very big beast like Daniel on their books, they tend to get way too big for their boots. Luckily I have some experience with these wretched people. Like undertakers, necessary, but not clubbable. See you tomorrow, Melinda.'

She looks around unobtrusively. She wonders who else has been laid off. She doesn't know how to tell her parents. They were so pleased when she was given a six-month trainee contract after winning a competition. They are great believers in the theory that children should be allowed to develop their imagination rather than being measured solely by exams and tests. There may be something self-serving in this theory, as neither of them made it to college, but they are on the side of Blake and Rousseau: children are born with an innate goodness and infinite possibilities. In a way they are more childlike than she is, and she can't bear telling them that she's had the chop. Twelvetrees Media's head office, somewhere in London, has decreed it. She knows that advertising revenue has fallen, but surely it will pick up when the crunch is finally over. The Cornish are pretty tight at the best of times; still, even they will be forced to spend on something. She will blog. Yes, she will. It's the future. She'll become famous. But is anybody going to care what she thinks? She decides to write a diary, with a few video clips and interviews, as a start.

'I am a number,' she writes. 'I am a statistic. I am a sacrifice on the altar of the free market. I have no power, except the power of words.'

She spends the rest of the afternoon thinking of her nom de plume. Outside, the evening traffic is approaching its stately climax. It is no big deal, but the locals love to complain about it: it is caused almost entirely by rich outsiders – the grockles – who all have a second home, and by rich farmers in Land-Rovers, who receive enormous EU subsidies. If the letter pages are anything to go by, the traditional Cornishman (and woman) thrives on bitter envy. She considers 'Cornish Lass' but it sounds like a brand of ice cream and far too twee. 'I tell you that which you yourselves do know,' Shakespeare. It has the right idea, but is way too serious for a blog. The truth is nobody gives a rat's arse about Cornwall, except as a place for the impoverished young to surf and get stoned when it's raining, which it often is, or as a place where the oldies want to recapture a mythical time when as children they went around in flannel shorts and sun hats picking up shells or sea glass or diverting streams to make doomed lakes or having their toes pinched by crabs. Good, cheap, wholesome fun. She toys with the idea of calling herself 'CornishPasty.com', but actually she is a little too fat around the middle – many Cornish girls are – and the irony might be lost on her readers. They haven't yet reached modern, let alone postmodern. Then she suddenly decides to call her blog It's-all-out-there-somewhere.com. It's good. It's got a little bit of conspiracy; it's got a little hint of mystery. It's-all-out-there-somewhere.com from Melissa Tregarthen. She can see the typeface and a little byline picture of her, from above the waist.

Next morning she's driving over to the Camel in her mother's car. There is no time to catch the bus, which involves three changes and takes ninety minutes. Cars can only be charged to expenses on urgent news stories – *Lifeboat rescues windsurfer, Sewage escapes into the Tamar, Oldest woman in Cornwall celebrates a hundred and two years young, Sheep loose on A30 after lorry overturns* – but not on features and definitely not on arts, unless some wasted old star collapses on stage while singing 'Moon River'. As she drives she wonders how to tell her mother that she has lost her job. Her mother has an old-fashioned idea of the job market: start work, work hard, get promoted, gold watch, die. It's no good trying to explain to her the new realities, what the prescient Max Weber (sociology, module 3) described as the move to a value-neutral rational society. The new realities have taken some time to reach Cornwall: Weber wrote that in about 1870.

Her mother was making a pie for her father's tea. It involved an almost forgotten substance, suet, a sort of tallow, without which no pie is sufficiently life-threatening, and some cheap cuts of meat. As Melissa was leaving she looked up from rolling the pastry. Her last words were heart-breaking: 'You're your dad's golden girl, you know. He's so proud of you.'

She smiled benignly, her face floured, the pastry clinging to her fingers.

Oh Jesus. She's got no prospect of leaving home and she's going to have to tell them the truth very soon.

*   *   *

Mr MacCleod is wearing a very small straw hat, and his side-hair is gushing strongly from under the hat in ringlets. His head looks like a frozen waterfall and he seems to be a little drunk. He's wearing a very old pinstriped suit with a brown satin shirt underneath it, and sandals. The threads on his cheeks are more pronounced than when she saw him four or five months ago.

'You're a lovely girl,' he says. 'I like a bit of meat on a girl. What Joyce called an armful.'

'Oh thanks.'

The boathouse is chaotic. His assistant is on sick leave, he says. He indicates a broken-down sofa for her to sit. It's prickly with what may be horsehair. He drags a wooden chair from a scullery where the lifeboat men probably made their cocoa. As it passes over the granite floor, it scrapes like fingernails across a blackboard. The floor itself has deep incisions, probably the legacy of being used for launching boats. Outside the tide is full and lapping the old slipway greedily. Here boxes of papers, set designs, beer glasses and wedges of scripts, held together with treasury ties, lie around randomly.

'Righty-ho. How about a drink?'

'I'm driving.'

'Tea is over there. Or coffee.' He points towards the galley, stacked with paint cans. 'I don't have any Lavazza Crema e Aroma. But there's instant. I can't drink the stuff. I was spoilt by living in Rome for a few years, of course.'

He pours himself a glass of beer.

'Scuppered. Scuppered Ale. From Scilly. I'm trying it out.'

He makes it sound like a public service, as if the world is waiting for his judgement.

'Right,' Melissa says, taking out her notebook, 'do you mind if I record this interview as well?'

'No, no. Go ahead.'

She sets up the small digital camera and recorder.

'OK, the first question is about your spring programme.'

'What about it?'

'It's *Thomas the Tank Engine*, I know, followed by *The Wind in the Willows* at Easter, I believe.'

'Yes, it's *Thomas the* fucking *Tank Engine* time again. For the kiddies. For the little, obese, pig-faced kiddies of Cornwall.'

'What about adult theatre?' she says, changing tack.

'Find me an adult in the whole fucking county.'

'You sound a little down?'

'Down? Down? This whole enterprise is doomed: theatre, touring theatre, Cornish-language theatre, Celtic theatre – all doomed. The spivs in London and Wall Street and Frankfurt have lost hundreds of billions pissing into the wind and now I can't even get my grant. Yes, I am down. Are you surprised? I'm going to set myself alight in a dinghy and float out to sea on the tide. Do you love Wagner?'

'Wagner? No. I can't say I do.'

'Brünnhilde is immolated.'

'Are you married, Mr MacCleod?'

'Not at the minute. I have been, three times. Alas, it never quite worked out. But I loved Fleur, my second wife. I shouldn't have let her go.'

He takes another huge gulp of Scuppered, and looks out to sea through the salt crystals encrusting the windows. Birds are flying by fast and low. The water is lumpy and green.

'Why hasn't your grant come through?'

'I don't know, they haven't told me. My lawyers are trying to get to the bottom of it.'

'Arts Council, is it?'

'Who told you that? No, we do get a pittance from them, but I have been funded by a charitable trust, until now.'

'Will *Thomas the Tank Engine* go ahead?'

'Yes, Binster's Pies and Pasties have stepped in to finance the production for one season. Do you think, Melinda, that Johnny Gielgud was sponsored by Fray Bentos?'

'Probably not.'

'Do you think he had to preface each performance of *Richard III* with, "and a thank you to Fray Bentos, our proud sponsors"?'

'Probably not.'

'Probably not,' he says, mimicking her voice, not cruelly but accurately, catching her Cornish vowels.

'You mentioned Daniel Day-Lewis on the phone.'

'Yes, I did. He and I have a project. Now I just have to wait while the agents out in Hollywood have their pubes nicely shaped into a Brazilian so that they can read the proposal comfortably without an itching in the depths of their Y-fronts.'

'*Thomas the Tank Engine* is booked out in Truro, Mr MacCleod.'

'Oh, absolutely bloody marvellous, darling, what wonderful news,' he says in a fluting voice which she assumes is Johnny Gielgud's.

They laugh. He's cheering up. He pours himself a whisky. Although the students at Exeter drank a lot, they didn't do it in this way, which she thinks of as theatrical: a lonely man sitting in a bar, bottle of whisky on the counter, sympathetic barman polishing glasses in the background. Hooker walks in. Heart of gold. *Maybe he thinks I am the hooker in this scenario.*

'So what are you going to do? Cornwall needs to know.'

'I don't know. I'm finishing my script for Daniel, and then we'll see what comes of it.'

He is at least fifteen years older than her father. How did he end up here in the lifeboat station, bankrupt and desperate?

'Mr MacCleod, can you tell me where your funding came from?'

'It came from a private charitable trust, a family trust of the Tubal family, who own the bank of the same name.'

'Are they sponsors of the arts?'

'Sponsors of my wife. To put it simply, Sir Harry married her, and I got the grant. But you can't write that. I don't want to antagonise them just yet, while legal proceedings are under way.'

'Will you keep me informed? Exclusively?'

'Yes, I will.'

'Can you tell me, off the record, a little more about your Daniel Day-Lewis project?'

'It's a film and theatre version of the life of Flann O'Brien, who observes life from a pub in Dublin. I see certain parallels with my life. O'Brien said his own identity – these are his words – was tangled with his art. Same for me. I am using his words, the immortal words from his novels, particularly *At Swim-Two-Birds*. Have you read it?'

'Sorry, I did philosophy and sociology. We only read set books.'

'It's a masterpiece.'

He scrambles around for some paper.

'This is the beginning. Flann O'Brien is in a pub: "One beginning and one ending for a book is a thing I did not agree with. A good book may have three openings entirely dissimilar and interrelated only in the prescience of the author or for that matter one hundred times as many endings." He snatches up another piece of paper.

' "People talk about true stories. As if there could possibly be true stories; events take place one way and we recount them the opposite way. You appear to begin at the beginning: 'It was a fine autumn evening in 1922. I was a solicitor's clerk in Marommes.' And in fact you have begun at the end. It is there, invisible and present, and it is the end which gives those words the pomp and value of a beginning." '

He looks up at her.

'You see, my life is not all *Thomas the Tank Engine*,' he pronounces. 'It is quite other.'

'I see.'

' "People talk about true stories." That's where the artist comes in. We don't have a beginning, a middle and an end. And that's why I have to complete this project. Because nobody has understood better than Flann O'Brien how absurd, poignant and inscrutable human life is. Did they teach you that in sociology?'

'That was more in philosophy. Modules 5 and 6.'

'Oh Jesus. Oh sweet Jesus.'

He adjusts his hat, and drops the papers on the floor.

'Let's go to the old sail room where we make our sets, and look at the props for Thomas. All being freshly painted. All bright and cheerful and ready to wow the little chubby-chops of our duchy.'

He stands up unsteadily: his legs aren't too strong; they are, after all, bearing a lot of accumulated mental ballast.

*   *   *

Back home Melissa listens to the recording. She is moved. There is a tragic gulf between that draughty shed where the lifeboats were once launched and the universe of big ideas in which he lives. Perhaps there is some equation between shabby poverty and high aspiration. He sat there in his absurd hat, a small wicker basket resting on his curls giving the impression of an inverted botanical still life, convulsed by some very big ideas about . . . About what, exactly? About art, apparently. Art, which, one of her lecturers said, cannot be privileged over other human activities. The academics loved the word 'privileged'. Mr MacCleod is perhaps the first person she has ever met who genuinely believes that art is something real, and necessary, something that should be privileged over any other human activity. She wonders if a story really can have many endings. There is something noble about Mr MacCleod; something suicidal. She thinks of him sitting on that one wooden kitchen chair, while she was virtually horizontal on the broken-backed sofa, his face charged, as though the currents of thought were causing his features to twitch. As they walked back from the sail room, he said, 'I want you to record this', and he began to quote. And she listens to it now.

' "I mean to say, said Lamont, whether a yarn is tall or small, I like to hear it well told. I like to meet a man who can take a hand to tell a story and not make a balls of it while he's at it. I like to know where I am, do you know. Everything has a beginning and an end." '

She has no idea what is going on, who is saying what, and why a story can have a hundred endings.

She writes:

Today I met a man who told me that there was no such thing as a true story. He told that Jim MacCool had an arse so big that it would halt the movement of men through a mountain pass. It was one of the most exhilarating conversations I have ever had, although I had no idea whatever what he was talking about. This remarkable man is Artair MacCleod.

She files this fragment away, for use in her blog. And then she starts on the story the editor wants about the all-new *Thomas the Tank Engine*, scripts revised, engines freshly painted (how tacky they looked in the paint room) and the generous sponsorship of Binster's Pies and Pasties in these straitened times, when Artair MacCleod's grant from a charitable foundation has inexplicably been cut. She talks about the essential role of the arts in the Duchy, and introduces a note of indignation: so this is what happens when bankers' greed brings the financial system down – children's theatre in Cornwall is threatened, Celtic theatre is threatened, and much-loved institutions are put at risk. We cannot afford to let this happen!

Outrage journalism, what fun. She appends the venues and the times of performances and emails it off to the editor.

It's after midnight as she starts her first blog:

Yesterday, I read a passage from Dorothy Wordsworth's Grasmere Journals, *and I wondered if she and her brother were incestuous.*

Dorothy wrote these words just after her brother William married Mary Hutchinson:

William had parted from me up stairs. I gave him the wedding ring – with how deep a blessing! I took it from my forefinger where I had worn it the whole of the night before – he slipped it again on to my finger and blessed me fervently. I kept myself as quiet as I could but when I saw the two men running up the walk coming to tell us it [the wedding] *was over I could stand it no longer and threw myself on the bed where I lay in stillness neither hearing nor seeing anything till Sara came up stairs to me & said, 'They are coming!' This forced me from the bed where I lay & I moved I know not how straight forward, faster than my strength could carry me till I met my beloved William & fell on his bosom.*

Funny, don't you think, that William rushed ahead of his wife to embrace his sister? Weird stuff with the ring. Strange that she should have thrown herself on the bed. Stuck out there in the fells, nobody to speak to except, occasionally, Keats, Dorothy utterly devoted: it all adds up to incest. I will come back to this topic. By the way, Dorothy suffered from migraines, at least two a week. Migraines are a modern plague.

I don't know what it means, but yesterday I met a man who believes a story can have many beginnings and many endings. And next week I will be asking, do children have natural integrity? What do you think? And finally, I have just discovered cupcakes. Utterly divine and recipes galore. I am trying them out as many as possible before reporting back to you. Yes, it's all out there somewhere.

This sounds lively, she thinks. She has never made a cupcake, but she has seen some recipes in full colour in the *Times Magazine* section. It can't be difficult: children were making them in the pictures. Admittedly, they were thin, overcoached children, expensively dressed. Probably in Notting Hill. While their parents were bankrupting the country, they were making cupcakes. She thinks this slightly ironic polemical style could work.

7

As Len ushers him into the back of the car, Julian feels an urgent need to see his children. The children. Whose innocence and unconditional love make him uneasy now. Len is pleased to see him, to be made whole by the Trevelyan-Tubal presence. Julian wants to see Alice's milk teeth and her pursed, amused lips, which look as though they are lightly rouged at all times. When at bath-time he sees her tiny innocent vulva, he finds it desperately poignant. God knows what's in store for her in the highly unpredictable sexual realm. He even finds the fine, vulnerable hair at the back of her neck moving. And he has, despite himself, a desperate hunger to embrace the children, to hug them. He longs to hold Sam's solid, small, restless toughness. It's not healthy: he needs them perhaps more than they need him, but at this moment he requires a transfusion, an implant – some bone marrow – containing their innocence, the innocence he, after all, helped bring into the world. Yes, he and Kimberly brought this about. Kimberly's genes are somehow uncomplicated and blonde and sun-struck. He hopes the children have received plenty of her DNA.

There are hundreds of emails for him. His assistant reminds him that he is supposed to go to a charity dinner tomorrow. He hates charity dinners, with all that bonhomie and the childish show-off auctions and those terrible jokey speeches. Dickens described the financiers of his time at a charity dinner: *sleek, slobbery, bow-paunched, overfed, apoplectic, snorting cattle*. Something like that. Now that he's more or less settled the future of Tubal and Company, Julian allows himself to admit that he was never at home in the City. The City has made him act in ways his younger self would have despised. Thank God things have eased a little. He sees his father's angry, distorted face as Estelle helped him hold the pen. He knew he was signing away his life. *Assets two thirds. Loans one third.* He knew he was putting his signature on his own death warrant. This betrayal may be the last thing he ever signs. And his son, who could have left him in peace under the umbrella pines, to listen to the song of the turtle doves, has harried him to his end, so that he can take himself and his children to another life, free from the bogus demands of history and tradition.

Julian speaks to Nigel. Have you told Eric? Yes, Eric knows that the balance sheet will show that deposits are strong. The auditors and the rating agency will get the news informally by the usual channels. The accounts won't be out for eleven months, and only then will they go to the Charity Commission, who are seldom in a hurry, but the agencies will know that Tubal's has come out of the recession pretty well.

'Just tell Eric to remind them that Sir Harry's dictum has stood the bank in very good stead: one third leverage to two thirds assets.'

'Or thereabouts,' says Nigel. 'Will do. They love a dollop of Sir H.'s philosophy. I've primed my old pal Clive at the *FT* with the good news.'

They only speak on encrypted phones these days.

'Well done. I'm going straight home. And I've got that Guildhall bash tomorrow. Are you coming?'

'I'll be at your side, Boss, bidding for a week's paragliding in Bulgaria, and hoping with all my heart I don't get it.'

Julian is dying to see the children. It's only been three days, but it is everything he loathes about corporate life – the meetings, the legal documents, the stale air on flights, the churning anxiety, the oppressive sense of importance, the dead coffee in insulated flasks, the portraits of all those crooks on the walls, the dull conversational conventions, the wilting sandwiches and above all – way above – the insistent belief that this money production is a superior form of activity and that those who deal in it are superior people. More and more he sees that these people have pulled a gigantic con trick on the rest of humanity. And now they believe their own myths. The Tubals have always had money since old Moses Tubal set himself up at the sign of the Leathern Bottle by Bread Street in 1671, and the family have carefully cultivated money for three hundred and fifty years. But these other people, who sliced and diced derivatives and recklessly lent money, believed that they too were entitled to millions. And the reason was that they thought they could make money appear from nowhere. Even Tubal's fell for it – we fell for it – and that is why the bank now owns – although 'owns' is not the exact word for this new class of debt – so many toxic assets. We don't even know which bits of these assets we own. Nobody does. And that is why he is selling the bank, and that is why his father, without knowing it, has given him power of attorney to get the job done quickly and cleanly. Legally, his father is now a child. Julian has to remind himself constantly of the rationale behind what he is doing.

Len asks him a few questions about the trip. He wants to know how Sir Harry is getting on – 'They don't make them like him no more' – true, and Julian is grateful for that. Len is glancing eagerly at the rear mirror, hoping to have a good chinwag on the way back to the house.

'He's not well, Len, but he seems pretty happy. His doctor is going out to see him. I've got to make a few calls, Len, but thanks for asking about Dad.'

I don't really know if he's happy. Maybe he is in a state of anguish, in hell.

His father liked a retainer. Len is part of a small tribe of cockneys brought into the palisade. They are agreeable, cheery folk. Back in the old days they had to sign a contract which forbade them *to embezzle, purloin, consume or keep any money and any other things whatsoever shall be entrusted to them.* In return they had a job for life, which could be passed on to their children. In later years they had a secure pension and free membership of the sports and social club, current president, Julian Trevelyan-Tubal Esquire. So it is in their interest to be dutiful and grateful. *Lovely jubbly, kushti.*

* * *

Kimberly has the children ready. It's an old-fashioned family scene: Kim, the two children in their pyjamas and Evija, the nanny, hanging back with Estonian diffidence. Evija has a lovely, pale skin, with something of the dairy in its Slavic pallor. Behind them the hall, vivid with paintings, and a huge contemporary chandelier made entirely, if you look closely, of old knives and forks and pewter mugs and plates; the rugs on the antique French flooring, the rather grand staircase curving sinuously upwards. Sam jumps at him and he catches him at about crotch height and hugs him. Sam's body is full of solid animal vitality, like an otter or a piglet, and he shouts slightly hysterically 'Daddy, Daddy' as Julian hoists him up into the air and then kisses him on the descent. From birth his children came equipped with distinct personalities. Also, both are unmistakably faithful to their genders, without any prompting. Alice waits her turn, waiting almost timorously, almost seductively. When Julian lifts her, there is a gentle, pliant submissiveness as if her only wish is to dissolve her self into his. These past days have been a strain, and he finds now that the tensions are released that he is on the verge of weeping.

'What have you brought us, Daddy?' shouts Sam.

'That's just a tad mercenary, little guy,' says Kimberly.

Julian puts Alice down, still holding her hand, and he kisses Kimberly. Then he hugs all three of them, corralling them.

'OK, bedtime. Straight to bed,' Kimberly says.

'Presents first?' Julian says. This is Kimberly's jurisdiction.

'OK, just this once.'

Len slips forward from the entrance hall with two exquisitely wrapped parcels.

'This is for you, Alice,' Julian says, 'and this is for you, Sammy Seal. Go to your room with Evija and I'll come up in a minute or two to say goodnight. Say goodbye to Uncle Len. OK, up you go with Evija. Goodnight, Len, thank you.'

Len never gets beyond the large doormat in the front hall. But he beams inwards, radiating hope. The nanny leads the children up the stairs. They – and she – sleep on the fourth floor, high above the gardens of Ladbroke Square. Julian likes it up there in the Peter Pan world, the trees below thrashing or oscillating or sighing.

'How did it go, darling?'

'Oh, fine. Some trust business in the place we never mention, and then on to see the old man. Fairly routine.'

'How is he?'

'On the way out, I'm afraid. Even the sainted Estelle admits that he's deteriorating. But I think he's happy. Anyway I hope he's happy, but it's hard to tell. It's actually tragic: he looks pretty well and he is still a snappy dresser, but it's like watching, I don't know, a shadow play or something. It's one-dimensional. Mr Abbott is going out to assess him formally. Kim, let's have a drink. I feel as though I need one, if that isn't a little corny.'

'It is a little cheesy – stressed exec comes home to little wifey and they hit the booze, but who cares? Not me. Welcome home, honey-bun.'

They sit in the small panelled study behind the drawing room. All his inclinations are towards the small and the cosy these days, as if size and opulence have conspired to diminish him. As if he's too small a figure in an expansive landscape. Kimberly sits next to him, very close.

'I saw your stepmother last night.'

'How is she? And by the way, please don't call Fleur my stepmother, not even in jest.'

'Oh, she was having a grand old time. We went to dinner around the corner.'

'Did she mention Dad?'

'She said she was going out to see him at Easter, I think.'

'Do you like her?'

'That's a strange question to ask now. Yes, I like her, but I think she's a little worried about what happens next. Why do you ask?'

'I don't know really. She's concerned, but her concern doesn't extend to going to see Dad.'

'Maybe, but it's more complicated. She's playing the role of lost soul. That's probably why they become actors, because they can't quite accept life as it is.'

'Do you really think that's true? I mean about actors?'

Julian feels a twinge of impatience: she's too ready with the obvious remark. But he also needs her optimism and straightforwardness more now than ever. Her eyes have an engaging openness; so many of us have wary, clouded eyes, he thinks.

'I'll just go up and kiss the kids goodnight. What's for supper?'

'An omelette and fruit salad. Is that OK? You said simple?'

'That sounds just perfect. I'll be right down.'

Sam is already asleep, but Alice is doggedly staying awake, clutching the rag doll bought in one of those dinky, scented shops behind the port.

'Have you given her a name, darling?'

'She's called Rosie.'

'That's a lovely name. Exactly right. Kiss kiss.'

She reaches up and he lifts her half out of bed.

'Kiss kiss, Daddy.'

He places her eager little body back and pulls up the covers so that she and the rag doll have equal billing on the pillow. The doll has buttons for eyes and a cat's nose of calico. It has a deranged stare, not necessarily suitable company for his precious daughter.

'I love you, darling,' he says.

'I love you, Daddy. More kiss.'

His heart is squeezed as he bends down to kiss her utterly innocent face. He wonders if his love for his children isn't the result of his own inadequacies, as if he sees the children as the guardians of his true self, the pointers to what he might have been or what essentially he still is.

'Go to sleep, darling.'

'Night night. I love you, Daddy.'

She closes her eyes determinedly.

It will soon be over. Tubal's with its portraits and handwritten ledgers and the Adam banking hall, its Wedgwood china, its rosewood tables, the panelled meeting rooms, the credit cards with 'Esquire' absurdly embossed after the customer's name, the buckram hand-bound diaries, and the little conceits that have brought in the newly rich in the last ten years – all this will be a memory. He won't even agree to stay on the board for two years, the usual arrangement for ensuring continuity and for securing some reassuring history for the new owners. In the City, private banking with Tubal and Co. is nearly as prestigious as owning a grouse moor or an Aston Martin. His grandfather said the bank's success would always be ensured by inviting their friends to join the club. Now Julian thinks of Bernie Madoff. And he sees some parallels.

'Thanks for letting them stay up, darling,' he says.

'You look tired.'

'I am.'

She goes down to the kitchen to make the supper. She's a very neat cook. In the old house there was always a chef, but Kimberly doesn't want someone else doing the cooking, except when they have lots of guests. Particularly she doesn't want some tyrant in her kitchen, cooking up the fatty recipes of Old Europe. She doesn't recognise – as his father once pointed out – the difference between servants and friends. And now the old boy is silent and his sarcasm and disapproval are locked away with him. Kim calls him from somewhere below on the stairs. This house, the trees outside in the gardens coming to life – there's still some timid light in the sky – the children tucked up in their Neverland, their night lights decorated with revolving fairies and toadstools, casting a softly curdled light on their sleeping faces – reassures him after his anxious, guilty journey. In the morning – it's Saturday – he will be playing tennis in the gardens. He's on the garden committee and they are debating some big changes, a new play area for children and a replacement for the fountain which was vandalised. There are foxes in the garden and at night they moan and scream. Nobody on the garden committee is worth less than ten or fifteen million, except for Mrs Purkiss, eighty-seven, who lives in a deep basement and is a protected tenant on a tiny pension, yet they all defer to her because they recognise the attachment to the past which she represents. *Maybe we are silently aware that she is the better for having very little connection to the world that has made us rich.* She has wild hair and wears a filthy green Barbour in winter and a plum-coloured Barbour waistcoat, equally dirty, in summer. She's an expert on shrubs and herbaceous plants. Her husband died in the last days of the campaign in North Africa and she has no family: the garden is her life. When she comes to garden meetings she drinks too much and takes supplies of canapés home in the waterproof pocket designed to transport recently caught trout. Her first name is Esmé and she says 'top hole' to indicate approval.

Down below in the kitchen he and Kimberly sit at a bar. His father once sat on one of these stools and said it was charming. He has a way of being extremely complimentary about things he dislikes. It is an Etonian habit, easily deciphered: 'charming' meant vulgar. Little Sam won't be going there. Kim says what's the point of having children if you send them away? He agrees although he thinks his reasons are more complicated: he doesn't want his son to be for ever an Etonian, which he thinks is a curse. When the bank is sold they are going to divide their holidays between Martha's Vineyard, where her family have a home, and Antibes. Kim's family house is on the beach at Gay Head, not far from the Jackie Onassis estate and near where John F. Kennedy Jr. – John-John – crashed his Piper Saratoga into the sea. Here the children can spend their summers free of Olde England.

Kimberly is looking for a house. On the water, but nothing too grand. Even nothing-too-grand is five million.

It's warm in the morning. That special kind of blessed spring warmth that gives you a presentiment of what's around the corner. The white wisteria is about to flower – it's taken six years. He walks through cherry blossom and hanging laburnum and on through their private gate directly into the gardens, and across the lawns to the court. His phone rings as he is almost exactly at the midpoint of the vast expanse of grass. It's his brother, the voyager.

'Hello, Simon. Where on earth are you?'

'I'm in Maun. It's up at the top end of Botswana.'

His voice sounds as though it is coming down a thin pipe, trickling uncertainly.

'All well?'

'Fine. We're going to traverse the delta in mokoros, local dugouts before you ask.'

'It sounds exciting.'

'It may be a little too exciting. Lots of hippos and crocs. Anyway I rang because I wanted to tell you, and you alone, that I met someone in the bar of Riley's Hotel last night. His brother, he says, is shagging our stepmother.'

For a moment, Julian is confused.

'Where?'

'In London. He's an ex-rugby player, turned personal trainer, whatever that may be. How is our pater, by the way?'

'Well, the good news is that he wouldn't be aware of it, if it is true. The bad news is that he's not getting any better. I saw him yesterday.'

'Poor old sod. The chap's name is Morné. The brother seems to think he's after her money. He's a game guide. The brother.'

'How exactly did the conversation come up?'

'I told him my name and he asked about the bank. I said why, and he said my brother is shagging the boss's wife. For a moment I thought he meant Kim.'

'Jesus, Simon.'

'Anyway, it's Fleur. Maybe you should warn her?'

'Simon, how the fuck am I going to do that? Dad's dying, she's all over the place. All I can do is make some enquiries about this Morné, or at least have somebody speak to him.'

'Has she got access to the trusts in any way?'

'No. I have sorted them out. But she's got plenty of her own with more to come. She's an adult and Dad is definitely not long for this world. I'll deal with it when the time is right. Are you OK?'

'Perfect. You won't be able to call me for at least three weeks. We're off in an hour. Just thought I should warn you.'

'OK, thanks. Strange world: I am standing in the gardens about to play tennis, and you are heading off to be a crocodile's lunch. Bye.'

'Different strokes for different folks.'

He says something in what is probably an African language. Wherever he travels he picks up a few significant phrases, so presumably this is goodbye, something like, *Travel well until the crocodile eats the sun.*

He wonders who his brother's travelling companions are. Julian's companions, his tennis chums, are already on the court.

Winter honeysuckle. He catches the scent now from the direction of the summer house. Each week they perform a sort of mummers' play on the tennis court, with the roles long ago set firm. Julian is not chairman of a bank here, but a man with a reliable serve and a suspect backhand, so he never plays in the backhand court. They always have the same partners, unless they need to call up one of the reserves. Julian feels oddly nervous before tennis, as though it matters how he plays. Although he doesn't think of himself as competitive, he feels strangely fulfilled by winning. Tennis demands aggression and control. You have to get the balance just right. He can't wait to get going, but experience has taught him never to start until he has hit at least five long balls, in and deep. He and Nigel face Freddie and Dieter. They stretch a bit now and then they spin a racket to decide who's going to serve. The gardens are still with expectation. The honeysuckle scent reaches them in gusts. Nigel calls successfully and hands the balls to Julian. Julian goes for his flat, down-the-middle serve and it comes off. Freddie is miles away from it. 15–0.

And in this fashion the game and the morning compose themselves. Julian's anxiety subsides into contentment; he forgets Fleur and the power of attorney and the £400m. sent into the ether, and tries to concentrate on hitting right through the ball, which is the secret of tennis. One of them, anyway. All around there's an urgent sense of promise, brought on by the sunshine and the rich scents of the gardens. In the distance he sees Esmé Purkiss, carrying her trowel and trug, head bent low, on a mission.

Later Kimberly and the children bring out some pecan cake and elderflower cordial: Kimberly lays these things on a Moroccan cloth, and they all sit on the grass. If you saw them sitting there, Sam swinging Julian's racket, which dwarfs him, trying to hit a passing bumblebee (it is in no danger), you would think what an idyllic little scene this was. And it is. It's shot through with Englishness, which has nothing much to do with reality. Although, of course, reality depends on where you are standing. Esmé Purkiss in the distance is English, one hundred per cent.

Sam misses the bumblebee and hits his own knee. He starts to cry but then he realises that there is no one to blame, and he stifles the second sob. Kimberly laughs and he comes to Julian for comfort. He sees, through Sam's hair, Kimberly talking animatedly to Freddie. She is a little too insistent; she's taken to England, but she is forever the homecoming queen, perky and upbeat, as pretty girls often are, right into old age.

'OK, let's play,' says Julian. 'Bye, ankle-biters, bye, Kim.'

'Bye, Daddy.'

After the second set he walks around the garden with Nigel.

'Nige, could you get Eric to find out something about an ex-professional rugby player called Morné? He played in England and he's South African, apparently, and is a personal trainer, probably at Fleur's gym.'

'Why do you need to know?'

'My brother heard a rumour that he's after her money.'

'OK.'

They pass two small children hanging upside down like bats on the climbing frame, and speaking French.

'Nige, I am not going to stay on when we sell. I'm going to propose you as chairman.'

'Let's talk about that. I don't think you should decide here and now.'

They walk back towards the courts through the whispering, fluttering, pulsing garden.

The family has always loved gardens. His grandfather gave Chisenbury Down to the National Trust in 1946. His great-great-grandfather built a grand house there and planted thousands of broad-leafed trees and dammed streams and designed temples and grottoes. The works almost bankrupted the business. Now, as he sips an elderflower cordial, Julian thinks maybe he will make some improvements to the garden of the villa when he's got more time.

Julian sees, too, that like his father he is surrounding himself with uncritical stooges, who in private probably blame him for what has happened. In his heart, he knew that the Gaussian bell curve was nonsense and he knew that credit swaps and diced mortgages were chimeras, but he did nothing about it because everybody said that there were huge amounts of money to be made. But how? These derivatives related to no assets, to no worth, to no human endeavour. They turned out to be imaginary. It's almost beyond belief that a huge industry was in thrall to fables.

'Come on, Julian. Let's finish them off.'

'Whose serve is it?'

I have always lived in these private spaces separated from the world by money. Simon is out in Botswana with his canoes in a real wilderness. He's hiding in the great expanses because he hated life here.

They go back on court but lose the deciding set when Julian's backhand flies off the frame up towards the warming, hazy sun, and lands finally in a clump of roses, just coming into bud. As they disperse with bonhomie into the late morning, Nigel holds Julian's elbow for a moment.

'Boris's cash for the boat has cleared. I've just had a message from Vaduz.'

'A chimera, Nigel, is a mythical beast made of the bits of mythical animals. That's what we are paying for: something which never existed.'

'Too deep for me. I banged my head against the wall too often at the old school.'

8

AMANDA STAPLETON DOESN'T often need to leave her office; the clients come to her as if to the shrine of an oracle. But for the Trevelyan-Tubals she will emerge. She arrives promptly at five minutes to four outside Mulgrave House and tells the driver to come back for her at five minutes to five.

Fleur lets her in and they kiss without warmth on both cheeks. Amanda is handsome but vulpine. She is dressed to kill, while Fleur is still in her tracksuit with the youthful pink trainers. They sit in Harry's library, because Fleur believes it will add some necessary gravitas to their conversation. Beneath the cold charm, Amanda has a barely concealed impatience, the fox eyeing the chicken-run. Fleur's voice is soft and uncertain.

'Amanda, thank you so much, darling, for coming; as you know Harry's not doing well. I have never talked to him about a will or anything like that. I just felt so safe with him.'

'And you are worried now, for obvious reasons.'

'I am. Very worried, not so much about money, but about my position.'

Before she can explain, coffee is brought in by the Filipina housekeeper.

'Great coffee,' says Amanda, sipping. 'I'm an addict. It goes with the territory. You were saying?'

'I wondered just where I stood. Do I get this house or have a share in Antibes? If Harry dies, I mean.'

'First a caveat. I can only disclose the outlines of the will as they relate specifically to you, and only the outlines, so don't ask me any detail about the rest of the estate. Of course if Sir Harry dies there will be a reading. I've looked at Sir Harry's will to refresh my memory and you don't get any property, except Tuscany, but you're well provided for. He's also designated some personal items for you, and you have a life right to use the villa, although you will have to share with the family according to any arrangement you agree with them. And you can stay in Mulgrave House with the permission of the trust. As I said, you inherit the cottage in Tuscany.'

Over the next forty minutes Fleur discovers that Harry has left her eight million from the family trust and an income of £200,000 a year, index linked, to be paid by the bank; he has also left her five of the pictures, mostly ones they bought together. But no Matisse or Bonnard or Seurat, and, obviously, not the Cézanne.

'Sir Harry has stipulated that the trust will only pay the income as long as you remain unmarried. A long-term relationship, these days, has the same force in law but you may be able to challenge this provision in the High Court if and when.'

She seems to be looking at Fleur, calculating her chances.

When Amanda leaves after one expensive hour, plus travelling and research costs, Fleur feels diminished. Perhaps it's the nature of the law to turn human life – love, emotion, et cetera – into a bill of goods. The human side of the transaction lags some way behind. Maybe these hotshot lawyers begin to imagine that they are the stars of any case and that the law is designed to give them an opportunity to show off their superior qualities. She thinks of those celebrity lawyers in Hollywood with the dead hair. She wonders why Harry would have stipulated that she doesn't go on receiving the income if she marries again. Amanda enjoyed telling her that: she can still feel the lingering appraisal. She's well preserved and having sex with a muscular young athlete; admittedly one with guttural English and some pretty bonkers ideas. Amanda has had two husbands and worn them out, Harry said. She lives with a Tory peer now. Eight million is nothing to Harry. It's the sort of money every Tom, Dick and Harry in the City has now.

It always happens with these upper-crust families: their instinct is to close ranks against outsiders. They shut up like molluscs. None of them has ever really liked her. And now she is probably too old to have children without help from an in vitro specialist. She had better go and see Harry as soon as possible. And she must turn down Morné's invitation to rugby. What was she thinking? Some journalist – even a sports journalist – would pick it up: *Rugby star squires ailing banker's wife*. The family has always been wary of the press, although Harry liked being seen at the theatre and the ballet. When she married him fifteen years ago there were headlines about the prince of finance and his showgirl. But the family has understood that you can't control the press and so you must try never to give them an opportunity. They sometimes write about Julian's hippy brother, but because he is so naturally innocent it is usually harmless.

She texts Morné.

hi thnk u for rugby invite but I must pass. have 2 go 2 France 2 see my husband. I will be @ gym tomorrow. lol

It's easy for her to assume a kind of carefree upbeat tone in a text. What she really wants to say to him can't be said: she wants to tell him that she has fallen deeply in love with him and that she has to pursue this relationship to its end, however disastrous. She wants to tell him that there is a madness in her blood. Already she sees a kind of appealing tragedy ahead: a tragedy of doomed love. When her friend Avril said that she knew before she had left her husband for an unsuccessful painter that it was going to lead to disaster, Fleur thought it was a shallow and self-romanticising claim. How wrong she was! But she has enough sense to see that she must wait until Harry has died, however long that takes. When Harry has gone she will live in Tuscany in the cottage. She looks at herself in the mirror. She wonders if the pink trainers aren't a little too stage school. Maybe the white ones would be better. She thinks her new skin-revitalising cream at £130 a jar is giving her face a healthy glow. Its effect is a little like going for a walk in a bracing wind. She's losing all sense of irony. She's turning into . . . what is she turning into? She doesn't know. Ahead of her she sees a void. Maybe she's become Emma Bovary, she thinks. She needs dramatic models to form a view of herself. When she was a little girl she was forever miming and dancing to pop songs. *What is it I lack, that I always need to pretend?*

She needs to get out. The gloomy Filipina, who also hates her, sees her to the door. She is definitely getting the chop when Harry dies. Fleur walks along the street towards the Royal Hospital, under the huge plane trees, just beginning to cast their deep, untidy shade. Eight million is a lot of money, but there was clearly some canny estimation going on when Harry drafted his will. He had calculated what he could leave her, just this side of looking mean. It isn't the will of a besotted lover, although in the depths of the night he had made extravagant claims: she was his muse; she had utterly changed him with her youth and (relative) innocence. Most of all he had loved having her lying next to him, a sort of captive wood nymph in his bed. For a while she had loved him too, basking in his fervour and happy to have been smuggled into the enchanted world of the very rich. And he had believed completely in her talent as an actress. More completely than the producers, it turned out, which cast some retrospective doubt on his judgement. But until she met Morné she hadn't really understood sex: sex with Morné was a revelation. Up until then she had seen it as a form of adulation, and she coveted adulation. Men had always wanted to fuck her. They responded to something in her with a sort of rutting instinct, as though she was unmistakably in season. Up for it. Now at the age of forty-three she has discovered the madness of true sexual passion. She thinks about Morné's body all day. She even thinks about the amount of sperm he produces, nothing like the thin watery paste her two husbands had projected. *God, what you think about in the privacy of your own mind.* She longs for Morné as though she can't be complete without him. But what it amounts to is about ten minutes a day in the storeroom. On the face of it this is demeaning, but the perfunctory nature of it, the awareness of borrowed time and of risk makes the whole business more charged. It's strange to her. But maybe to him it's routine. It's not something she can rationalise; she's having sex with a huge, hairy Afrikaner, an epigone of Harry, an uncultured, shallow and faintly hectoring athlete. It's possible some hidden need of hers has been unearthed although she doesn't want to explore exactly what that could be. At the Shirley Simms Stage School they had a voice teacher who set them exercises, which involved howling and uttering. The exercises were supposed to locate your core, because once you had found it – for example, by howling like a wolf on the tundra – you would become a better actor. She wondered why Ray Taplow – who taught the howling – wasn't himself a famous actor. At the time she thought the whole thing laughable, but now she thinks she understands what he meant. Sex with Morné has stripped away many layers of pretence and artifice, just what Ray, who wore a bull-terrier spotted neckerchief, was aiming for. Now she thinks of herself not as a complex being, but as elemental, in touch with a few basic truths about life. An obsession that has taken her over. It's exhilarating but at the same time she can see that it is doomed: what's she going to do, run off with Morné to the veld?

Morné is disappointed that she can't come to the rugby. His disappointment gives her hope. She calls Estelle to tell her she's coming down next week.

'How is my darling Harry, Estelle?'

'He's happy. He likes the spring sunshine. Oh, by the way, the consultant is coming down on Monday, so we'll have a better idea.'

'I've missed Harry. Has he mentioned me at all?'

'Yes, quite often.'

She wonders what he has been saying about her. Of course Estelle is now the official interpreter. Fleur hopes he hasn't noticed her absence.

'OK, Estelle, I will be at Nice Airport at 11.25 p.m. on Saturday, BA. Could you send the driver?'

'Of course, Lady Trevelyan-Tubal. Jean-Marc will be waiting. And when will you be departing?'

'Probably Tuesday or Wednesday. And Estelle, get Mr Abbott to ring me as soon as.'

She can't bear to miss even a few days with Morné. In the little storeroom, lying on the mats this morning, their skins fervid and moist, he asked her if she would consider donating to his sports foundation.

'I could make a small donation if it helped.'

'You a doll,' he said. And demonstrated that he could make love twice in a few minutes.

It was predictable that he would ask for money, but she tries not to think it has any relation to the sex in that windowless room, and she tries not to think that he sees himself as offering a service in return. As she quickly discovered when she married into the family, the rich always find it difficult to know how genuine their friends and acquaintances and flatterers are, but she's happy to help if it ties him to her for a while longer. She's lost all dignity, but at the same time she knows that this isn't going to last and perversely, desperate though she is, it's comforting to know. It's like a play, the information in the first act – Chekhov's gun on the wall, et cetera – always gives clues to the third act. And there are plenty of pointers in this first act.

When Harry is dead she's going to buy a small house in London and do it up quite differently. She will spend much more time in Tuscany, too. Mulgrave oppresses her with its stuffy magnificence. It was never hers and she was never able to decorate it as she would have chosen, more like Kim and Julian's house. Although Harry adored her, he said that Mulgrave House was not the sort of place you could 'muck about' with. The only major change she made was to the kitchen. Harry hadn't been brought up to think of the kitchen as part of the family domain; generations of cooks reigned in this *terra incognita*. But she had made a comfortable breakfast bar with a small television and brightly coloured banquettes and put in steel German ovens and a huge gas range. Harry was happy to let her cook simple suppers on the few nights they weren't going out or were without staff. He called it her Petit Trianon. She smiled, and later looked it up on Wikipedia: she was deliberately slumming, apparently. And she sits there now, as if in retreat from the French tassels and gilt frames and Aubusson paysages and Sheraton card tables and Boulle side tables and gloomy ancestors – less Mitteleuropa with each passing generation as they married fair people – and the perfect flowers, sent in by the bushel.

Around her the house is very quiet, although there's always a little groaning in the pipes and at intervals a distinct rumble from the Underground. There's also a subdued whisper, the noise of old fabrics and curtains responding minutely to draughts, but also there's just the sighing and settling of an old house in the way that elderly people make little noises as they move or bend or sit – a sigh here, a groan there, and sometimes the small whoosh of an involuntary emission. All the noises are much louder now that she's alone. She plays some Chopin on the CD but it doesn't calm her. Instead it seems to isolate her: it's like a small waterfall of piano notes, and she is standing on the other side, behind the water. Her thoughts are becoming disordered. What had happened to her for eighteen years was a form of embalming. She was embalmed by Harry, and the unguent was money. In the old days – she's a bit vague about millennia – the Egyptians used spices; now the embalmers inject wealth straight into the aorta. She's been lying in her own tomb. She thinks with sympathy of her old father and his boyfriend; maybe he felt he was entombed in heterosexuality. This cultural/artistic gulag she's been living in is not so noble. It's nothing more than the product of money. She has the feeling that Julian also finds it oppressive, but he is far too buttoned-up to admit to anything like that.

Amanda calls. It's after eight, but she's still in the office.

'Can you talk for a moment?'

Oh God, Amanda has found out about Morné. She's got a hotline to the tabloids. Somebody at the gym must have been talking. Or maybe Morné has been boasting.

'Yes, I can,' she says brightly. 'Fire away, Fi.'

'I wanted to ask you what your understanding was of the settlement with your first husband. I wasn't working here then, as you know. But Artair MacCleod – that's his name, isn't it? – has sent a letter via some rustic lawyer to the bank asking why he hasn't received his grant. It was pushed on to me, as a family matter. Before I go into it with the trust, it looks as though it wasn't an award in court, but a grant from one of Sir Harry's arts charities. Is that your understanding?'

'I don't know anything about it. Harry simply said, as I recall, that he had made a settlement which would keep Artair going for the rest of his life.'

'Have you spoken to Mr MacCleod?'

'No. Not once in eighteen years.'

'Well, don't speak to him under any circumstances.'

'I wasn't planning to.'

Amanda isn't really listening.

'No, but he may try to get in touch with you,' she says as though this is a given, which people like her, wised-up, realistic people, understand without help.

Amanda rings off.

Fleur is so relieved that the call has nothing to do with Morné that she feels light-headed, like somebody who has survived a car crash. She cancels gym for tomorrow, leaving another message for Morné, which invokes Harry's doctor: she feels she should be on hand in case he wants to speak to her. The truth is that a deep survival instinct tells her that it would be an absolute disaster if it was ever revealed that she was having sex with a rugby player at the same moment as a top neurosurgeon was examining her stricken husband. Amanda's call has reminded her of her real status in this family which, despite the title, is precarious: she's Harry's indulgence, an old man's infatuation with a fluffy, failed actress. She's tried to fit in, but without Harry's protection they could easily gang up on her if she displays fear. Morné would say that that is the law of survival. He's keen on natural laws.

She calls Kimberly, to tell her that she has been thinking about her project, organic food grown on bits of spare urban land, to be donated to soup kitchens and schools... And so on. She says how keen she is to help.

'It sounds like just such a great idea. So fun.'

'That's so cool, Fleur, I am soo-oh happy you can do it. We've budgeted for a thousand starter kits and we've already identified nearly forty sites in London alone. Can you come round tomorrow for coffee? About ten? I really, really need someone with your presentational skills. You would be totally awesome talking to schools.'

'OK. I will be speaking to the doctor who's going down to check out Harry, but it should be cool. He has my number.'

She's copying Kimberly's upbeat manner. She wonders how her presentational skills are. Or what they are. She's now agreed to sell the virtues of organic vegetables to dreadful children, to provide herself with cover during Harry's twilight; Harry's back-somersault into oblivion. She realises with a stab of guilt that she has accepted the fact that Harry is not the same person he was. Of course it's to do with Morné and his body, but by what law is she required to continue to love a man who is not the man she married? And now Artair is asking questions. When Harry dies, she will be able to see Artair again. He must be seventy-six by now, and probably as full of mad schemes as ever. When he'd had a few drinks his mind became a virtual battlefield of forces he couldn't control and the conflict spread to his face which became beatific and anguished by turns. She finds herself smiling. He lives somewhere in the sticks now, his universe shrinking. Once he had worked at the Old Vic and talked passionately over drinks with Larry and Johnny. But nothing ever worked out quite as he predicted: there would be some fatal disagreement, some unpaid bills – he was always let down by a third party – followed by the lavish expenditure befitting a titan of the theatre and once or twice there were rumours of misappropriation, but he would come back full of conviction and certainty to hold an audience rapt with his glorious, helter-skelter conversation, the emperor of the snug bar.

9

ARTAIR IS LOOKING at the liver spots on his hands. They
seem to have launched a takeover bid for the available skin surface.
They're moving fast. He thinks of those maps his father showed
him of the progress of the panzer divisions across France. They were
living in Dublin then. Little Artair was worried that 10th Panzers
would arrive in England, but his father was looking forward to the
defeat of the English. He was an advocate of a free Ireland. In fact
almost anywhere the English had turned up in the world would be
better off if they went home. It was as though the only purpose of
the English was to patronise and annoy the subject people, from
India to Scotland. He sees that the liver spots are moving to occupy
his brow as well. He'll soon look like a Dalmatian. When he was a
boy he and his friends would say to the kids with freckles – there
were plenty, as you would expect in Rathmines – *When they join
up you will have a nice suntan.* It's happening to him. He's steadily
going brown.

He's still waiting for Daniel Day-Lewis's agent to get back to him,
which means that he has to go each day into town to use the library's
computers. He has no hope of making his own computer work because
he can't afford to get in a boffin until he's paid. He is also waiting
for his lawyer to receive a reply from Tubal's. 'Lawyer' is a generous
description of Gerald Barnecutt, who shares his two-room office
with his assistant and mistress, Lowenna Biddick, creating a dense,
concupiscent atmosphere under the low ceilings. They are rumoured
to have a rich sex life. Gerald prefers the papers he is working on to

be spread on the floor and Lowenna does a delicate lobster quadrille among them, applying her long acquaintance with Gerald's mind to guessing where the papers have ended up. They have generous lunch hours and close early on Wednesdays to recover from the rigours of Monday and Tuesday. Lowenna is a handsome woman, with broad hips and barely-under-control blonde/grey hair which suggests to Artair that she is sexually avid.

Artair rings Gerald to see if he's heard anything from Tubal's.

'No reply yet, Artair. You know how it is with these grand banking families and their lawyers.'

'I do,' he says, but he's pretty sure Gerald has no idea.

'We'll give it another week or so, and then I will unleash –'

'Would it be the hounds of hell or the dogs of war?'

'That's the sort of thing. Probably both at once. Or maybe just a stiff letter.'

'In the meanwhile I am living on free pasties from Binster's.'

'As long as you don't try to pay our bill with pasties. Got to go, she who must be obeyed is waving papers at me for signature.'

Gerald doesn't like talking on the phone. God knows why he went into the law. Funny phrase, *went into the law*, as if you just trotted in one day. Went into the Army. Marched in, *Morning, Sarge*.

Artair walks to the bus stop and waits until a bus appears like a wraith out of the rain that is sweeping in from Nova Scotia and he settles down for the ride into town. The rain is shot-blasting the windows. Two old people huddle on the worn, weary seats. (Artair does not see himself as old; the life force runs strongly in his veins.) At the library he discovers that the posters are already up on the advertising board: *The Wind in the Willows, all-new Easter Holiday Production*, and that cheers him up somewhat. There is a notice of an extraordinary meeting of the town council to discuss the financial shortfall after some disastrous investments in Credit Default Swaps, which he has heard of but doesn't fully understand. But then it seems the bankers didn't either. The council tax is going to have to go up. But there is no email from El Camino Drive, not even an acknowledgement that his letter has been received. He knows that these people have assistants who have assistants, so it's probably in the works. As he leaves the library, he sees that little shit from the bank and without moving too suddenly – his acting training helps here – he turns to examine with deep interest the offer of a savings scheme from the Spanish bank which has apparently taken over the Devon & Duchy Building Society, which once invested the council's money. In his mind (it is method acting) he's considering where to place the Tubal money when it arrives. He may place it with these sensible Spanish fellows. He's instructed Gerald to go for punitive interest on the two and a half months unpaid. He's also posted his copy of *Richard III*, signed by Gielgud, Richardson and Olivier in 1953, to Fraser's in the Strand, who sell autographs, for appraisal. On their website he found that their top sellers were Angelina Jolie, Brad Pitt and Michael Jackson, but he was pleased to see that they were offering a publicity still of Olivier and Vivien Leigh for £1,500 so he has high hopes that his *Richard III*, signed by all the top theatrical knights, is worth double, at least. And this is the life of the actor-director-manager or, he thinks, a heroic but precarious roller-coaster ride. Art and finance – not many men have the mettle for it. The *Richard III* was given to him by an actor called Fléance Conyers who was keen to sodomise him when he was at drama school. Fléance played Lord Grey, the brother of the Queen's consort, for two performances in Olivier's production.

Back at the boathouse he eats an onion-and-potato pasty, his eleventh of the week, and looks out across the estuary, which has been flattened by the rain. The seabirds are flying in low, grimly defensive. The wheelhousing of the fishing boat is half submerged. He imagines there are palm trees on El Camino Drive.

At first when he looks at his script it seems to lie lifeless on the page, inert like the cast-off skin of a reptile. But as he reads, it comes to life. He has a sudden idea: he will set the whole work within the first Bloomsday, which Flann and his friends initiated, a shambolic and drunken walk which started at the Martello Tower, in the presence of

Sylvia Beach, who first published *Ulysses*. Also Flann's friends, Patrick Kavanagh and John Ryan, and the author's nephew, Tom Joyce, a dentist.

He writes:

16 June 1954, 10 a.m. Flann O'Brien is already drunk. It is the very first Bloomsday, celebrating Joyce's great novel, Ulysses.

This is a far better start.

Flann is standing in for Stephen Dedalus and A.J. Leventhal, the registrar of Trinity College, is standing in for Bloom. Leventhal's only qualification is that he is Jewish.

> *FLANN: We are here to celebrate a great writer who was illiterate. His every foreign-language quotation in any of his works known to me is wrong. His few sallies at Greek are wrong, and his few attempts at a Gaelic phrase are absolutely monstrous. But he was, as T.S. Eliot said, the greatest master of the English language since Milton.*

Now out on the silver verdigris estuary, the skeins of birds appear again, flying fast, and the fishing boat completes is twice daily U-boat dive and Artair is caught up in his script and he has turned himself into Flann-O'Brien-Daniel-Day-Lewis as the magic of creativity consumes and sustains him.

Melissa is writing her second blog. The Dorothy Wordsworth blog has been picked up by a literary magazine and she has had nearly one hundred hits. Some are from feminist groups who think that Dorothy was shabbily treated by her brother. Two are from men who accuse her of being a dyke. But the overwhelming theme is that women are always exploited by men and that the phallocracy will invariably try to keep control. She wonders if some of the writers are lesbians, regarding the phallus as an instrument of oppression, like the knout. It's amazing how many of the writers don't know how to spell.

Blogs should be fun. She writes about cupcakes, about their sexual connotation, their bright colours and childish appeal, their resemblance to small breasts, and she writes about the Americanisation of sensibility. This leads to her thoughts on changes in language: 'It's so fun' is one she admits to using herself and is probably a lost cause, but she doesn't approve of nouns like 'impact' being used as verbs and she hates phrases like 'going forward', which businessmen seem to think lends weight to their every other sentence. She reflects on the increasing use of compound words like 'counter-intuitive' and 'age-appropriate'. The explanation she has heard is that, because so many Americans are of German extraction, it is natural for them to link words. She also attacks the use of the word 'comfortable' to mean 'happy', and 'characterise' – a Donald Rumsfeld favourite – to mean 'describe'. Her point is that the English language is infinitely rich and it is a crime to thin it out in this way. She puffs the local production of *Thomas the Tank Engine*, and decries the drying up of funding, under mysterious circumstances, for that ornament of Cornish and Celtic culture, Artair MacCleod.

But just in case she is sounding too pious, she ends with another little riff on the joys of cupcakes and just how perky and nubile they are, food porn. She puts the blog into the system. Her friend Steve in graphics says he will sort out the layout. She needs a template. Steve seems to be keen on her, but he is just below her threshold of acceptability, admittedly a rather fluid standard.

Then she Googles Lady Trevelyan-Tubal. She finds a picture of her with her husband, Sir Harry. They stand side by side outside a porticoed country house looking amused in a restrained sort of way as if it's jolly clever what these photographer chaps can do, despite their frightfully common clothes. Fleur looks a little foxy, definitely a trophy wife. It's hard to believe she was ever married to the rumpled and insanitary Artair MacCleod, pillar of Cornish culture.

The editor summons her. At least you can't be fired twice, she thinks. He's staring gloomily at his screen. His face is layered, an impasto created by the journalistic life and sixty cigarettes a day.

'Melissa, I like your blog. I am going to print it and I want another one next week or sooner. And your piece on Artair MacCleod was spot on. How is he holding up without his money?'

'Binster's are sponsoring him for the Easter run.'

'Poor sod. Keep tabs on him.'

She goes back to her desk and looks at some more pictures of Fleur. There's one of her in a soft-porn film twenty years ago. She's dressed as a stewardess in a very short skirt. In another she is wearing a gingham dress with a scalloped blouse and her hair is in bunches. In another she is wearing a sort of Lady of Shalott medieval dress. *Long fields of barley and of rye, That clothe the wold and meet the sky* . . . She has quite large boobs, and they are featured in every picture. In one comedy still she has a surprised-inn-keeper's-daughter look, her eyes wide in mock horror. Her mouth is strange, pursed like a flower puckering hopefully for the kiss of a travelling bee. Like devoted fans, maybe the people who take these pictures love theatricality more than theatre. They are obsessed with the symbol rather than the thing itself. This comes to her straight from a lecture on Hegel, module 7.

Artair is on the phone.

'Hello, Melinda, I need to talk to the editor.'

'It's Melissa.'

'Melissa? Yes, you are probably right. You should know. Is he there?'

'I will see if he's free. He is probably in conference.'

She rings through.

'Mr MacCleod wants to speak to you.'

'Melissa, Artair MacCleod is one of those higher loonies, whose whole life is a paranoid performance. In the theatre this is just about acceptable. But we live in a harder world. I haven't time to listen to his ravings. Just say I am in conference and see what he wants; ask him to write. That usually shuts them up. By the way, I like your blog so much I want two next week. I've had some emails, well, four at least, saying how good it is.'

'Thank you.'

'Mr MacCleod, the editor says he is in conference, but could you write to him? Or to me? By the way, I saw a lovely poster for the show in the community centre. Can you tell me what you want to speak about?'

'No, it wouldn't be appropriate.'

He sounds a little subdued now.

'Oh, OK.'

'Melinda, we are living in dangerous times.'

He rings off.

As she's waiting for Steve in graphics to finish the layout on his professional Power Mac, she finds a message in her inbox from an address she doesn't recognise, Alan39@hotmail.com

To *melissa@It's-all-out-there-somewhere.com*

I have information that you may find helpful on the Artair MacCleod grant situation. If you are interested email me at the above address. Alan is not my real name. You must understand now that I am in a very risky situation, so we can only communicate on my terms.

He may be a crackpot. But there's nothing to suggest that he is really interested in sex or a date.

To *Alan39@hotmail.com*

From *melissa@It's-all-out-there-somewhere.com*

Alan39, I would be very interested. Please send it to me as soon as you can. And I can guarantee your anonymity. Melissa

She will protect her sources to the death. She waits, staring at the screen, but nothing comes through. Her mother rings.

'Hello, lovely. Auntie Florence met a woman who says that you are a blogger. What is that? Is it one of those people who writes on the netweb?'

'Oh, it's just a sort of column which gets posted on the internet so everyone can read it.'

'That's marvellous. Why didn't you tell us?'

'Mum, I'm freelance now.'

She can almost hear her mother's thoughts in the silence.

'Does it mean you don't have a proper salary?'

'From the end of the month I get paid per piece I write. But the editor likes my blogs and he's printing them.'

'What a shame.'

'It's the way journalism is going, Mum. Everyone is freelance.'

'Don't worry, darling, there's always a home for you with us.'

'Thanks, Mum. It's not all doom and gloom.'

'Will you tell Dad?'

'Don't worry, I'll tell him this evening.'

'All right, my lovely.'

She feels tears in her eyes. They were so proud of her when she went to university, and even more proud when she got a job on the famous *Globe and Mail*, and now they have discovered that she, like everybody else, is subject to disappointment and setbacks.

And then, into her inbox comes a long email from Alan39. Her source. Her source. She wants to tell someone she has her first SOURCE!

'Mr Tredizzick, Mr Tredizzick, I have to see you.'

'Come to my office in five minutes.'

10

JULIAN LIKES THE bank best on holidays. It is deathly quiet today; his ancestors gaze down on him benignly or vacantly, the banking hall is empty, the air is still, the tellers are all at home or at the sports and social club in south London and only the duty security is here. Until just after the war, one of the directors always slept overnight at the bank. This was a precaution, introduced after the River Plate bubble of 1849, when the original building was burned down by angry investors demanding their money. The PR people have declared that this was the earliest example of twenty-four-hour banking. For years the bank has traded on its rich history, making a connection between longevity and integrity.

He drives himself in Kim's Mini up to the anonymous archway off Bread Street, presses his remote and enters. Security, in the form of a very plump young woman he hasn't seen before, is waiting for him. She wears the semi-military uniform that has evolved from the days when the doormen were batmen to the directors in two world wars.

'Morning, sir.'

'Hello, are you new?'

'Yes, sir. I am Jason Newell's partner, Jade.'

'Very good. Well, welcome to the bank. How's Jason?'

'He's fine, sir. He hopes to be back to work soon.'

Jason Newell works in the post room; he was injured playing football for the club's second team. He severed a cruciate ligament. Despite himself, Julian does feel a responsibility for the staff and he's always pleased to see a new member. His father would have asked Jade when Jason was going to make an honest woman of her. Julian doesn't like the word 'partner', but not necessarily because he's in favour of marriage for the staff.

'OK, good. I will be in my office for about two hours, Jade. Let my visitor in when she arrives, won't you?'

'I'm not going nowhere, sir.'

'That's the ticket.'

He wonders briefly why he used a phrase of his father's. Years ago all the directors were family members and they sat together in the directors' room. When the bank started it was a precaution against family cabals. There's nothing as destructive as family jealousy. This communality ensured that the members of the family developed a team spirit. Harry was the first chairman to have his own office, and now Julian has it. It looks down across the secret Italianate courtyard to the directors' room, where, to this day, the five managing directors, as they are now called, sit. They still meet for lunch in the directors' dining room, watched over with Old Testament rigour by Moses Tubal, his portrait said to be by James Thornhill. It was painted in the period when Moses Tubal raised money for Queen Anne to build Blenheim Palace for John Churchill, 1st Duke of Marlborough. Churchill had in turn recommended Moses Tubal to the Emperor Joseph, one of his patrons, and the family fortune was established. When he's in the directors' dining room Julian feels the weight of Moses's seriousness. Dickens said that there are only two kinds of portraits, the serious, and the smirk. Moses, very definitely, didn't do smirking.

Julian lets himself into his office. On the wall he has one of Hockney's Yorkshire landscapes and behind his desk, a commissioned Howard Hodgkin in those wonderful deep blues he favours. The paint flows down on to the frame. The picture hangs where his father kept his Matisse. *French Window at Collioure*. His desk is a wide, blond piece of Scandinavian design, a huge slice of birch resting on two elegant trestles. All part of his attempt to come out from under the deep shade of heritage. The Italian garden below – box hedges, gravel, bay pyramids and a cruciform pond – has unnaturally early tulips in the squares of box, black and white alternating.

The consultant's interim report – full report to come – sent from his Blackberry, says that there has been significant deterioration. His father may also have developed a clot that could require the removal of a kidney. He needs a scan.

Julian calls Estelle who answers with that receptionist's voice, obliging but dutiful, the vowels a little over-articulated as though she is speaking to the mentally impaired.

'Estelle, hi, it's Julian here.'

'Hello, Mr Trevelyan-Tubal.'

'Julian is OK with me, Stel. How's Dad?'

'Did you get the consultant's report?'

'Yes.'

'He wouldn't tell me anything, except to say that he seems to be deteriorating.'

'How does he seem to you? You're closest.'

'He seems fine. I mean he's happy. He's enjoying the sun. Lady Trevelyan-Tubal is here and she is with him now. They're sitting in the garden.'

'Oh, when did she come?'

'She came last night. Do you want to speak to her?'

'No, not at this moment. Give her and my father my love. You haven't told him the yacht is sold, I hope?'

'No, no, I haven't.'

'From what I have in front of me, it looks as though my father may need an operation but I think I should speak to Mr Abbott tomorrow. Tell Bryce that the boat is now officially sold and Boris Vladykin's crew will take possession some time next week. They want Bryce as skipper, but that's up to him, of course. And tell Bryce I think he should do it until the end of the summer anyway. I will call him if I can. I am coming down with Kim and the children at Easter. We'll stay in the guest house. I don't want Dad to be disturbed. OK? Speak soon, and don't forget to give Dad and Fleur my love, as I said.'

'I won't.'

'Oh Stel, the children are looking forward to seeing you.'

'Bye, Julian, thank you.'

He wonders if she resents Fleur turning up. He's not going to take his brother's tip-off about Fleur too seriously. He knows what is in the will: she will have more than enough and she can do what she likes with her money. He stares out of the window at the parterre and the globules of water emerging from Pan's pipe to fall on the water, where briefly they bounce and explode. Pan has the legs of a goat. The marriage between the goatish legs and the human torso is not a good one.

Jade rings up to tell him his visitor has arrived. She says her name is Anne Porter.

'Show her up, Jade.'

'Yes, sir.'

Amanda is dressed in her weekend clothes, jeans and a waistcoat over a plaid shirt. He's never seen her in jeans before and he thinks she is like one of those people who give up glasses for contact lenses but forever look as if they are missing something.

'Thanks, Jade. Morning, Mrs Porter.'

'Morning, Mr Trevelyan-Tubal. Good to meet you.'

She's no actress, that's for sure. When Jade has gone, he says, 'Don't give up the day job.'

Amanda, ever businesslike, smiles coldly and produces two huge files from her bag. They set to work on the deeds of the family trust.

'By the way, Julian, I spoke to Fleur. She asked me to let her know what she was entitled to. Where she stood, is how she put it.'

'With my power of attorney, I don't think she can make any decisions without us, do you?'

'No, anything that affects the trust, no, nor anything that your father put in place.'

'Look, I hate to get nasty, but if she cuts up rough, I have something on her.'

'Let's keep that on the back burner. On a need-to-know basis only.'

'OK. Just put the documents in front of me.'

He signs, and she witnesses that he is signing on behalf of his father, incapacitated, attested to by Mr David St John Abbott, FRCS in a medical report, attached. It takes just half an hour. As ever, she's well prepared. No ethical questions are raised or discussed. Amanda deals strictly in the law. Julian calls Jade to show Mrs Porter out. As she leaves the office he looks at her rear. It's not out of prurience but simple curiosity; it's usually hidden by jackets and pleats. She's wearing the expensive kind of jeans that, with all their stitching and tailoring, seem to be apologising for being jeans at all. Amanda's bottom is apple-shaped, he now knows. A large, cooking-apple shape.

When she's gone he wonders how long it's going to take to cleanse himself. Amanda said that Fleur wanted to know where she stood. Those were her words. And he, the last of the Tubal dynasty, where does he stand? He has done things he is ashamed of and yet he knows that his shame is in some respects a pretence, because what he is doing will soon end the drawn-out hypocrisy. It was different back in Moses's day when the little outsider dealt fairly with the Gentiles, so that they trusted him and he built up a fortune on his reputation. Now the family are not even Jews any more – and much taller – and what they are doing is utterly pointless: they are charging a premium, a kind of snob appeal disguising the very basic business of retail banking. And they are the establishment now: *from Estonia to Etonia* as some wag put it. The establishment is now a marketing concept. His father lavished tens of millions on art and ballet and theatre to disguise the fact: his philanthropy gave him access to a world – and women – he loved, but it didn't really give him a grain of credibility. The Royal Opera House, Glyndebourne and various galleries fêted and flattered him and the crazy thing was he believed them. He saw himself as a prince-patron, not merely a rich man.

I don't want any of this for my children. This rotten crumbling indus- try resting on greed and half-truths; this pretence that Tubal's itself is somehow special, that the people who work in banking are particularly talented, that the government is principled, that the old country still possesses ancient wisdom and deeply bedded human standards.

It's all a sham: the ludicrous royal family in their castles and palaces, the Army pounding away hopelessly at mud houses in recalcitrant villages far away, the wretched government with its desperate determination to save its skin by issuing more and more ineptly populist statements of intent and benchmarks and guidelines and tables and unenforceable laws. And worst of all, we, the bankers, believing we could produce money out of thin air. Instead we lost nearly £600m.

He sometimes lies awake desperate to enquire where the money went. Not a banking question, of course, more an existential matter. But the money simply imploded. It no longer exists. Nobody can explain it. The fucking Gaussian bell curve – the formula is branded on his brain – proclaimed that this was impossible. Even now he feels himself drenched with the shame as he remembers briefing financial managers in smug confidence, all of them eager to learn how the risk could be taken out of investing. And now by borrowing from the family trust, by depositing Koopman's money in the bank, and by hiding the transactions in a blizzard of paper, he has saved the bank and the clients who invested and the bank will go safely where it belongs, into the haven of a vast commercial bank. The topcoats, the directors' apartment, the stocks of old port, the bored portraits – the higher boredom – the handwritten ledgers, the free lunches – will all be history–history in the American sense, meaning gone and forgotten, an ornament, but not a prescription.

And he may finally be able to shake off the rumour that his father's donation to the Finch-Kerr Institute eased him into Cambridge. Oh, of course, there's always a way for these rich boys to get in, they said. As long as the candidate isn't completely useless a place can be found at some impoverished college that was once a hall for the sons of clergymen and where the qualifications for admission remain, as with religion, subjective.

It's time to call Cy. He uses another unregistered and encrypted mobile. Cy is in Palm Beach. As soon as Cy gets there from New York he changes out of his suit – lapels a little boxy – and slips on shorts, white Gucci loafers and a cap, and he assumes a maritime air. His cap has the word 'Captain' stitched on to it; it's the sort of thing George W. Bush wore when he proclaimed *Mission accomplished*. Julian likes Cy. Cy treats him with the deference his eleven generations demand, as a member of banking royalty, but neither of them is under any illusion about their relative importance. Cy wants to buy the bank. Even now, when he has taken a few hits like everybody else, acquiring Tubal's is a very small investment.

'Cy, morning. Julian here. Not too early for you?'

'No, I'm just about to take the boat out for the first time. How's your lovely old tub?'

'Great. New engines, complete refit. I took her out a couple of days ago.'

'You ready to sell?'

'The boat?'

'Duh. No, Julio, the business. That's why you're calling.'

'At the right price.'

'That's the tricky part. Always. Can I have my guys look at the latest balance sheets?'

'Of course.'

'Can you get them to me by the end of the week?'

'Absolutely.'

'How's our old man?'

'He's very ill.'

'That's a shame. A real shame. They don't make them like him no more.'

'They don't.'

'Julio, it would be good if you and I had a private conversation someplace. We are going to exercise due diligence of course, but it would be good if you let me know frankly of any difficulties you have had. Everyone is running about trying to shore up their assets and find new capital in China and so on. I don't want any surprises. You can talk to me in private, you know that. By the way our friend Elstrevier has lost his shirt on Madoff. I warned him six years ago. What a schmuck. But you know what, the old saying is still true, if it quacks like a duck and walks like a duck, it is a duck, but these guys are so greedy they tell themselves it's not a duck, it's a nightingale. Do you like Keats? I love Keats. When are we going to meet? And where? Maybe it's better we meet in Chicago. I'll fix something and get back to you. A coupla weeks after we get the stuff from you. OK, I gotta go: a drowsy numbness pains my sense. Hey, Julio, see you soon. By the way, have you squared the family?'

'All done.'

'Good boy.'

Julian calls Nigel.

'Yup, Cy's up for it. He needs to see the latest balance sheet of course, so can you get that ready by the end of the week?'

'It's almost done. Looks pretty good considering the conditions out there. The agencies have had off-the-record briefings. Old-fashioned virtues have triumphed.'

'OK, Nige. Don't overdo the bullshit.'

'Jules, you are doing the right thing.'

'I hope so.'

> *Fade far away, dissolve, and quite forget . . .*
> *What thou amongst the leaves hast never known,*
> *The weariness, the fever and the fret . . .*

That's Julian's Keats. But it's probably true of Cy that he has never known the weariness, the fever and the fret. Every day for him is, in his telling anyway, an adventure and he never forgets that he started with nothing on Coney Island. He can become lyrical about the sounds of the roaring, screaming, falling Big Dipper that punctuated his childhood and he still goes out there sometimes to buy a hot dog, the best in New York, he says. Owning Tubal's will remind people of just how far he has come. He is in love with life. Life is to him the multiple opportunities the world of money offers him to demonstrate his combative/charming qualities. He's the sort of man who spends very little time in introspection. Julian thinks that in order to succeed in business you need, like his father and like Cy, to have limited imagination. If you were aware of life's possibilities would you really choose a path of endless problems, disappointments and treachery? Would you choose to wear white Gucci loafers without irony? Moses Tubal was probably the same, but he was driven by the ferocious desire of the outsider to belong. But the

Tubals are safely on the inside. They're woven into the fabric. Their bums are deep in the butter.

He asks Jade to open the gate, a Victorian Gothic wooden door, studded with fancy medieval ironwork – Cy will love this – and as he arrives at the car park she is waiting, sturdy, beside the gate, plumped up defensively like a hen, as if she is ready to repel the oiks.

'Thanks, Jade. Give Jason my best, won't you?'

'Yes, sir.'

'And tell him from me, you are doing a great job.'

'Thank you, sir.'

She's as happy as a Labrador. He's aware as he drives out on to Bread Street – completely deserted apart from two Japanese or Korean tourists looking at a map – that the staff are going to be angry. They have a proprietorial feeling for the bank, carefully nurtured by his forebears over three hundred years.

The river is high. He loves these few hours when the weary old Thames looks grand and imposing, the water lapping at the huge granite blocks of the Embankment and the bridges, the tourist boats, the restaurant boats and *HMS Belfast* all riding high in the water, and today the spring sun is titivating the water and turning the familiar murky khaki into something lively and active. As he slows for a traffic light, he sees small dinghies sailing, anxiously escorted by a man zipping about in a Zodiac inflatable. All the sailors wear fluorescent life jackets. Julian has a friend who lives on the river at Limehouse and he claims to swim when the tide is full; the detritus, the dead bodies – traditional in Limehouse – have sunk and the mysterious stray chunks of lumber have come to rest, so that the water, he says, is perfectly clean. He says he has seen a man catch a salmon near by. When Moses Tubal was alive the river ran between fields and swamps and groves of willow and drifts of celandine. The sweet Thames ran softly then. And in his subdued state, Julian wonders if all the massive works and cranes and bridges are really a tribute to man's energy and vision. Could they just be one huge delusion? At least the Victorians were making something, something that existed and that you could stumble over, something very different in fact from the Gaussian bell curve.

He shouts, 'Where are our fucking alligator swamps? *Où sont les crocodiles d'antan? Where the fuck are they?*' And he laughs.

As he passes the stretch of green at Cheyne Walk, presided over by a statue of Sir Thomas More, he sees a man in a tweed jacket practising his fly fishing on the grass, his lurcher sitting watching patiently. The gillies in Scotland taught Julian and Simon to cast on grass with a button in place of a fly. What is it about the English upper classes that it is still so important to associate themselves with the country-side? Lurchers, rabbits, tweed, Viyella shirts, caps – flat caps are back – and those Dijon mustard trousers. Signifiers. Signifying that these people are the true people of England. You never see a Jew in these togs, accompanied by a lurcher, although that Home Secretary chap used to dress up in new green wellingtons and corduroy trousers in his constituency. God, he looked like a twat. At Eton the thickos with inherited acres regarded themselves as far superior to the merely rich or intelligent.

He turns up through Chelsea, away from the river, and heads up to the park and Notting Hill. They have a large garage round the side of the house in a mews, where he pulls in. Kim has taken the children to an open day at one of her urban gardens, scraps and corners of land butting up against railway lines and disused gas holders, all being lavishly manured. She is making a speech. She is now a vice-president of the Soil Association: it all starts with the soil and spirals upward towards heaven. Their food at home comes from known sources where the farmers are kind to the soil and the crops that are grown in it and the beasts that feed contentedly on this superior fodder. They are contented until their big day when, as Joyce put it, their heads are poleaxed and their brains spill out.

11

FLEUR WALKS ACROSS the terrace. She is wearing green shorts to allow her legs to catch the sunshine, which is falling on the front of the house. At the height of summer the terrace throbs with heat. Long after the sun has gone, you can feel the trapped heat escaping from the terracotta tiles. Harry is sitting under the umbrella pines, looking out to sea. She walks over to him and puts her hand on his shoulder. He glances up at her and says something that she believes is 'Fleur'. His face is powdery, mildewed. His eyes are laced with strings of blood.

'Yes, darling?'

His face is contorted now and his legs in the pale-yellow trousers are mortally thin. He doesn't answer. She sits next to him and holds his hand. His fingers are stiff; there is no answering pressure. If he knows he's dying, is she frightening him by being here? Since she arrived yesterday his face has become more anguished, but she can't identify the cause. He may be trying to tell her something. Or possibly he wants to ask her why she has neglected him. Even Estelle says she can no longer understand his words. He's deteriorated in the last few weeks.

'I'll get some coffee, Harry, and I'll come back very soon.'

He doesn't react. In the house she finds Estelle.

'He's not good, is he?'

'No, he's not.'

Her demeanour is tightly under control.

'Do you think we should call the doctor?'

'Julian said he would speak to Mr Abbott tomorrow and see what should be done.'

'If anything.'

'If anything.'

They are two women doing, she thinks, what women have always done, taking charge of the dying and competing for the priestly role. A sort of solemnity has seized them. It's uncomfortable.

'Estelle, could you ask Chef to make some coffee. What shall we order for Harry?'

'He's on a fairly strict regime now. We can't really give him drinks as usual, because his kidneys are not working too well. He gets another drink at one o'clock. *Treize heures*, as the French say.'

Treize heures? Why is she saying that? She doesn't speak French.

'I'll ask the chef to prepare you your usual, Lady Trevelyan-Tubal.'

'Estelle, please, call me Fleur. It's sort of oppressive now, at this time. This formality I mean. We're in this together.'

Estelle walks stiffly and squarely towards the kitchen. She doesn't accept Fleur's offer of camaraderie. Her feet clatter on the flags as if they, at least, are protesting. There's a strong scent – an oily gust – of rosemary from the garden where one of the Algerians is cutting and weeding. She walks to the hall and looks at the Matisse, which Harry said he would leave her, but obviously changed his mind. Maybe they could get him on to the boat and take him around the bay that he loves. The painting, he was fond of saying, was a revolution in perspective, drawing the eye through the window and out into the distance. Matisse liked the sense that the infinite space came seamlessly up against the domestic, to make one space. The focal point is nothing specific, but you cannot help searching. Perhaps now he thinks that the far distance, the cheerful blue sea beyond the masts of the moored boats, is where he is headed.

She finds Estelle in the kitchen. A tray is laid with coffee and *tuiles aux amandes*.

'Estelle, I have had an idea. Wouldn't it be nice to take Harry out on the boat? Do you think he would like it?'

'The boat's having a refit. Julian wanted it done.'

'Julian? It's his father's boat.'

'Apparently the engines weren't working and Julian sent the boat to the boatyard. He asked me to tell Sir Harry.'

'Oh. OK.'

She sits with Harry and nibbles a *tuile aux amandes*. Harry may never have another chance to go on his beloved boat. Harry looks out to sea and grimaces. Fleur sees that all her paths to the family are growing over. Estelle speaks for Harry; Julian bypasses her; Amanda gives her the brush-off, and Estelle does not want to enter into an alliance of any sort with her. She wonders what Estelle is planning to do when Harry passes. She remembers cringing when her mother, with fastidiously pursed lips, used the word 'passed' to describe a death. Now she thinks that it is the right word. Harry appears to be ready to pass through the window of the house and out on to the limitless, hazy Mediterranean beyond. There's another Matisse that used to hang in his office in Bread Street; now it hangs in the morning room. Last night Harry sat in front of it for an hour. It's called *French Window at Collioure* and is three panels of colour, but still clearly a window with a stone frame. The stone of the window is in lilac, the shutter – if it is a shutter – is of a wood bleached by exposure to the sun and on one side of that is a lintel of greeny grey. It could be seen simply as beautiful blocks of colour. But in the middle, where you would expect the view beyond, there is a large rectangle of darkness, absolutely black. And maybe that's what Harry sees, the looming nothingness. Her lips are minutely littered with almond crumbs, and she brushes them with the back of her hand. Harry said to her that Matisse believed the artist should see with the eyes of a child throughout his life. Could that be what Harry was doing, staring at the blackness with childish apprehension?

She reaches for his hand; her heart, her little gingham actressy sentimental dishonest heart, is full. He turns towards her. There is a small aggregation of greenish scum at the corner of his mouth. It's the colour of the lintel in the painting. His pills – there are many – have given him a strange scent, somewhere between the bottom of a mouldy biscuit tin and a doctor's surgery. Even as she inhales this for a moment when he turns, she longs for Morné with his warm, vital scent of sweat and youth. She looks at Harry, adjusting his hat – slightly askew – and kisses him. But instead of being pleased or comforted, his dimpled, dry, veined, fungal, Somme-landscape face becomes contorted, and his cold parchment hands come up to his cheeks; he clutches them in unmistakable horror, his eyes are rheumy and liquid as tears – or a random expression of bodily fluid – gather in the corners.

She jumps up and runs back to the house. The turtle doves are at full volume. The cicadas are tuning up. Even the avian and insect life is telling her to fuck off.

Il faut regarder toute la vie avec les yeux des enfants.

Estelle has seen the kiss and Harry's reaction: Fleur is tormenting him.

As Fleur strides into the house, Estelle says, 'Is everything all right, Lady Trevelyan-Tubal?'

'What do you think? He hates me.'

'Oh I don't think he's . . .'

'He hates me and you have turned him against me.'

She is crying now. And as she rises up the grand staircase Estelle can hear a gulping sob. It's a baby's sob. A spoilt baby's sob.

Estelle goes out to Harry. He turns, staring, fearful; but he smiles when he sees her.

'Dear Harry,' she says, 'how are you? Lunch is nearly ready.'

'Fleur.'

'Yes, she's here. She's gone to her room.'

As she wipes the foam from the corner of his mouth she realises that Harry thinks she is Fleur and he has no idea who this other woman is.

Harry sleeps downstairs, so that in an emergency he can be rushed to hospital and also to avoid the stairs. Up in her old bedroom, Fleur lies on the covers. Out to sea the pale haze has thickened, blurring the distinct line between the horizon and the water. She wants to ring

Morné and tell him how she feels, but she knows she can't. Down below a gong is sounding to indicate that lunch is ready. It's from Burma, mounted on a teak stand, and belonged to Harry's maternal grandfather. Eventually she goes down. Estelle is waiting anxiously.

'No, I'm not having lunch, thank you. I'm going for a walk. I want the gate opened now. Immediately.'

She walks across the gravel crunching it noisily. She sets off for the port. The Villa Tubal is squeezing the life out of her. It has until now been a place where she felt free and happy. From the villa there is a narrow lane of high walls. A Russian billionaire has recently bought Villa Floriana next door. He paid an enormous amount of money for it. The locals are upset: they think that €150m. is an absurd amount of money and will destabilise the place. The sums of money washing around are toxic, but then there is money everywhere, despite the banking crisis. When she first joined the family she couldn't comprehend the amounts they had. She saw an invoice one day from John Lobb for two pairs of handmade shoes: £8,000. For two pairs of Harry's shoes! It was shocking. But you adjust: good shoes, after all, are an essential. For the locals the idea that people who are basically criminals should have so much money and use it to belittle them is offensive. The locals are minor, look-the-other-way rascals, not criminals.

The midday heat is bouncing back at her from the walls. By the time she reaches the port she is calmer. Perhaps Harry is simply scared of what's to come: the truth is he doesn't really recognise her and she shouldn't be so upset. She orders a coffee and a glass of wine at Le Voilier. The patron knows her and he comes out from the dark depths to offer some olives and propose – *Je propose* – a very light *bourride*. 'No thank you, Jean-Loup.' His name is a lot more *sportif* than he is.

'*Comme vous voulez, Madame. Milord s'améliore?*'

'*Oui, je crois, un peu mieux chaque jour.*'

Actually, Milord is not ameliorating himself at all. Quite the reverse.

The yacht basin is coming to life after the winter. In their self satisfied way the yacht owners and crews are ferrying supplies out to their boats in small dinghies; decks are being varnished, sails pulled from lockers and the restaurants all around are sweeping and polishing and cleaning. There is a nice domestic atmosphere. The big motor yachts now tie up at a huge quay built to accommodate a Russian oligarch's new boat. Graft is suspected.

The Bar Sport opposite is always busy with locals – who don't own villas or yachts, but make a living supplying them – toping away from seven in the morning. Sometimes they take a whole hardboiled egg with their *petits vins blancs* or *petits vins rouges*. The prevailing fiction is that lots of small glasses of wine don't add up to anything much. Their faces are fired like bricks. They laugh a lot, but it's the whistling-in-the-dark laughter of drinkers, tinged with self-knowledge. Around them, at home and here in the bar, are sensible women who clean and cook and tidy and are always, in contrast to their men, bustling. These people – the last peasants – are united in their dislike of North Africans: the narcissism of minor differences, Freud called it.

She sees Bryce walking up towards the bar. He catches sight of her.

'G'day, Lady Fleur.'

'Hi, Bryce.'

'Drinking alone?'

'I'll buy you one.'

'Bonzer.'

She thinks he must get his Aussie slang off the web.

Jean-Loup appears smoothly. Bryce orders a beer.

'Jeez, I'm hungry. I could eat the crutch out of a low-flying duck. Let me have the *bourride*, Jean. What about you, Fleur, why don't you have lunch with me?'

'*OK, moi aussi, je prends la bourride.*'

'So, how's Sir Harry?'

'Do you want the official version or the truth?'

'You choose.'

'He's not doing well. He may have to have a kidney removed.'

'Oh, jeez, that's crook.'

'Bryce, could you lay off the Aussie schtick. I know you were at Geelong Grammar.'

'Geelong Grammar, my arse, I was at the school of hard knocks.'

'That's not what I heard. How's the boat?'

'All done and dusted.'

'Can we take her out?'

' 'Fraid not. It's sold. Oh, you didn't know?'

'Why? Who sold it?'

'Julian, I suppose. I don't know. Boris Vladykin, your new neighbour, bought it. And me. For six months anyway. I don't think it's his kind of boat. He will want something way more like a floating hotel soon.'

She wants to protest that it is Harry's boat, her boat, and that Harry loves the annual classic boat regatta at the port; he hasn't missed the *Voiles d'Antibes* for forty years, but she sees that this is not the moment. It's pretty obvious that nobody really thinks of her as part of the family. Anyway, it may be a family boat, owned by the trustees.

'No, nobody told me, but then why would they?'

'I can think of plenty of good reasons.'

'Actually, so can I.'

'Shit happens.'

'You're a philosopher. I hadn't realised.'

He laughs.

Bryce is that rare thing, a happy person. It's not fashionable to be unconditionally happy. You have to have suffered and then to have got your life back on track, in this way enjoying a certain amount of self-admiration, which passes for happiness. But Bryce is genuinely happy: everything he does from sailing boats to eating a *bourride* – which now arrives in deep earthenware bowls – makes him happy. The *bourride* is fiercely red with tomatoes and in this unctuous redness two small local rock fish are half submerged along with some mussels and langoustines; crab limbs break the surface. Jean-Loup places a smaller bowl of *aïoli* on the table and a basket of sliced baguette. The French always cut baguettes in exactly the same way and place the slices in exactly the same little baskets. Jean-Loup says there is some turbot in the depths. He speaks conspiratorially: turbot is reserved for the best customers, he seems to be suggesting.

'*Un peu de vin, Monsieur, Madame?*'

'Let's have a bottle of your Goats do Roam.'

'*Côtes du Rhône, bonne choix, Monsieur Bryce.*'

Bonne choix. Fleur wonders if it's possible to make good choices. Sure, a bottle of wine or a *bourride*, they are easy, but on what basis do you really decide you want to spend your life mucking about in boats or speaking other people's words? Or marrying Harry. She would like to ask Bryce but he is sucking enthusiastically on a small langoustine. Could she have made other choices? In theory, she could have. But when her mother sent her to stage school and when Artair came along and when Harry began to pursue her, nearly smothering her with flowers, the die was already cast. Where does Morné fit into this pattern? It's too early to tell, but it's sure that having an affair with a personal trainer is utterly predictable and will appear pathetic with hindsight.

But now, becoming a little flushed as the chilli in the soup sweeps through her and the red wine races indiscriminately about, she feels a surge of optimism.

'Great *bourride*,' says Bryce.

'Bryce, do you ever worry about the future?'

'Never. I just go from day to day.'

'You just go from day to day? That's it?'

'More or less.'

'And women? Girls?'

'Loads of those wherever possible.'

'And what are you going to do when that stops?'

'Why would it stop?'

'Well, slows down.'

'Plan B.'

'What's that?'

'Dunno. I'll think of it when I have to.'

'Great.'

He stops eating, a loaded spoon suspended against the harbour.

'Fleur, what's your real question?'

His eyes are hidden by his dark glasses and his lips, permanently flaked by sunshine, are lightly smeared with *aïoli*.

'I just don't know what's going to happen to me if Harry dies. Now you tell me the boat's been sold, that and one or two other things have upset me.'

'You'll be OK. You are a lovely woman and rich. You'll be fine.'

'Will I?'

'Of course you will. You'll find someone in minutes.'

She wonders if this can be true. She understands that she is one of those women whose purpose seems to be to live through men. She hears her friends talking of how they want to be independent and study literature or travel to the Hindu Kush, but she has noticed that these elevated thoughts usually arise only after some man has let them down. It's particularly true of those who have made disastrous choices, which all the friends could see would end in a train crash. And it's something to do with getting a little older, that you can see this sort of thing a mile off, even when the protagonists can't.

'I've always thought you were totally gorgeous,' says Bryce, in a matter-of-fact way.

'Bryce, what a lovely thing to say.'

'But I couldn't do anything about it. As we say in Australia, never dip your pen in the company's ink.'

'But now that you are employed by a Russian oligarch . . . Is that the sort of thing you were thinking?'

'Spot on.'

When she gets home, the turtle doves are winding down. Their calls become more liquid and diffident as the sun begins to set. The sea is darkening and that wonderful haze of gold, beaten to thinness, is lying beyond the Cap, so that the Mediterranean looks as though it is encased in a dome that doesn't extend beyond the limits of the classical world.

She rings the bell at the villa's gate: Emma Bovary is home. The housekeeper lets her in.

Estelle comes quickly across the gravel, almost running, no – scuttling, like one of those creatures that went into the *bourride* – and she knows that while she was in bed with Bryce in his small apartment behind the port, Harry has died.

Our lives run on rails.

But Estelle tells her he has had another stroke and the air ambulance is on its way. Estelle has ordered it after talking to Mr Abbott. Estelle has had the last word.

12

FROM DOWN THIS end of England, London looks alien and very distant. Melissa's only been to London twice. Her mother is advising her. She took a course in London for six months in 1981 and retains some expertise. She is concerned about Melissa's clothes. She thinks Melissa should have a suit and has seen just the thing in Marks & Spencer. It's elegant. Against her better judgement Melissa has agreed to go with her to see what's on offer. She favours the single-breasted, notch-lapel suit, with slacks, but her mother thinks that the single-breasted, one-button, chevron, dark suit is more classic, although Melissa isn't sure what she means by 'classic'. Linguistic philosophy, module 11, Ordering the Language of Philosophy, has made her sceptical about the loose use of ordinary words: 'classic' could mean anything. Like 'boring'. It's £55. The skirt is another £45. She tries it on and thinks that maybe the skirt is a little tight, emphasising her plumpness, but the assistant says that she looks great, it only needs letting out, and they buy it on her professional recommendation: *It's a real classic. You can't go wrong.* They try on a white silk-look blouse to go with it. Then she hurries to the office, leaving her mother marvelling at the elegance of the classic suit, with the assistant nodding enthusiastically.

The editor wants to see her.

'Come.'

He is smoking and his office is in a low fog.

'Sit down. I liked your blog on Pamela Anderson and Shakespeare. Very good. It's a freak-show out there. Anyway, I want you to record your conversation with your source tomorrow for accuracy and I want you to phone me just before you meet him. Let him talk. Don't ask too many questions. Sources are usually people who have a grudge and they can't wait to tell you what they know. Just be as sympathetic as you can and take a few notes for authenticity. And bail out if he seems like a nutter.'

There's a harsher note to his voice than any she has heard before. Tougher. He has suggested the meeting place, the courtyard of Somerset House with a view of the fountains, and her source, Alan39, has agreed to meet there. The editor thinks it will be safer to meet in a public place.

'Now, Mr MacCleod, you haven't told him about this?'

'No, you mentioned that.'

'Just checking. We need to be sure that there is something in this story before we go public. But go and see him again now and find out, discreetly, if his money has come through. Go and see him and say that the paper wants to send someone to photograph the cast and slip in a question about his money. See what you can find out. OK, here's some petty cash for the ticket and here's a hundred for incidentals. If you go over let me know when you come back. Don't speak to accounts. I've arranged cabs to take you to Mr MacCleod and to the station. And good luck tomorrow.'

He's made her uneasy with his talk of nutters and public places and the vow of silence regarding accounts.

Artair's usual transport refused to move the sets to Newquay when he couldn't pay in advance and the new man, who is supposed to be moving them in a horse box – he's guaranteed that it has been mucked out – has broken down in a lay-by on Bodmin Moor. And the Royal National Lifeboat people, his landlords, have written to him, despite accepting his offer of free tickets, asking him to vacate the lifeboat station within thirty days, unless payment, plus interest, is made by the end of the week. The bank has refused him an overdraft, despite the twenty years he has been a customer; he probably shouldn't have written to that little shit the manager, Trefelix, to say that he was a money-grubbing intellectual pygmy. The manager wrote back saying that the bank had a zero-tolerance policy towards any form of racial and religious denigration. The word 'pygmy', Artair replied, was used as a metaphor for small-minded; it was not in any way a reflection on the heroic race of small people inhabiting the dense and unforgiving jungles of Central Africa. The manager did not take up the challenge of a long intellectual correspondence. Only Binster's Pies and Pasties have remained loyal, sending him a box of their product each week.

But there is some good news from the autograph people, Fraser's: they will accept the *Richard III* for sale with a reserve of £500. Also on the plus side, *Thomas the Tank Engine* is playing to almost capacity audiences of cynical little fat children and their obese, fleece-clad parents, and he has been able to pay the actors. But he wonders how it is that at the age of seventy-six he is obliged to go himself to the scene of the breakdown to pay cash for a tow-truck. His assistant is still away with back trouble, a well-known symptom of depression. Also he has received an email from El Camino Drive. In fact, it is more in the nature of an automatic response, acknowledging receipt of his email, than a reply, but he has high hopes for the life of Flann O'Brien, starring Daniel Day-Lewis. The Bloomsday framework for the piece has given it coherence. He will have to explain it to Daniel in person, but you have to allow agents the conceit that nothing can happen without their assent. Their true life's work is to prove that they are as important as their clients. When they wake in the night they understand that they are just the pimps in the real relationship: the panders, the go-betweens. They have no talent, and they know it. The transformative power of art is a mystery to them. To Artair it is everything. His life has been a string of triumphs and disappointments but he has always been sustained by the certainty that life is for living according to your highest aspirations. Life is for burning up. And a life lived in the pursuit of art is the only one worth living. On any rational assessment, he is at a low point – penniless, under threat from landlords and banks, stabbed in the back by the Tubal family, and with his clapped-out production of *Thomas the Tank*

Engine and its poorly painted sets stuck on the A30 in a horse box. A certain unaccustomed desolation surrounds him as he looks out at the green, ceaselessly motile tide and the hulk of the fishing boat, which lends a suggestion of memento mori to the view; yes, he is at a low point, but he knows that Flann O'Brien is a project that has unlimited possibility. He has tried to contact Fleur direct, but the letter has obviously not found its way through the security that these rich families employ to protect themselves; they have battalions of lawyers and gatekeepers. Wealth makes them nervous. He nibbles the crust of a cheese-and-onion pasty. He has acquired a pasty aroma: there's something farinaceous about his piss, too.

Fleur. He wonders if she is happy inside this cocoon of wealth. What he remembers of her most vividly is her awareness of her own girlish sexuality. It was as if she took more pleasure in the excitement she aroused in men than in sex itself. There are many forms of self-affirmation, of course. More and more he hears people speaking the language of self. Their lives are a work in progress, as they attest to becoming more confident, more assertive, more independent and happier. It's a delusion fostered by lifestyle and celebrity babble on television. Celebrity on the Daniel Day-Lewis scale, for example, depends not on having your breasts enlarged or going to parties, but on possessing a real transformative talent. Fleur, sadly, was no actress. He had wanted her to be great, but her acting was not intuitive; it was more an imitation of acting than acting itself. Great actors, like great writers, draw you into their world. They reshape the world minutely by their work. How do you explain that to a bank? He rings his lawyer, the legal eagle, Barnecutt, but of course it's a Wednesday and he's relaxing at home with his sex animal Lowenna, after working his fingers to the bone on Monday and Tuesday.

A taxi arrives. He opens the door allowing a seagull-speared and wind-racked day to enter briefly. It's Melinda from the *Globe*.

'Melinda. How are you?'

'Melissa. Windswept but fine, Mr MacCleod. And how are you?'

'On the record, I am fine, and *Thomas* is playing to packed houses. But I have to accept that – off the record – things are not good. On the plus side, Daniel Day-Lewis's agent has replied. Obviously, I can't tell you the contents at this stage, but let's just say there is hope. I'll put some coffee on. I managed to find some of Signor Lavazza's Crema e Aroma in the cupboard. My favourite. Sit over there by the window and look at the heron-priested shore. My assistant is still AWOL. Ah, here we are, Cre-ma e Ar-oh-mah.'

He proclaims as if he's Richard of Gloucester: ' "Now is the winter of our discontent made glorious summer . . ." ' Melissa is amazed at how many vowels and their little subsets he can find in a phrase. She looks at the half-submerged wreck out in the estuary while Artair puts the Bialetti on the stove and spoons in some coffee. His hair beneath the little hat is like the eaves of a thatched house. He is wearing a crumpled but vividly green T-shirt which bulges over his stomach.

'You know as I was waiting for you, Melinda, I was thinking of past lovers. There's nothing quite so melancholy as lost love. And do you know why? Because it's not recoverable. At the time you move on, but you leave something of your innocence behind. It's leached out. OH FUCK.'

'What happened?'

'I burned my hand on this miserable little Eyetie gizmo.'

'Are you all right?'

'No, but I will survive. Just a mild scorch. Right coffee – caffé espresso – first the crema then the aroma.'

He pours into two chipped cups, one from the Royal National Lifeboat Institution and the other from the National Theatre. She sips: she's never had coffee this strong before.

'Espresso. The finest.'

'It's strong. Oh my God.'

'It's supposed to be strong. It's supposed to hit you right here.'

He makes a chopping motion with his hand against the back of his neck and takes it in one.

'*Puttana di merda*, as the Italians say. Right, fire away.'

She feels she is being underhand, but she sees that this is the way journalism works.

'Well, I wanted to know a little bit about your plans. The editor wants an update and he'll send a photographer tomorrow to Newquay. He thinks you could be photographed outside the theatre. He's very keen that you should be funded properly. And personally, I would like to know about your film project.'

'The first few dates have been a huge success. We open tomorrow night in Newquay, as you rightly said, and I'll be going down there this afternoon just to keep an eye on the production.'

'Did you suggest that there was no progress on the grant?'

'I've not had a reply from the trust, but my lawyers are on to it. It must be a foul-up. You know what these big organisations are like: we're barely a speck in their eye. It will be sorted out soon, I am sure.'

But Artair seems to have been diminished in the days since she last saw him. His voice is confident but his eyes are cowed.

'Have you tried speaking to your ex-wife?'

'I did send her a message through the family solicitors, but so far there has been no reply.'

'I saw on the wires that Sir Harry Trevelyan-Tubal has been flown to London for treatment. He's had another stroke, apparently.'

'Yes. Poor Fleur.'

'Why poor Fleur?'

'She's a dependent person, very needy as they say now. She needs the admiration of men. Like Blanche Dubois. Pauline Kael said nobody else in theatre had this quality of hopeless feminine frailty.'

Later, she Googles Blanche Dubois. She is not a real person. Melissa wonders if Artair isn't being harsh on Fleur because she left him. Also, Pauline Kael, she finds, was a famous film critic.

'Could your taxi give me a lift into town?' he asks. 'We could talk on the way. I have to sort out one or two small problems with the production en route.'

As they drive along the estuary, he talks. He talks about Gielgud and Richardson and *At Swim-Two-Birds*. She has only a limited idea of what he's talking about or what decade he is traversing in his mind. It's like listening to someone speaking a foreign language you barely know, with only the odd phrase having meaning. It all seemed to have happened so long ago. People of his age find it hard to believe that she was born in 1989. To them, that is yesterday. But his strong face and deep, damp eyes and the comical hair are all engaged in the telling and she listens not to the sense but the music. Larry said to Ralph and Johnny had a hissy fit and then Brendan somebody or other vomited on the dinner table and heckled his own play at the Abbey and the Crowned Bard of Porthmadoc turned out to be a transvestite and she feels strongly that after all this heroic struggle he deserves better than to be cut off, penniless and homeless, unless the grant comes through. Which, in her opinion, is not likely to happen. She leaves him at the bus station. He's picking up some money. One of the actors is making a detour to bring him the takings of £600. Two hundred has to go to a tow-truck driver, although she couldn't follow the whole story.

'Bye, Mr MacCleod. And congratulations on your production.'

'You're a sweet girl, Melissa.'

'You got my name right, Mr MacCleod. Hurray!'

'You'll be at the first night. I will introduce you to Daniel. I can see you don't believe me, but I will.'

'I believe you. Honest.'

And she does in a way. She has to collect her clothes and take the taxi to the station in time for the London, Paddington train. The hotel the editor has recommended for its proximity to the meeting place is included in a shoppers' special at a discounted fare. It's designed to attract the peasants from the outlying districts to enjoy some shopping in London.

Artair arrives by taxi at the scene of the breakdown. The driver of the horse box is unapologetic. As far as he is concerned it's a natural disaster and nothing to do with him. He says it's one of those things. The tow-truck arrives and Artair hands over the money, a third of the previous night's takings. He sits with the driver in the cab of the horse box as they are towed in the direction of Newquay. He uses the time – they are moving slowly – to think about Fleur who will soon be a very rich widow. He has never allowed money to dominate his life. It wasn't his idea that he should receive a pay-off, but Harry's. It was humiliating, done with a forensic coldness. But the arrangement has allowed him to run his theatre company and live modestly.

Fleur, Fleur. Once a film festival had invited him to Brittany as a judge and he and Fleur had stayed in a dilapidated but grand chateau. The place had excited her: there were a lot of important directors with younger women. She had pulled up her skirt and sat astride him against a background of crumbling plaster and scraps of tapestry – he remembers a maid carrying a cornucopia of fruits – and they had arrived downstairs for the opening dinner – all the richness of the Breton coast was on display – in a febrile state. He was seated next to the Mayor's wife and they discussed oysters and crustaceans. His French was not up to more detailed conversation and anyway she had none, although like most French people she respected something called '*la culture*': '*La culture de la région est très forte*,' she said confidently. Across the table Fleur was charming a fellow judge, a man who had won the Prix Goncourt twenty-five years before, and had dedicated his subsequent life to smoking and young women. Fleur sucked oysters lasciviously and glanced suggestively at Artair as he struggled to find something interesting to say about *araignées de mer* and *huitres*. On the wall behind Fleur and the laureate, who was working hard on his Gallic intellectual act, was a fishing net adorned with crabs and lobsters. From this distance it was impossible to tell if they were real, but in front of the net there was a huge table on which mountains of seafood were piled in that quasi-artistic style that the French favour, so that lobsters reared up in heraldic contest with spider crabs and thousands of shrimps advanced on the mussels; it looked like a battle panorama – the Battle of Waterloo, recreated by seafood. Probably, he thinks now, the festival was funded by the Société de Pisciculture de Bretagne. And he sees a certain symmetry: he is funded by Binster's; a few pasties are not in the same league as lobsters and spider crabs rampant, but they are also in the cause of art.

Fleur, he saw then, was particularly excited by escaping the suburbs where she had grown up. This was it: sitting next to an elderly French literary man who was describing to her one or two of his many sexual encounters, trying to pique her interest, irredeemably and for ever vain, in this magnificent but tired chateau overlooking a wooded creek of some unknown Breton river. Her mouth – how clearly he remembers it now – was glistening with oil, and the literary man was (she told him) trying to stroke her leg under the table. She winked at Artair. Later she also confessed to having brushed the front of his trousers with the back of her hand, but she found no sign of life. She and Artair made love again in the huge brocaded bed after the dinner; a fine cloud of ancient dust rose from the tapestries and the bed coverings. Above all he remembers Fleur lying on her front, carelessly, innocently, knowingly provocative. And he feels the loss keenly in the horse-scented vehicle as it is towed down the A30. He's allergic to horses and their by-products. The owner of this malodorous horse box, who himself has yellow equine teeth and a huge earring, looks at him disdainfully as he starts to sneeze. Artair feels an urge to kill him, as they trundle along behind the tow-truck.

13

BEFORE HE WENT to the hospital, Julian tried to summon his brother from the Okavango Delta, but there was no obvious way of finding him. He has delegated to Nigel the task of getting him a message somehow, although he knows Nigel is busy with the accounts.

In the hospital his father lies wired up. His head, still a very bold presence, moves and smiles, or seems to. But Mr Abbott says that the scan reveals that there is no significant brain function. He has the sort of handsome, intelligent look that seems to develop in the higher reaches of professional life.

'Can you keep him alive until we are all assembled?'

'We can. Unless there is another catastrophic brain event.'

'He squeezed my hand.'

'Yes,' says Abbott, 'but that is, I am afraid, simply an involuntary reaction, a sort of spasm.'

Mr Abbott has a hieratic and soothing manner, as though over years of giving bad news he has perfected the words to a point where they have almost become a litany, the sort of familiar and comforting formula believers like to hear in church.

'Are you saying there's absolutely no chance of recovery?'

'None. I'm sorry and it's entirely understandable and commendable that you would wish to take any possible opportunity to help your father, but this is, sadly, the end of the road. Your brother will be here soon, you said, and I think then it would be best to end this process. Of course the final word is yours and Lady Trevelyan-Tubal's.'

'She is coming in from France this afternoon to see him. Can you be here?'

'I'm in theatre, but I will send one of my senior registrars to answer any questions and accompany Lady Trevelyan-Tubal. Just let my secretary know when she is coming if you can and he'll be waiting. I'll alert him.'

Mr Abbott and the Matron escort Julian all the way to the front steps where nurses in their dress uniform sometimes assemble to wave goodbye to recovered members of the royal family. Rather brusquely he hands his file to a junior doctor. The Bentley receives Julian and only then does Mr Abbott turn back. Vulcanised hearts, Julian thinks. Where has he heard that phrase? He knows by the backward glances that Len is anxiously waiting for news of the governor as Julian rings Nigel. He relies too heavily on Nigel.

'He's not going to recover.'

'Oh, I'm so sorry, Jules.'

'The strange thing is he looks more alive than he has for months. He grins and squeezes your hand and his eyes are looking around eagerly. It's horrible.'

'It was the same with my mother, Jules. It was very painful. You feel guilty when they ask you to agree to turn them off. By the way, we're making some progress with finding your brother. A small aircraft has located him and they have found a safari camp that will send out a boat to intercept him. And also, Jules, the rating agency is not considering a downgrade.'

'Good news.'

'Just by the way, the FSA have sent us a letter asking for some detail on the assets, but it's pretty standard stuff; don't worry, I can handle it. As long, of course, as Cy comes up with the cash fairly promptly.'

'OK, thanks. Tennis, Sunday?'

'Absolutely. It's the highlight of my week.'

'Me too. Sad bastards. Mr Abbott says that we should turn him off when my brother has been, and you and I should go to Chicago as soon after as we can. The funeral will be the following week and we'll plan for a memorial in October. Can you work out a schedule?'

'Of course. And another thing, Estelle wants to see him one last time.'

'I'll call her. I'm not sure this is a good moment, loyal though she has been. Do you think I can say family only?'

'Probably not, Jules. She came over in the air ambulance with him and what she wants more than anything is to feel part of the family.'

'One of us. You're right. I'll try to make sure she doesn't meet up with Fleur or Kim and the children. She has a sort of holy possessiveness. Yes, I know what you are thinking: you're thinking she bore the burden for months. All true.'

'Jules, the staff have asked me to tell Mr Julian how so sorry they are about the governor.'

Julian is touched. They all loved the old tyrant. In the hospital he felt a sense of utter futility. His father – the tenth generation of Tubals, chairman of this and that, philanthropist, lover of the ballet, driven around all his life in a huge Bentley – ends up a sea creature, brain dead, his hands flexing and unflexing, mouth opening and closing as though he is sieving the water for minute particles of plankton.

That afternoon Fleur is shown in by Mr Abbott's registrar. She is wearing dark glasses, although it's raining outside. She's struggling with her demeanour. She spoke briefly to Bryce before she left Antibes. He understands. He's a great bloke. Everything happens for a purpose, he says. He thinks that is just about all the philosophy you need. There's a long tradition of great blokes south of the equator, where both her lovers originate. Great blokes hide their feelings and their highest ambition is to be chilled. Life is a sort of enjoyable progress that can only be ruined by introspection.

'I understand, Fleur, you don't have to worry about me blabbing. Just bad timing. See you one day, yeah?'

'Thanks, Bryce, thanks.'

'No worries. You're a real honey.'

She wondered exactly what the qualities of a honey were. Now the registrar takes her into the ITU and she sees her husband lying on his back with his eyes blinking and staring as if he is trying to find something he has lost. She starts to cry. The registrar brings a chair. It's one of those chairs you only find in hospitals with curved blond-wood arms and functional blue plastic seats, designed to provide no hiding place for human secretions or germs. She's not yet quite grasped the notion of widowhood. She feels as if she is grappling with the role, working her way into it. She wipes her nose and sniffs. She removes her huge dark glasses, which have inlays, almost mosaics, in the side-pieces.

'Can he hear anything?' she asks.

'He can't process the sound even if he can hear it. Shall I leave you for a few minutes?'

She's floundering. She remembers the look of horror on Harry's face when she held his hand and kissed him in the garden. She wants to touch him but she's frightened. It was the kiss that caused his disgust, as if she was engaged in the preliminaries of necrophilia. His eyes are reddish: she thinks his soul has been crying. She tries to imagine what it's like to be barely alive. Is there some primal instinct still urging Harry not to die? He moans now and she wonders if he is suffering, not via his conscious mind, but simply suffering pain on the invertebrate level, an overwhelming headache, for example. Julian said that they were advising that there was no point in keeping him alive artificially. Harry's hand is contracting and she reaches out to hold it in the faint hope that he will take comfort. It closes on her fingers with the simple-minded grip of a crab. She wants to call the doctor to release her, but then a spasm seizes Harry, his mouth gapes, closes, his eyes open and close again and then they roll upwards and around the perimeter of his eye sockets as if he's having a fit.

Oh God, oh God.

'Goodbye, dear Harry,' she whispers, but not too near the agitated head; she fears it could snap at her with those regular and youthful teeth, the work of Harley Street's finest implantologists. She sees now that her eighteen years with Harry have been peopled by flunkies. His relationships were always one-sided; everyone deferred to him and he knew no other way. And in those years she, too, has been drawn into a sort of seine net of privilege, with hairdressers, florists, drivers, pilots, doctors, dentists, gardeners, tennis coaches and boatmen all eager to serve, all trembling with the desire to be touched by the holy mystery of great wealth. The truth is that Harry was a coldly ruthless, determinedly selfish but charming man, who never questioned this fawning. It wasn't his fault: the family name carries too much weight and gives off the low humming sound of immense privilege.

Her new life will be simpler. She sees the way forward. It's not too late for her to adopt the more democratic life of people like Bryce and Morné, although she has hints that Morné sees himself as a bit of a philosopher. Sport has given him an insight into motivation and he believes he can harness this energy. When he first told her this, she wondered if he was thinking of producing his own electricity, but he was referring to dynamic qualities, like leadership. And now, next to the dying, blindly semaphoring figure of her husband, she finds herself thinking of her lovers, naked: Bryce, cheerful, relaxed, small-ish cock emerging from reddish pubic hair; Morné all long hard limbs and fibrous muscles, with pubic hair that fades gradually to under-brush on his stomach. His cock is darkish at the end as if someone had been drawing on it with a marker pen. Bryce treats sex as a pleasant pastime, a bit of a laugh, but Morné sees it as a test of his masculinity. She has come – so late – to appreciate the connection between youth and sex.

She understands now, as she sits by the grinning, gurning, contort-ing, wild-eyed body that is Harry, that all his relationships were conducted on his terms. It was his contempt that drove Simon to be a gentleman explorer, a career choice that enabled him to put a huge distance between himself and his father. He once told Julian that he felt there was not enough air for him in a room occupied by Harry.

Harry's geniality was of the iceberg sort: below the surface there was a lot more implacable coldness. His views on the theatre always had to prevail over hers; his choice of restaurant or acceptance of invi-tations or choice of hotel contained the premise that only he had the taste and the experience to make these judgements. She was supposed to be forever grateful to be admitted to his charmed world, but now things have changed: *j'ai deux amants*. And Harry is dying, right in front of her eyes, his power over her lost, and she is elated by and frightened by what is to come.

But still, she loved Harry. She believes it. She loved him. She loved his urbanity and his charm and his passion for her body; she delighted during those early years at how she aroused him. At times it seemed obsessive, as though by feasting on her youth he could ingest some of it. Like the cannibals in Melanesia who wanted to acquire their victims' qualities. Maybe that's what she's doing now.

She sits with Harry, increasingly desperate. Kim has said that she is not coming to the hospital because she doesn't want the children in the presence of death. It's a lively death, punctuated by moans and horrible broad smiles and small convulsions.

Later, when the hospital is dimmed and subdued, and the pools of lights at the nurses' stations have become the lights of a necropolis, Estelle arrives.

She sits by the bed and she tells Harry about the villa and the colour of the sea and the calls of the ring-necked turtle doves in the umbrella pines. He doesn't interrupt, but he is definitely listening. His face is tinged with blue and his mouth moves, trying to speak.

'What is it, Harry?'

He makes a noise but she can't decipher it. He's smiling. She continues with her account of the work the gardeners are doing, planting lavender to replace the plants that have died – some always die inexplicably – because she knows these are the things that please him. She opens a parcel wrapped in brown paper and holds the picture of the port of Collioure in front of him like an icon at a Russian orthodox procession, and he gazes at that intently for a while before falling asleep. She puts the picture away and sits with him for a few hours, until a nurse comes in and asks her if she wants some tea. But as she's asking, the nurse notices that Harry is not breathing. He's dead. Estelle feels guilty; she too has dozed off. But she is thankful that his last sight on this earth was of his beloved picture. When the nurse has left the room to call a doctor, Estelle kisses Harry on his forehead.

'Goodbye, dear Harry. I loved you.'

Is she saying this out loud, or has she, too, slipped into a world where small facts don't matter?

She leaves the hospital before the family can be recalled, to stay with her sister in Queen's Park. As she walks down through Marylebone, looking for a taxi, she wishes she had been born beautiful, and she weeps.

When Simon appears from the Okavango Delta, he brings with him his boundless innocence. He's strangely cheerful because he doesn't subscribe to the idea that death is a downer. It's in fact uplifting, perhaps something to do with recycling. When he first enters his old room in Mulgrave House he is a little surprised to find that his things, for example his books and school photographs, have been moved. Fleur says they are all safely stored in a box room. He sees the point immediately. He says he must go off to buy a suit for the funeral. And he's not upset about arriving after his father has died, because, quite honestly, he wouldn't have known how to handle it. He proposes to walk from Chelsea, wearing his khaki shorts, to Gieves and Hawkes at 1 Savile Row, even though Fleur says that a driver would be delighted to take him. He's very brown, but brown in a speckled way, like a chicken. His legs look as if they have been shot-blasted with African sand.

He smiles at Fleur warmly, indulgently.

'No, no, no need at all. My constitution is geared to the outdoor life. You're a beautiful woman, Fleur.'

She remembers that he often makes guileless remarks. The natives probably love him for it.

Julian arrives on his way to work to discuss the funeral arrangements. He stands in the hall waiting for Fleur.

'Fleur, you can stay here as long as you wish, as you know. Technically the family trust owns the house, but Dad made it plain when you and he were married that you would have a life-right to the house. And we wouldn't want to disturb that arrangement without a reason. It's entirely up to you.'

He's off to work, but already looking tired and drawn. By contrast his brother is rudely healthy. If it was intended to make her feel secure, Julian's little announcement, delivered rather mechanically, has the opposite effect. It's as if he is asking her to consider her position carefully.

'I can't think at the moment, Julian. People go into a state of shock after bereavement, don't they? How are you, poor love?'

'I'm fine. I think I am fine, thanks so much. It will probably hit me later. Where's the intrepid explorer, Sir Simon?'

'Sir Simon. Ah yes, he set off to renew his contact with Gieves and Hawkes.'

'Why?'

'Why? Because he needs a suit now that he is a baronet. All his clothes are in Johannesburg, or perhaps he said St Petersburg. He seems quite excited.'

'He doesn't react like normal people. Which can be both good and bad.'

She knows that Julian bears Simon a grudge; because Simon couldn't be in the same room as Harry after their distracted mother, Eleanor, committed suicide, he left the country and Julian had to go into the bank: he had no choice as he was the next in line after all those generations. He was in his second year of a postgraduate degree at the John F. Kennedy School of Government, Harvard, when his father summoned him. He was studying public policy, whatever that is. Kim was at Radcliffe.

Julian suggests that Estelle should be kept on until all Harry's papers and pictures and so on are located and accounted for. She could also help with the secretarial side of the funeral arrangements and do some forward planning on the memorial service. He produces some notices of Harry's death for her approval. She is moved by the line 'the devoted husband of Fleur'; she's always depended on other people's kindness and it never fails to affect her deeply.

'Julian, does it have to be so quick?'

'It does, unfortunately. Shall I get Estelle to help?'

'Yes, please do.'

'I'll set her up in Bread Street and she can consult with you and help you for as long as it takes.'

'Thank you. You're a darling.'

She has a very good line in old-fashioned, theatrical female help-lessness. Like Blanche Dubois.

'Fleur, will you and Simon come and have dinner with us tonight? Kim says we should keep close. Don't worry, we've got cassava nuts and grilled yams for Simon.'

'I'll come regardless. When he comes back I'll ask him. He doesn't appear to have a mobile.'

'No, he doesn't believe in them.'

'In what sense doesn't he believe in them? They don't exist?'

'They're the devil's work, standing between people. Are you genu-inely all right, Fleur? Please don't feel you're one against many in any way. You are more than part of the family. See you tonight, about eight-thirty.'

When he's gone she thinks this is the warmest thing he has ever said to her. Death seems to release unexpected emotions as though it makes us all more human and causes us to huddle together as the finality of mortality sinks in.

Julian has gone to Bread Street to address the staff and to have a talk with Nigel about their disclosures to the FSA, which – Nigel said at tennis – may be a little more difficult than had first been thought.

Len is adopting a frozen, sombre look. His face is set as if he is determined not to dishonour the governor's memory by speaking out of turn, or smiling. Julian sees that Len is demonstrating his grief and respect to him, and he's driving the Bentley as though it's a hearse and he is the chief undertaker.

Julian feels a pang of anxiety whenever they pass the griffins on the Embankment that mark the City's boundary. It's the same feeling of loneliness and foreboding he had on Sunday nights at school. The tide is low and there's no water visible until they turn up Farringdon Road and, briefly, he can see down the bend in the river to Tower Bridge. The river is wearing its dirty-brown aspect, and agitated seagulls are wheeling overhead. But then who knows what a seagull thinks? Who knows what other humans think, come to that?

He would like to go back to Cambridge, Mass when the bank is sold. He met Kim there at a party given by the editors of *The Crimson*. That was the happiest he has ever been.

All the staff gather in the banking hall, which is closed until lunchtime out of respect for Sir Harry. He stands under the grim-faced Victorian portrait of Joshua Tubal.

'Sir Harry died peacefully on Saturday morning about 3.30 a.m. We, the family, are devastated, and I know already that you are too. My wife and I and Lady Trevelyan-Tubal are very grateful for all the messages you have sent us. My father, as I am sure those of you who knew him don't need reminding, was not an easy man, but he had a passion for this place and a devotion to the staff. He impressed on me from a very early age just how important it was that the bank should run not solely to make money, but to make a contribution to society. And we have always tried to follow his example of probity and prudence. His motto, often repeated, was "Loans one third, assets two thirds". In a sense we are all standing on the shoulders of a giant. The funeral will be across the road at All Hallows next Monday. All Hallows has been the bank's and the family's church since my ancestors converted. Incidentally, my grandfather played an active part in its restoration after the war, when the chancel was destroyed by a Luftwaffe bomb. The bank will be closed all day as a mark of respect, except for the dealing floor and the IT department. All staff are welcome to come to the service, or to take the day off in private memory of my father. Drinks and refreshments will be provided here after the service. Thank you very much, once again. I feel Sir Harry's death is not just the family's loss, but a loss for every one of you. Now, as my father would undoubtedly have said, it's noses to the grindstone.'

What a lot of tosh. Hypocritical crap. He walks up the directors' staircase with Nigel.

'Great speech. Spot on.'

'Thanks.'

They are passing a thirties portrait of a great-uncle in tennis kit, long white trousers and a cricket sweater, holding a wooden racket.

'Jules, we need some coaching. That's twice in two weeks we have lost.'

'Maybe they are better than us.'

'That can't be possible. Never.'

'I played like a drain.'

'No, you weren't at your dashing best, but under the circumstances how could you be?'

Julian hasn't been sleeping. He's been taking sleeping pills. He's blamed it on his father's death, but the fact is that he is nervous about the FSA probing and the deal with Cy. Nigel is far cooler.

When they reach Julian's office, he says, 'OK, the FSA want some more detail. It's purely political; banks are everyone's hate figures and the government and the FSA need to look tough. All you have to do is sign a letter that essentially says that we have understood and we are taking steps to implement the new rules about liquidity. I have had to produce some more figures. But I have drafted a reply that includes upcoming ratings informally. The FSA can go to their masters to tell them we have responded and that will be that. We could delay things by asking counsel to draft an opinion as to whether the new rules apply to us at all, but is that worth it? It might just attract attention. Let me read what I have said.'

He reads.

'Brilliant. OK, let's sign and send it off.'

'And can I fix a flight to Chicago?'

'Just run the dates by Cy's office.'

'Of course.'

Sitting under the Hodgkin he signs on behalf of the bank. They discuss the funeral. Fleur has rung to say that brother Simon, back home, will come to dinner and wants to read a poem or two of his own and an extract from his award-winning travel-trade article, 'What's the Point of Travel?' Perhaps his thinking is that his father is going on a journey. He has also recommended a coffin of woven hemp.

Estelle arrives and Julian feels less lonely, as though in her busyness she is bringing a necessary quotidian quality to proceedings. She's wearing a sober business suit. Her new blue glasses are large; she looks as though she is peering out of two portholes. He wonders if she ever hoped to have an affair with his father.

'Thanks, Estelle. I know what you did for him and I appreciate it. I'm so glad you were there at the last.'

'He was a wonderful man. It was an absolute honour to work for him.'

It's one of those remarks you can't decently argue with.

'Have you spoken to Fleur?'

'Yes, we are going to draw up the lists together. I have already made a draft.'

'How do you think she is?'

'She's coping.'

She doesn't like Fleur. It's a kind of jealousy over possession of the essential Harry. And now she has trumped Fleur by being there as Harry's soul departed his body. *She's trumped us all in the devotional stakes.*

The soul, with its more high-minded approach than the body, departs on death a little fastidiously. Some people report a breeze; a little flutter of wings. Or a draught, as weak as the draught the engines of model planes give off. Plato believed that the soul headed out of the door as soon as the body died. You were born with knowledge, he said, which proved that you had a soul. Those tiny engines, fuelled by ether, would splutter and whine and cartwheel along the grass more often than they flew. When they did fly, they were doomed to nose-dive almost immediately.

His mind is wandering erratically. It's stress. He longs for the moment when he has the bank sold and the trusts paid back. He's tried to tell himself that he has just been pragmatic, but the speech to the staff about values, followed by signing the FSA's forms, has rattled him. He can't say the word 'fraud' to himself. But he's aware that he is not too different from Leeson and the Enron people and Lehman Brothers who tried to hide their debts with something called Repo 105. He has to repay, or he's going the way of the crooks. The sleeping pills have caused him to dream, and he's been dreaming about his pony, which is a very bad sign.

Estelle has set up in what was the directors' smoking room, a panelled room with a huge fireplace. Her old-lady smell has infiltrated the room. It's a combination of face powder and subtle decay. But why it should happen is a mystery to him. His grandmother also had this sickly, insidious aroma. Anybody who believes in God would need to explain why he cruelly allows (or causes) elderly women to moulder in this way. And much more insane arbitrariness. In this room the men of the family would smoke clay pipes and in later years Cuban cigars from Davidoff in St James's Street. The panelling has been lightly roasted in the process.

Earlier he had noticed Estelle looking, mystified, at the Howard Hodgkin behind his desk. She sees me as a usurper, he thinks. The smart-alec son who thought he could do better. And he deserves her disapproval. He can't wait to hand over this nicotine-stained old pile of English heritage to Cy who absolutely loves the directors' apartments and the smoking room, although his doctor warned him off cigarettes years ago. The way he tells this story, or any story, is characteristic of a self-made man – every banal detail of his life and times – even being told to give up smoking – is part of an epic. He's the hero in the narrative of his own life.

14

ALL THROUGH THE night Melissa tried to sleep in the overheated dog kennel of a room which opened onto a blank wall – finished for some reason in greasy off-white tiles. All night Melissa heard the sound of police and ambulance sirens, heavy rumbling from beneath the streets like furniture being dragged in another room, the detached shouts of drunks and, from the hotel's pipes, anguished moaning, followed by clunking and juddering and also there was muffled speaking in tongues – maybe of sex between strangers – and below and around all this, a constant thrumming from deep beneath the crust of London with mysterious electrical and gaseous qualities, as though she could hear the power lines and gasworks and sewers all in constant flux and surge and spurt. Her thin, dirty, mustard curtains flickered as lights of unknown origin played on the walls of the soiled well outside her room, sending her an anxious but obscure message of distress.

By the time morning comes, she believes she is exhausted. *I am in no state for what's to come. I am in no state to meet a source.* But the thought of her source revives her. She gets out of bed, showers in the thin but scalding trickle, and dresses in her classic Marks & Spencer suit. The dining room is staffed by a single Eastern European waitress with very dry blonde hair, wearing a shiny black uniform with an apron, so that the pre-glasnost look, if that's what is intended, is complete. Melissa's breakfast is included in the out-of-town deal. A laminated card on the table reads: *The Full English Breakfast is specially designed to set you up for some serious retail therapy in London's famous West End.*

The waitress has wary, trafficked eyes. She brings the scrambled eggs and tinned orange juice of the designer breakfast and inspects Melissa coldly, as if trying to assess what this young and chubby girl is doing all alone in London.

'Coffee, you like?'

'Oh, yes please.'

She comes back with a metal jug of coffee and pours it. Artair has spoiled her for coffee; she wants to say that she only drinks Signor Lavazza's Crema e Aroma. There is no cosy West Country chat, which Melissa would have liked; maybe the waitress sees only competition in some obscure way, feminine competition for economic advancement. After breakfast she looks for the tenth time at her Google maps. She wants to make sure she knows exactly where she is going. Time spent in reconnaissance is never wasted, says her father, who was in the Territorial Army for a time, driving a Bedford truck, which he says was the workhorse of the armed forces. He likes phrases like 'armed forces' and 'naval power' and 'deadly force'.

She wonders, as she passes through a magnificent archway, if she doesn't look a little overdressed for the assignment. She doesn't look like an ace reporter but a nervous provincial. The courtyard that opens out to her could be in St Petersburg, or what she imagines St Petersburg to be. Fountains play in front of elegant façades that enclose a huge piazza. She's nearly forty minutes early, so she walks back out under the arch, her suit snagging in places, and finds a simple café up a small side street in Covent Garden – the sort of place she is used to, with bacon rolls and milky coffee and sandwich fillings in metal trays. She sips a latte – 300 calories – watching London in all its variety and weirdness go by. She can see that there is a huge difference between Londoners and West Country people. West Country people favour fleeces and vocational shoes, and the younger ones also like frayed string amulets and hoodies, whereas Londoners have a more hard-boiled look and their clothes are astonishingly varied and their hair looks expensive. Down her way people have a cheerful, calf-like expectancy. Early days, but there doesn't seem to be much of that here. Londoners stride purposefully and grimly; bicycles flash by, going in every direction and through every traffic light and over every pavement, and nobody seems to complain. She feels as though she is the foreigner here in this vivid current. In half an hour she's formed the idea that it's time she moved to London. She asks for her bill; before it comes, she turns on the recorder in her inner pocket.

As she walks the short distance back to Somerset House, worrying that her source will not turn up, she thinks that she is now, for better or for worse, in the real world. When you are young, even when you are at college, you see life through gauze. What politicians proclaim, what multinationals do, what older people say and think, comes through a filter that removes the possibility that it applies to you or has any meaning for you. It's just the white noise of a dimly perceived world, heard like the sound of a carousel over a hill. But now she's walking – awkwardly, her classic skirt riding up – to meet a source, a snitch, a man with a grudge, a person from the unfamiliar other-world. The fountains in the middle of the piazza are throwing jets fifty or sixty feet into the air, rising and falling in rhythm against the grandeur of the buildings all around. The whole place speaks of urban sophistication, as though big cities belong to an elite club where art and public works and probably even journalism have a sensibility that doesn't exist out in the provinces. She sees herself as one of those Austen heroines who leave the sticks to stay with the snobbish aunt in London, or a French heroine who departs some stunned, silent town for Paris, wearing the wrong bonnet and shawl. In her silly suit with the cheap shoes and clutching her pink see-through Ryman's folder, she sees herself as a hick. Self-knowledge is painful, but there must be some redemption in recognising it: she's a plump, badly dressed, underprepared amateur. A *rube*, as they say in those American novels they were taught at school. There are generations of British school-children out there who have read *Of Mice and Men* and *To Kill a Mockingbird*.

She sits at a table on the terrace and looks around. She feels even more like a foreigner than the tourists who are wandering about, their children braving the narrow gaps between the fountains, the water rising and falling, in a game of chicken.

'Hello,' a voice says behind her. 'Are you Melissa?'

She turns.

'Alan?'

'You're very young.'

'Sorry.'

He's about forty or a little less, she guesses, wearing a grey suit and a blue spotted tie. His dark hair is thinning at the temples and the crown. He sits. They order some coffee. She hopes the toilet isn't too far away; she's becoming her mother. She takes out her notebook.

'I need to ask you a few questions before I tell you anything. Is that all right with you?' he says.

He has a private-school accent, with – perhaps – some London vowels, she thinks.

'Of course.'

He's nervous too, which helps; there is a faint line of sweat on his upper lip, although it's not hot.

'You work full-time for the *Cornish Globe and Mail*?'

'Yes, I am on a contract, although not staff. Staff jobs are more or less gone in the newspaper world because everyone's getting their information –'

'Yes, I know. My point is, if I tell you why Tubal's haven't paid your man, I need a guarantee that it will be printed. I'm taking a risk.'

'What's the risk?'

He has a thin face, appropriate for a source. He looks around briefly.

'My job prospects. For starters. So I don't want some freelancer hopefully punting this information about.'

'No, no. The editor himself sent me to meet you. Mr Tredizzick.'

'Will he vouch for you?'

'Yes, of course.'

'OK. This is how it works. I give you some information, you publish, and then you make sure it's uploaded on to the net, or picked up by bigger newspapers than the *Globe*, no offence.'

'Can you give me the outline of what's happened with the bank and the money for Mr MacCleod?'

'OK, Melissa, I am going to have to trust you. Tubal's is basically bust. The hedge fund went tits up – belly up – and they are trying to cover themselves so that they can sell. All the philanthropic trusts – charity –'

'I know what "philanthropic" means.'

'All the grants have been cut, assets sold, money moved around the world to hide the fact that the bank's value has fallen. They want to avoid a run before they sell.'

'Can I ask you a question?'

'What?'

'Why are you telling me this?'

'I have my reasons. The less you know about me the better for us both. But I can steer you in the right direction.'

He looks around again and glances at his watch.

'As I said, they are padding the assets. When you come to sell something like this you don't want the purchaser to think there are all sorts of vanity payments and projects and nasty surprises on the books. You cut them. You try to improve the asset ratio. Tubal's is still owned by the family trust and it has some amazing clients. But they fucked up big time when they stepped out of their comfort zone. The son of the old boy is a real upper-class twit. He lost a bundle of their clients' and their own money. Now they plan to sell, but they want the bank to look like a going concern. Follow me?'

'Yes, I think so. What I don't understand is why you are telling me this.'

'You'll have to trust me. What I am telling you is all absolutely true, but you don't need to know anything about me, or why. I will give you proof that they are moving money around fraudulently. It's huge.'

'What am I supposed to do now?'

'Here's the deal.'

But for a moment he says nothing. He seems to be wondering if he can really trust her. She wants to know who he is and what he does and whether he has a wife or a girlfriend, and above all what his grudge is.

'OK, here's the deal. I give you – not now – some paperwork which you show to the editor. It will just be a starter of what I can provide. Then your editor and I speak on the phone at a time I have set. I'm not going over your head, it's just that I need his absolute assurance. I could go straight to the *FT* or the *Journal*, but that's not the way I want to do this.'

'How did you find me? Do you mind me asking?'

'Just an alert: anything to do with Tubal's. Dead simple. I liked your blog, by the way.'

'Oh, thanks.'

'No sweat.'

His narrow face is pale and his flat voice is more estuary than she first thought.

'Yeah, I liked it.'

'But what's in it for you?'

'Does it matter? You don't need to know. Believe me, Melissa, it's better you don't. All you need is rock-solid info, which I can provide, OK?'

But she does need to know. He's proposing to bring down a famous bank. Why? What's his angle? She needs to speak to Mr Tredizzick to get advice. She tries to keep calm, but she's completely out of her depth. Her thighs look fat and rustic and her skirt, which is becoming alarmingly creased, rides up. Her skirt is rising as her confidence is falling.

'Go and talk to your editor. Text me to say he will talk or he won't and we'll fix a time. But wait until you receive the new number that I will text you. I will call him to get the assurances I need and then I will send you the information to get you started.'

'Look, I'm new to this. I don't want you to think that I'm some investigative journo.'

'I know. But I also researched your editor. He's no mug. He got burnt in the Maxwell business, but he knows the game. This is a big opportunity for him.'

'He said his antennae were buzzing.'

'That's good news. OK, so tell your editor that I will provide some transaction printouts that you can then chase up. My suggestion – but

I'm not a journo either – is that you innocently bring up the bank's problems in your blog in relation to the grant business. There will be a firestorm after that – your editor will make sure of that, and the good old *Globe and Mail*, founded 1862 by Sir Josaiah Twelvetrees, will be ahead of the game. You will have the inside story. Don't worry, your editor will understand what this means.'

'And me?'

'You'll be young investigative Cornish journalist of the year. Got to go.'

He seems quite cheerful now.

'Bye.'

He walks off towards the fountains, and she catches sight of him once more, heading for the street, refracted by the water. She sits wondering what to do. God, she's babbled away so unprofessionally. She tries to get a grip. She hopes the recorder has worked properly. She writes down everything she can remember in her notebook.

Now she calls the editor.

'Tredizzick. Ah, Melissa, how did it go?'

'He came. He said that Tubal's is basically bankrupt and he can give us the proof, documents I think, about fraudulent –'

'Let me call you back. Just wait.'

He calls back on an unfamiliar number.

'Sorry, we need to be careful. Go on.'

'Yes, he can give you documents about fraudulent movements of money to boost – I think he said – the asset value so they can sell the bank. And that's why all the charitable grants have been cut. They got out of their comfort zone, he said.'

'Why is this bloke telling us this? Did he say?'

'No. He says he will give us all we need after he's spoken to you, but we mustn't ask questions about him.'

'There are two possibilities. One is revenge – he may have been fired – the other is some sort of scam. Short selling is one of those, but the bank is not publicly quoted. I'll ask around discreetly. I still know a few people up in London, you may be surprised to hear.'

'He said you were something to do with Mr Maxwell.'

'Did he? Interesting. Well done. Come in tomorrow early for a meeting. Come at eight.'

Her train doesn't leave Paddington until mid-afternoon. She goes back to the hotel and changes out of the classic suit in the ladies' lavatory. She walks down to the river, pulling her bag behind her. How's all this going to help Artair MacCleod, she wonders? Her phone rings; it's the editor.

'Did he mention the death of Sir Harry Trevelyan-Tubal?'

'No.'

'OK. There may be a connection.'

He rings off. Does he mean murder? Surely not. She remembers something her mother says: if you put it in a book nobody would believe you. But actually the things her mother believes should be in a novel – true love and nice people, for instance, are way less believable.

She walks down the river towards Tower Bridge and the familiar skyline. The water is high and lapping the granite of the Embankment. All the energy of the country seems to have congregated here along this river. *The rest of us are just the extras, without speaking parts, just filling in the blank spaces in the frame.*

15

THE COMEDY OF history has found its way to this wild estuary. Some idiotic bankers fuelled by testosterone have made ridiculous decisions and he is the victim. For a week the rain has been striking the front of the boathouse like bird shot. (He thinks of the late Sir Harry shooting a pheasant: it falls with a soft mortal thump for the Labrador to pick up.) But he hasn't let the grass grow under his feet. He has been working. And now, in the middle of a squall, he has written the last, resonating line of his screenplay:

> LAMONT: I mean to say, whether a yarn is tall or small, I like to
> hear it well told.

He sees his financial problems now as the product of hubris; the classical failing is behind all this. His problems are nothing. The script is money in the bank.

The gale is smashing against the soon-to-be-repossessed boathouse. He has withdrawn the four free tickets in a petty, but satisfying little revenge. He sees that his troubles have freed him. In the past week, stoked by two new varieties of Binster's pies and encouraged by the last of his good coffee, he has finished a masterpiece. Daniel will love it. No more children's drama, no more horse boxes and horse-induced rashes. The rashes still linger, but the itching has eased. He will have proper meals.

The postman, Brian, arrives; he sees himself as some sort of heroic explorer to have driven the few miles in his van with one letter.

'Shocking weather, isn't it?'

'I like it,' says Artair.

'Artair, can I use your toilet?'

'Go ahead. Straight through the kitchen.'

He looks at the envelope, and his heart lurches as he sees the handwriting; you never forget handwriting.

Dear Artair

Thank you so much for your wonderful letter about Harry's death. I loved the couplet from 'Morte d'Arthur'. I can hear you reading it. Do you still have that lovely voice?

As you can imagine, I am in complete shock, but your kind and compassionate letter – despite our history – has reassured me that there really is love and kindness out there.

When I am settled, let us meet again. I believe your grant has been terminated for some reason and I enclose a cheque for £25,000. This is not out of guilt or regret but because I know you have a heroic spirit which I once shared. The funeral was at the family church, All Hallows, on Monday. It was very beautiful, but I am still down.

With fond regards and with warm thanks for your generous letter,
Fleur

The Tubal's cheque is in the name of the Lady Trevelyan-Tubal Trust. He holds it for a moment to see if there is more to be gleaned. He hears paper tearing and the lavatory flushing. God, the postie has been having a dump in there. When he emerges, doing up his shiny serge trousers, Artair summons him.

'Brian, I need a lift. Are you going back to town?'

'It is against the rules.'

'Bollocks. This is a matter of great urgency. Anyway, it's against the rules to smell up my kitchen.'

'I have to make a delivery or two on the way.'

' "Once more unto the breach, dear friends . . ." '

Artair pulls on a huge trawlerman's sou'wester. Indeed it belonged to a real trawlerman once, the skipper of the *Cornish Maid* who gave it to him in return for four tickets to *Postman Pat*, one of his early forays into children's theatre. They stumble towards the little red van, bent against the ferocious rain.

'Pull your hood up,' says Brian, when they are in their seats.

'The Post Office, if it hasn't been sold to Dubai this week – oh, I forgot, Dubai is bankrupt – the Post Office, the Royal fucking Mail, is a national organisation serving – as I do – the people. I am entitled to be driven anywhere I like.'

'Bloody hell. What a load of bollocks. I could lose my job.'

They stop at Caruan Farm to deliver a parcel of useless catalogues and at the Three Bells to deliver some rate demands and other bills; the envelopes are familiar to Artair. Brian tries to stop him looking into his mail bag.

When they reach town Brian insists on dropping him down a small blighted street behind the old jail, now closed.

'Brian, it's raining. You can't see the end of your fucking nose, let alone a man in a sou'wester. I could be the Pope or the Postmaster General in here and nobody would be the wiser. Anyway, thanks for the lift.'

Almost before he has closed the door, the van is off. Artair walks in the direction of the High Street, the cheque deep inside his clothing. The rain is lashing the sou'wester futilely. He feels like Peter Grimes. He sings, 'Peter Grimes, Pe-t-er Grimes', with a falling octave. He marches into the bank and the effect on the waiting customers is just like the scene when Grimes bursts into the pub as the storm is breaking. Or was it after the boy was drowned? Peter Pears, buggery, Aldeburgh 1959.

'I would like to see the manager.'

'I'm afraid he is in a training seminar, Mr MacCleod,' says a cowed teller.

'I want to see him now. If he's not fully trained, I will overlook it.'

'I'll try and interrupt him.'

He stands, a colossus, carved by Rodin, close to the counter. He's dripping on to the floor.

'Mr MacCleod, I am afraid I can't –'

'I want to apologise unreservedly for calling you a pygmy. It was not my intention to insult that fine people by the comparison.'

'I am in a seminar.'

'I want you to take this' – he delves for a moment and holds up the cheque – 'I want you to take this and deposit it in the account of the Lifeboat Theatre Company immediately.'

Trefelix looks at the cheque.

'Oh, that is good news, Mr MacCleod.'

'But there is some bad news. As so often in life.'

'What is that, Mr MacCleod?'

'As soon as the cheque is cleared and all my outstanding commitments are met, I shall be closing my account.'

The manager doesn't look unduly concerned. In fact he looks quite sanguine.

'Yes, the thing about pygmies,' Artair says, 'is that, because they live deep in the forests, they are unable to see the wood for the trees. That is perhaps their only defect. You might consider the moral of this, if you have ambitions to progress in the world of banking. Goodbye, or, more properly, adieu.'

He strides out into the teeming rain. *Peter Grimes, Pe-ee-ee-ter Grimes.* He walks one street back from the High Street to the modest offices of his legal counsel, the uxorious Barnecutt, and gives him the good news.

'What a surprise: I may get paid after all,' says Barnecutt.

'Raise your eyes from the gutter for a moment, Barnecutt. Art has triumphed. Let's go and have a celebratory drink.'

Barnecutt clears it with his mistress, and they head for the Cross Keys where they get very drunk.

'It's the comedy of history, Barnecutt.'

He's becoming Flann O'Brien and Barnecutt is his creature.

'Is it?'

'Call off the dogs, Barnecutt, we have won.'

*   *   *

In the morning when his hangover has retreated, he wonders how he got home. And he wonders if he wasn't just a little high-handed with the bank. Twenty-five thousand pounds isn't going to last for ever, after all; he should perhaps have seen the cheque as a bridgehead. But there is a rosier aspect: the show has been playing to good houses in Newquay and his assistant has promised to come to work. Her back has healed with the promise of a salary.

He calls Barnecutt.

'I have changed my mind. Keep up the pressure on Tubal's. I see a chink in the armour.'

'Pressure? The phrase a flea on an elephant's arse comes to mind. Pay up for work done first.'

'You drank most of it last night.'

'And I paid for a taxi to take you home. That's what we call "disbursements".'

16

A NIGHT AT home has calmed Melissa. Her mother's habits, so often irritating, are strangely soothing now. Her own narrow bed with its candy-striped duvet cover received her warmly. Her mother is making breakfast. She will undoubtedly think Melissa needs extra nourishment.

'Morning, lovely. How are you?'

'Sleepy.'

'How was the suit? Just the thing? I thought it would be. I'll send it to the cleaner's. You'll be needing it, I shouldn't wonder. It's a classic. Who were you interviewing exactly? How is it in London these days? Meg says you never see a white face from one week to another. She went up for *Mama Mia* with the church last November. You remember, when I couldn't go because of flu?'

She's constructing her own narrative, but for once Melissa doesn't rise.

She eats fast.

'Mum, I have to go and see the editor right away. Thanks for breakfast. No, no more, I'm on a diet.'

'Since when?'

'Since this morning.'

Her father beams at her fondly from across the table. As if she's made a little jest. If she were to be murdered, he would say after the trial, *Melissa was our special little angel. She lit up our lives. Forty years in jail is not enough for that monster.*

Now he says, 'You don't need to diet, my lovely.'

On the bus she can't help noticing that her fellow burghers have a rather lumpy, placid appearance. But then, so does she. Still, she's travelled the road to Damascus.

The editor is in his office with the smoke rising. For some reason he's wearing a tweed overcoat. She has noticed that his fingers are stained. He opens the window and stubs out his cigarette.

'Terrible vice. Right, tell me all.'

Melissa gets out the recorder.

'Do you want to hear this first? I recorded the whole conversation.'

'No, I'll do that privately later.'

'OK, well, I made notes after he had gone and I transcribed the recording on the train. I tried to summarise.'

She hopes he is impressed by her efficiency. On the recording she sounds very unsure and nervous.

'He wants to speak to you, to get your assurance of confidentiality and a guarantee that you will publish before he supplies the full information.'

'I think it will be best if we run your blog first, if there's anything solid in his information, and publish later when there's a reaction.'

'He also thought the blog should come first.'

'Do you know why?'

'Not really.'

'Because he wants to put as much distance between himself and the leak. If he works for the bank he can't afford to be exposed as the source. That's why he wants my assurance, because he knows that no journalist will reveal a source.'

'So what do we do now?'

'Tell your source that he can speak to me at 10 p.m. tonight and give him my new mobile number.'

'Oh, I forgot, I can't text him until he sends me his new phone number to use.'

'OK. And I'll take a little drive at lunchtime and listen to your recording.'

'What about Mr MacCleod?'

'Don't tell him anything. It's not really about him. This has all the makings of a very big story and the last thing we need is the Celtic bard blundering about. We should leave him out, as far as possible. What we have to nail down is the fraud at Tubal's, if it exists. If it does it's huge. Tubal's has been in business since the time of Queen Anne or maybe earlier. The family is the absolute cream of banking. Almost the last of the private banks and very much of the old school and, thanks to you, this newspaper is going to expose what's going on. We have had nothing like it since we broke the Cornish pasty scandal.'

She wonders if he is being ironic about the Cornish pasty scandal. Probably not, she thinks. She remembers it: the EU ruled that there was no such thing as a unique Cornish pasty which could be granted protected status, like Camembert or champagne. 'Cornish pasty' was a generic term. European gastronomic snobbery was suspected, particularly by the newspaper, which ran a long campaign. There's an appeal in process in Brussels.

'Also, Melissa, do not use the paper's phones for any of this and do not at any cost tell our colleagues anything at all. You and I will handle this completely alone, at least in the early stages.'

'Is it dangerous?'

'I don't think so. But when a story like this arrives you can't afford to get a single thing wrong. And here's some petty cash for a new phone for you and for transport. OK, get the phone, text your source when he gives you the number and tell him to ring me tonight. And let's see what happens. I haven't had so much fun since –'

'Would that be since the Cornish pasty scandal, Mr Tredizzick?'

'No, that was good, but not as good as when a crew member told me that Robert Maxwell had jumped off his boat the *Lady Ghislaine*. Nobody believed me, but it turned out to be true.'

'Why did he jump?'

'Well, Melissa, it's a long story, but let's just say he wasn't going for a midnight dip. He had stolen the *Daily Mirror*'s pension fund. Funny how these things come round. I wonder just what Julian Trevelyan-Tubal has been up to.'

As she goes back to a spare station, she imagines some of the others are looking at her keenly, wondering why she is closeted with the editor. From a carrier she takes a box of beautiful, brightly coloured macaroons bought in Piccadilly, and offers them around. She wants a taste test for her blog. They are from a little shop which has walls of beaten and shaped gold foil and displays these macaroons in exquisite rows of pistachio, coffee, fruits of the forest, salted caramel, orange blossom, two strengths of chocolate, raspberry, wild strawberries and some she's forgotten. The colours are screaming, but in a curiously tasteful French way, like French fabrics or lacquered furniture.

What are they? They are the latest thing in London, try one. They bite. She doesn't tell them that these little roundels of French sophistication cost her nearly a pound each. She notes the comments. She can see the caption: *Multicoloured Macaroon Mania Hits Cornwall.* She wonders what it is that makes people in capital cities prize good pastry and baking. Down here the pastry looks like something your mum could make, or not even that good. The height of sophistication is to stick a few Smarties on to the icing.

She sits down and starts her blog.

Yes, it's all out there somewhere. A couple of days ago I went up to London – shoppers' express – and I discovered macaroons. They are absolutely the latest must-have-munchies. They come in fourteen flavours and each one is as brightly but as delicately coloured as the wing of a tropical bird. Think macaws, think humming birds. These macaroons look less like something to eat than miniature works of art. An unscientific – and uncultured – taste test in the newsroom produced these comments from the hungry hacks: 'Bloody fantastic' (crime reporter), 'An orgasm on your tongue' (sports editor), 'Utterly, utterly divine' (fashion and leisure), 'A small explosion of taste' (farming and business), 'Beautifully designed' (graphics and layout), 'Utter rubbish' (unknown delivery driver).

For myself, I'm completely hooked. Heaven knows how they produce that intense colour or the extreme subtlety of taste or the astonishing lightness of texture. One moment you are chomping down, the next the whole thing has vanished, hardly a calorie in sight – I hope. Brace yourself, Cornwall, it can't be long now before the macaroon invasion kicks off.

I'm starting on a diet today, and I would like you to send in your diets, but only successful ones. By the way, remember the Cornish pasty scandal? Well, Naples have been granted protection for the name pizza by the EU. What have they got against Cornwall and our pasties? What do you think?

Melissa thinks this girlie persona is good camouflage for what she's doing in league with the rumpled but increasingly obsessed editor. She, and Mr Tredizzick, of course, are going to expose some criminal dealing in London. Down here nobody has a great opinion of London anyway, but since it turned out that overpaid and self-important bankers didn't have a clue about what they were doing, they have been happy to be confirmed in the belief that London is a sink of iniquity, double-dealing and miscegenation. They thank God there are still some real English men and women out on the margins. But Melissa knows it's not that simple. Why, if London is such a hellhole, does London have the art and the theatre and the taste? Down here they throw us a bone, like the St Ives Tate, which has a few interesting daubs hanging on the walls, but mostly people are just doing rubbish watercolours and making wind chimes and seagulls on sticks. Why are people more stylish, worldlier and generally way more interesting in London? And why do people from all over the world want to live there? It's the no-hopers with low horizons who find it convenient to hate London.

But she feels uneasy. Does she really want to be responsible for humiliating a family like the Tubals just for a story, for the sake of the *Globe and Mail*, which is already holed below the waterline? Or is it for the editor, who couldn't hack it in London? She goes out and buys a cheap phone and a few hours of airtime. As she's walking down Market Street, Alan39 texts her; she replies and soon he rings back from yet another phone.

'He says you can call him tonight at ten.'

'OK. Give me the number.'

He doesn't say another word. Who is he frightened of, she wonders? She takes the phone back to Mr Tredizzick.

'Ten is fine.'

'OK. Well done. We will speak tomorrow.'

She feels lonely now. She can't talk to anybody, she hasn't got a boyfriend and she doesn't think she has the ruthlessness for this. Yes, it may be that the boss of Tubal's has committed a fraud, but she wonders whether that's so uncommon in the financial world. They all seem to have been guilty of a kind of fraud by pretending they knew what they were doing with other people's money. She read that in the dealing rooms they would shout 'OPM' gleefully as a deal went bad: *Other people's money.* It was exciting until she met her source; somehow his desperate seriousness, his grudge or whatever is driving him, has taken the whole business out of the realm of an adventure, into something more ugly, more banal. She has made a category error (philosophy, module 7) by confusing one sort of thing with something entirely different. But the editor is like an old warhorse – she understands the phrase now – trembling with anticipation at what's to come. Perhaps after the humiliation of editing a pretty poxy provincial newspaper – *Two Redruth boys make Ripcurl surf final in Durban* – he sees bringing down the high and mighty Trevelyan-Tubal family as a last hurrah.

She rings her best friend from uni, Ruth.

'Hello, babe.'

'Hello, slapper.'

'Do you want to have a bite tonight?'

'Who's paying?'

'Me.'

'Have you come into money?'

'No, I've fiddled me expenses.'

'Pizza Express?'

'Lovely. I'm free at six-thirty.'

'OK, babe, see you there.'

'Mel, is anything wrong?'

'No, I just felt like a girlie chinwag. I haven't seen you for – what? – a week?'

'OK. Love your blog, by the way.'

'Really?'

'Totally. Everyone's talking about it. I've told them that I give you all the ideas.'

'Oh, thanks.'

'See you then.'

She calls her mother.

'Hi, Mum, I won't be home for tea. I'm having a pizza with Ruth.'

'That's all right, sweetie. I was only going to make some spag Bol. You used to love it. Your suit's back from the cleaner's. See you later.'

'Don't wait up.'

'If the light's on, pop in to say goodnight to the dinosaurs.'

Her mother has become a little desperate since her brother took a job in Winnipeg. The gravitational pull is deserting the family and she can't bear it.

17

ESTELLE SITS IN the former smoking room. She's enjoyed her ten days back at Bread Street. The place has changed, but she recognises that it is for the better in many ways. When Harry was still chairman, everything had to wait for him. It wasn't that he couldn't delegate, it was just that he couldn't see the need to discuss anything. His idea of delegation was a strict order to be carried out by a minion. In his mind he and the bank were indivisible. So the directors, including Julian, were terrified of confronting him. For thirty-two years Estelle was the gatekeeper to his office. She knew exactly how to approach him; memos and suggestions and policy papers were always presented to him through her and phrased so that he would make the right decision. The directors knew that there was no other way and some of them muttered that she was running the show.

But it wasn't that at all; although he wouldn't have admitted it, Harry needed her, her organisational ability and her protective feelings for him. It was also true that his vanity – and if she's honest, his snobbery – would never allow him to acknowledge her publicly. She knew that he sometimes said 'The dragon-lady has decided', but she understood him too well to take offence. When Julian suggested to his father that they start a hedge fund, she reminded Harry of what had happened to his friends in Baring's. She asked him if after three hundred years he wanted to run a casino instead of a bank. Now the phrase 'casino banking' has come to haunt the City. Harry believed that he had coined it. A year before his retirement, speaking at the Guildhall, he said, 'It is my belief that banks like ours would be serving our customers very poorly by embarking on casino banking after three hundred years.' It was widely reported in the financial press. They were her words. He was impossible, but she misses him: she feels his brooding spirit hanging over the bank. She tries to speak to him when she's alone in bed at her sister's poky little house.

In the last ten days, busy though she has been with the funeral, the memorial service to come and all the tasks to do with Antibes and Harry's possessions and Fleur's future, she has seen the evidence of what she had guessed, that Julian and Nigel have lost tens of millions with the hedge fund and with some other risky financial manoeuvres. Casino banking came to Bread Street after all.

The funeral, she thinks, as she checks the invoices for flowers and transport, catering and funeral directors, was a wonderful occasion. The memorial service in October will be the social event with the City, family friends, staff, the guilds, the clients (as they are now called), the law, some Rothschilds, Prince Andrew, politicians and the Business Secretary – if his party is still in power – a trustee or two from Koopman's, and representatives of all the charities Harry has supported – they always turn up in their sackcloth, begging bowls barely concealed. But the funeral was very intimate: the Bishop of London gave a fine eulogy, and Julian spoke movingly. Her heart broke as they carried out the coffin for cremation as Harry had specified. She had to walk at the rear of the important people, just ahead of the office staff, but she understood. They didn't want to accept how close she was to Harry. She had confirmed that he wanted his ashes spread in the sea beyond the villa. Alas, he had also asked that the ceremony be performed from *Niobe*.

The flowers were wonderful, simple but lavish. All Hallows is seldom used these days but when it was first consecrated in 1382 it was one of the most important churches in London with a huge nave and towering stained-glass windows. Every pew was full. Harry's father commissioned Chagall to design the window behind the altar blown out in the Blitz and it is a thing of beauty, bathing the mourners in sub-marine blue.

From the smoking room she sees that this is the end of the line for her. It is a curious vantage point. She can't camp in her little house in Antibes if Julian and Kim are going to use the villa. Simon has also expressed an interest. He feels like settling down. She was anyway only living there to be with Harry in his decline and she will always cherish her conversations with him as they became so close. Poor Fleur: Harry hated her at the end. With all his artistic interests and love of life, being cut off by the stroke was unbearable to him. By giving her the Matisse he has made it plain that he loved and valued her; the painting was something he treasured most, of all his possessions. She was reluctant to accept, but he insisted – he could still speak a few sentences – on her writing a note, which he signed: *For my dearest Estelle Welz, I bequeath my Matisse painting of the open window at Collioure.* The note is in a safe-deposit box along with the picture.

Julian and Nigel are going to be away for a week and Julian has asked her to stay on at least for another six weeks. She wonders why they are going to America. She can't ask. She has established an iron grip on the arrangements for the memorial service and she has her inventory ready. She's been given the privilege of joining the directors for lunch and now she makes her way from the smoking room though the drawing room and across the corridor to the dining room, which looks down on the courtyard. In the past lunch was a formal occasion with Harry presiding. Now it's more relaxed; the food is laid out on the long refectory table and you help yourself, although a wine steward and a waitress are on hand. A young man and a young woman come in. The woman – she knows her name is the Hon. Charlotte Stammers – is only the second woman director the bank has ever had. Estelle has noticed that her picture – long neck, striking Tubal eyes – appears in all the bank's promotional literature and she is described as 'highly qualified' as though this might come as a surprise.

'Estelle Welz, a legend. I'm Charlotte Stammers, the token female. What an enormous pleasure to meet you.'

'Thank you, I knew your mother. How is she?'

'Oh, gardening away. The Vita Sackville-West *de nos jours*. She's sixty-six now. I'll tell her I met you. Estelle – may I? – I believe you were wonderfully kind to Uncle Harry.'

'Well, I did work for him for over thirty years. I got to know his ways.'

She wants to say to this elegant and slender creature that she loved him and that he loved her. They chat through lunch: she has two young children, Buzz and Flea – they must have proper names – and fortunately a wonderful nanny. She has the engaging quality of appearing to be interested in other people. Most of the family find it hard to believe that someone like Estelle could have a history and a family and some aspirations of her own. Estelle finds herself telling Charlotte about her sister in Queen's Park, her little house in the grounds of the villa, and her last conversation with Harry. She tells Charlotte that she's sure the family don't really believe Harry could speak to her towards the end.

'Oh no, I am sure he could speak to you. Don't you think that when you know someone so well you can almost anticipate what they are saying? I do. My father used to say to me that he could tell from the way I said "Hello" just why I was calling him. No, I am sure you knew exactly what Harry was saying and thinking. Doctors are far too ready to ignore those parts of the brain and the intelligence they can't see on a screen, don't you think?'

'I agree. You're absolutely right. It's as if once you're severely ill it's in everyone's interest to write you off.'

She thinks she may have gone too far.

'Of course I am not saying that is what the family wanted, far from it, but the doctors are always in a hurry to clear the decks.'

'Fleur has not taken it well.'

'No, she's in a very poor state.'

'But I hear you are helping her sort out her affairs. That's so kind.'

Her keen eyes, above the almost freakishly long neck, are looking at Estelle closely.

'Yes, I'm trying. She is a woman who has always relied on others.'

'Do you think, perhaps, she's the sort of woman who finds expression through men?'

Estelle thinks this is a coded way of saying that Fleur is a tart.

'Well, I think it's because she was an actress. She plays roles and feels happier when she knows exactly what the role is.'

'That's so-oh fascinating. I had never thought of it like that, but it explains a lot. Do you think the merry widow could be the next role?'

Estelle sees that the family is wary of what Fleur may do. The old boy's indulgence. Charlotte eats fastidiously.

'Estelle, it was such a pleasure to meet you, but I have to go off now to help keep the show on the road.'

She departs smoothly, without causing a ripple in the air.

After lunch, Estelle finds a message from Amanda Stapleton.

'Estelle, I hear you're back. How marvellous. Would you give me a ring?'

She knows that Amanda is not calling for a chat. She rings her.

'Estelle, hello. Can we talk tomorrow? There are some questions I need to ask you. The family trust requires absolute clarity about Harry's intentions. Would you mind coming in to me first thing, say about eight? I'll send a car.'

She takes a note of the address; Queen's Park is evidently about as familiar to her as Ouagadougou.

'Good, see you tomorrow. The car will be with you at seven-fifteen.'

You can't say no to Amanda. This will be about Fleur and possibly the paintings and Amanda imagines she can intimidate her. Intimidation and bullying are what have made her such a success. You don't mess with Amanda Stapleton, they say.

She goes back to her lists and prints off the inventories for her meeting with Amanda.

Nigel, always neatly and modestly dressed – no satin linings for his suits, no velvet on his overcoat – comes in to see her. He was the first director ever to be appointed from outside the family. She's heard that Julian relies on him for everything. They play tennis every weekend.

He's sitting on the edge of her desk now, one leg on the floor, the other showing an inch of skin above the socks.

'What's it like to be back in the old place, Estelle?'

'I love it. Those years were the most exciting of my life.'

'I bet they were. From what little I know of him, Sir Harry was a hard man to work for.'

'He was sweet really. I just think that when he took over here times were different. It was more paternalistic. Oh, I met Charlotte Stammers today. Sir Harry would have had a fit. But what a lovely girl.'

'I'm proud to say I had a hand in her appointment. By the way, Julian and I are not going to the States until next week now. I hear you are seeing Amanda tomorrow. Good luck, she scares the pants off me.'

'Do you know what she wants to ask me?'

'No idea. Have you noticed that we work for her, rather than the other way round? Anyway, lovely to have you back.'

He swings lightly off the desk.

Estelle goes back to her sister Kay's little house in Queen's Park. It's a doll's house, one of many, all contained within a few blocks, all just a little different. But strange and surprising, like finding a series of woodcutters' cottages in the middle of London. Her sister was married to a butcher who died at the age of fifty-one of a heart attack; she has lived alone for twenty years. Nothing ever changes in the house. Estelle can see just how tacky and tasteless it is. Her sister is sitting in front of the television. It seems she doesn't distinguish fully between real life and television shows these days. And who can blame her? The television is a lot brighter and livelier than real life, as she lives it. She's very strong in her opinions on television presenters and the characters in soaps.

As Estelle enters, she says, 'Look at this, the little rascal's only gone and nicked her bike. It was a new one and all.'

Estelle doesn't know who she is talking about and hopes not to find out.

'Kay, I brought some things for our supper on the way home.'

She knows her sister refers to the evening meal as tea, but she can't bear to say it after her years of close association with Harry.

'Oh that's lovely, you are a darling. Just let me finish this and I'll help you lay up.'

Estelle has always suffered for being competent: people take advantage of her. Even here in these gloomy and mean surroundings. Kay shows no interest in her day, but wants to talk about a new dance competition. She fancies an ex-cricketer to win. She never looks up from the screen, and is chuckling away as Estelle lays out the supper.

After supper – Fortnum's pâté with *cornichons* ('Oh, very Continental,' says Kay) and a good quiche – Kay returns to her armchair, already plumped up with anticipation, and Estelle heads towards the little staircase and her bed.

'Nighty night, Stel,' Kay calls out. 'What time you off out in the morning?'

'Early, I have to see a lawyer.'

'That's nice. Oh, look at him, he's a good jiver. But he's best on the Latin-American. One judge give him ten.'

Amanda favours big cups of Starbucks coffee in the morning. There's something appropriately aggressive about these huge buckets of coffee. She looks up briefly as Estelle is shown in and carries on reading an email.

'Right, Estelle. Great to see you.'

Her hair is curiously arranged in a mannish cut, parted on the side, but with two leaves of hair hanging down in front of her exposed ears.

'Good to see you, Amanda. What can I do for you?'

'I have ordered you a latte, by the way. Is that OK? I hear you have been doing a great job sorting out Harry's possessions. And thank you so much for the inventory of Villa Tubal. Particularly the pictures. My job is to try to make a determination of what belongs to the trust and what to individuals for probate. As you know, holdings by the trust, based – as you also know – in Liechtenstein, are not subject to UK inheritance tax. Sir Harry's pictures were his alone, I think. Anyway, I'm going on that assumption until anyone tells me different. Sir Harry has made a very decent provision for you in his will, forty thousand a year for life – he also topped up the pension personally – and use of the cottage at the villa for four weeks a year.'

'Yes, he said.'

'Now, I want to get on to a question of some delicacy. Did Lady Trevelyan-Tubal know that the trust owned the villa?'

'Yes, I think so. She was under the impression that Sir Harry owned the house in Chelsea and that she would be left that for life, although it was to go to Julian and his children if Fleur predeceased Julian.'

'That's absolutely right. Julian thinks it's too big for him now and thinks it would be better sold. But at the end of the day it is her decision.'

'I suppose it would be.'

'Here's your coffee.'

A timid assistant places it on the desk. Amanda doesn't acknowledge him. Estelle never drinks from paper cups but she sees she has no choice.

'Now, there's one more thing. A very small newspaper in Cornwall, we have been told, is claiming that the family trust has cut Sir Harry's grant to Lady Trevelyan-Tubal's first husband. What do you know about that?'

'Nothing. Sir Harry never mentioned it.'

'Look, we just need the background to this story.'

'As far as I know, Sir Harry simply set up a standing order on one of his charitable funds for Mr MacCleod. I knew nothing more about it and Sir Harry never discussed it with me.'

'OK, thank you. Now, I see that one of the paintings, the Matisse of Collioure, no longer appears on the inventory.'

'No, it doesn't.'

'Why not?'

'Sir Harry gave it to me.'

'He gave it to you? Under what circumstances?'

'He saw that I had looked after him and he wanted, I am assuming, to show his appreciation.'

Amanda is staring at her. She is transfixed.

'Do you know what that fucking painting is worth?'

'I do, but I am never going to sell it, so it's irrelevant.'

'Are you serious? He was struck by a major stroke, he couldn't utter a single intelligible word for eleven months, and you say he gave you a painting conservatively worth £20m. at the time. Are you out of your mind? You will find yourself in terrible trouble if you are shown to have stolen this picture, which seems to be the only logical conclusion. You will spend years in Holloway where, I am told, older women suffer appalling mistreatment.'

'I have a note from him bequeathing it to me.'

'The deathbed will. Oh wow, now I've heard it all. I suggest you hand over the picture today, before I get on to my friends at the Met. This isn't some fucking colour-by-numbers picture of spaniels, you know, it's a national treasure. The French want it, the Met – not our boys in blue, but a gallery in New York – would kill for it, and you are saying a dying man, who couldn't speak, gave it to you.'

'I have a letter in a safe-box and with it I have a copy of the deeds that authorised £250m. to be taken from the family trust and another £150m. from the Koopman Foundation, with the dying man's signature granting a power of attorney. Postdated. I was a witness. They brought the papers from Liechtenstein for a little work. I wasn't happy, but I had no choice.'

'Are you saying that you are prepared to blackmail the family? I can't believe it, after all they did for you for years.'

'No, all I am saying is that Sir Harry gave me the Matisse. I looked after Sir Harry, he spoke to me every day until the end, and I tried to make him happy. He appreciated it.'

'He was out of his mind. I'll get Abbott to testify.'

'And I'll produce his letter with his signature on it. And if that isn't enough, I'll produce the deeds of the transfers. This isn't blackmail, but I can make a guess as to why the £250m. was taken from the trusts in Liechtenstein. And it's probably the same reason why the yacht was sold and the charitable trusts were choked off and now the Chelsea house is going to be sold, if only Fleur can be turfed out. And I can also guess why it needs to be done quickly. I'm quite happy to say these things if I am forced to.'

'That is fucking blackmail.'

'Shut your face, you foul-mouthed, toffee-nosed bitch. I'm not going to be walked over by you just because you went to some posh school and I only studied bookkeeping at night. Do what you like.'

'Don't worry, I will.'

'Good luck to you.'

As she goes down in the lift, Estelle is shaking and queasy. She stops outside, facing Lincoln's Inn Fields, wondering where she should go. No doubt Amanda is already speaking to Julian. God knows what's waiting for her at Bread Street, but she decides she must face it. She takes a taxi. The doorman, Bill Saddleton, greets her.

'What a lovely day, isn't it? Spring has sprung.'

She hadn't noticed. She goes up to her desk and sits down. It calms her to make lists and she starts revising the arrangements for the memorial service. But soon Julian's secretary rings. Could she come to his office?

Julian is sitting under the messy blue picture: she hasn't noticed before that the paint has even spilled over on to the frame. Julian looks drawn, as though he has flu.

He stands up. 'Ah, Estelle. Have a seat. Tea, or coffee? Tea, if I remember.'

He orders.

'Thanks so much for coming to see me. Amanda Stapleton has been on the line, ranting, as is her way. She says that my father gave you the Collioure Matisse of the port. Is that true?'

'Yes, I have his note.'

'The thing is, what date is on it?'

'It's before the power of attorney, if that's your question.'

'That was going to be my question, yes. But look, Estelle, I know how much he valued you, but I honestly don't think that any court will uphold the validity of this piece of paper. Even if he did intend to give it you at that time, he had suffered a catastrophic stroke. If you think about it, he left you a pension of around £40,000 a year and any court would find it strange that he would give you a painting worth millions when he was very ill, if in his rational mind he had already made provision for you.'

'He spoke to me every day, Julian. I sent you his thoughts on the business. Some of them were not really coherent but, as you know, some of them made a lot of sense. Asset ratios, for example.'

'Can I tell you something, Estelle. We were not the only people who were mistaken about the markets. We believed, like the Nobel Prize winner who advised us in setting up our main hedge fund, that it was possible to take the risk out of investment banking. What we didn't realise, and I regret bitterly that we were so foolish, is that the markets have no logic – unlike mathematics – and they can be thrown by all sorts of random events, human events. We lost a huge amount of money. It just vanished. So what you apparently said to Amanda is true; we are trying to boost our capital. The boat has gone, the Chelsea house will go – Fleur's agreed – the charitable trusts have gone and the family trust has lent the bank money.'

'Without Sir Harry's consent, and his vote on behalf of the relatives.'

'Without my father's consent. He was not competent to give his consent, according to Mr Abbott. That's why we had the power of attorney drawn up, that you witnessed.'

'The problem is, you are trying to mislead the regulators and the ratings agencies.'

'We are just holding them off. This is a matter of life and death. The bank is on the line.'

'And the Koopman Foundation?'

'Amanda said you mentioned that. It's not just Koopman's if we go under. But in fact we have discretion over Koopman's investments, renewable every year. I know that they probably wouldn't have liked them to be put into the bank's funds if they knew the situation. But that's where we are. We didn't want to be here, but we are. You know the City runs on rumours. If you spread rumours about breaches of fiduciary trust, the whole thing could implode very quickly.'

'You're selling, aren't you?'

'There are a number of options open to us, but not for long. I am asking you, in the family's name, to help. We need the picture, but more important, we need you on side for obvious reasons. Amanda wants to injunct you, but I have called her off. Actually, she admitted that she had gone too far, talking about prison. It would be point-less and it would make your life utter hell. I don't want that. Estelle, there's more to life than this. My father and I didn't get on well, as you know, but I always appreciated the way you handled him. What people said was true: you were more or less running Bread Street. I should never have allowed myself to be sucked into the bank in the first place. It isn't the life I wanted. What I do want, Stel, is that we all get out of this with our reputations intact. Including my father's. I know you loved him. Can you please help me now? I beg you. What I have told you, only Nigel and I know. Not even Kim knows. You are one of the family, you were closer to him than anyone, and this is a family matter.'

He's trembling and she is shaken.

'Poor boy,' she says. 'I'll help you.'

She holds the hand he is extending to her and squeezes it.

'The painting is in a safe-deposit box in Mayfair. I'll give you the key.'

He smiles, although tears are running down his face.

'Did you really call Amanda a foul-mouthed-bitch?'

'I'm ashamed of myself.'

'Don't be. Somebody had to do it.'

He hugs her. They are both snuffling like children as they recover themselves. All she ever wanted was to be part of the family.

18

'She's on side,' says Julian.

'How did you do it?'

'I can't tell you, it's way too personal. Just accept that I gave her what she wanted.'

'And she's giving the picture back?'

'Yes, she's actually given me the electronic key of a safe-deposit box. Nigel, this is killing me. I wasn't cut out for this kind of thing. Also, why is Cy delaying?'

'I don't know. It's possible he's got wind of something. The big guys have informants everywhere. He hasn't commented on our disclosures. And maybe due diligence has taken longer than he expected. Or most likely he's just trying to rattle our cage.'

'Nige, can we take a walk? I'm going to get the painting myself. I don't need Len.'

They leave the bank through the car park, surreptitiously, down towards the Mansion House. Julian loves the names, Little Trinity Lane, Garlickhythe, Watling Street; when Moses Tubal was alive these poetic and beautiful names were far more prosaic. Garlickhythe was the landing stage for garlic and St Andrew by the Wardrobe was the place where Edward III's state robes were kept. Cy loves all this history, but Julian thinks he loves it as you might claim to like Siena or Venice, as reflecting your own self-importance in being able to claim familiarity with another culture. Harry did it too. Everything he did was designed to demonstrate his superior taste. He was a monster. In the *FT* the other day he read an interview with a Canadian banker who explained how Canadian banks had avoided the worst of the problems: *We are boring and we don't go to the opera.* Like Simon, Julian thinks, he should have refused to have anything to do with the bank. It's turned him into a liar and a fraudster, not much better than Madoff and Ebbers. Nigel takes a more pragmatic view: you have to do what you have to do. In his book it's fine if it all turns out for the best. They walk down Little Trinity Lane, choked with cabs and delivery vehicles, and away from the bank Julian feels more calm.

'Nigel, Estelle seems to think we have borrowed some money from the Koopman Foundation.'

'Holy shit. Fuck. Fuck. Is she just fishing?'

'She says she copied the papers we signed in Antibes and Vaduz.'

'Why? How did she get her hands on them?'

'She had them for an hour or two before I left.'

'But you are sure she is on side?'

'Pretty sure. She doesn't want money, that I am sure of. Also I am not convinced someone in the bank is leaking. I think Estelle knows the bank well and the asset situation and has put two and two together, what with the boat and the charities. But why are people asking questions about Fleur's first husband? Is that sinister?'

'I really wouldn't worry too much about that one. There was some local paper in Cornwall saying that Artair MacCleod hadn't received his grant. At first they thought it was the Arts Council or something, but then they heard it was from a bank. Big bad capitalists snub Cornwall, et cetera. I suggested to Fleur that she pay off her ex-husband. And she's done it.'

'OK. If there's been a leak we must find it, in the meanwhile we should tough it out, as you say.'

'Good. It will be over soon.'

'Let's hope so. I'll get a cab now. I've spoken to Kasimir about a private sale. No publicity at all. He says it's got to be thirty million.'

'Just two hundred and twenty to go. Oh, I forgot, with the boat, two hundred and twelve.'

'I'm glad you can laugh.'

'You gotta laugh, gov'nor, don'tcher?'

It's not a good attempt at a cockney accent. They part reluctantly, like lovers, not wanting to break out of the cocoon of affection around them. Julian knows, although he could never say it out loud, that for both of them real friendship is a masculine state. It's impossible to have a woman as a best friend.

But Julian doesn't get a cab immediately. He walks on right through to the river at Blackfriars. Trees are coming into blossom and the clouds are higher. Weak sun seeps through suggesting that winter is over. It's like the sun in the Arctic winter, not sitting high enough to cast shadows, but creating an even, directionless and diffused glow. He and Kim spent a few days at the Ice Hotel for an anniversary and he has never forgotten the light. The whole trip was magical, from the moment they travelled in a sleigh pulled by huskies from the airfield to the hotel. The huskies had strong muscles on their hind legs, as though sausages were buried beneath the fur. They ran in their manic, unstoppable wildness through this empty and eerily beautiful land-scape. The runners of the sleigh sometimes susurrated and at other times scraped on ice. The driver called to the huskies and helped them on the uphill stretches by scooting with one leg. Huskies could run for six hours non-stop, he said. Unless something was lost in translation.

It was before they had children and as he and Kim snuggled under reindeer-skin blankets she undid his trousers, opening at the same time the possibility of dangerous frostbite.

He hails a taxi. How strange this light is as they approach Mayfair; it has a preserved-fruit quality, lightly coloured and refracted by a syrup.

He remembers that they ate a lot of reindeer – stews, burgers and dried. Kim is mostly vegetarian now. He was happy then. He feels a certain melancholy for the time he's wasted pretending to be a banker. Only after the whole place was crumbling did people in the City begin to question the true value of what they were doing and already they are forgetting. It was a conceit of the market that by operating at its diktat they were helping human progress. Nobody had read Keynes. He wishes he could claim he had been immune to the *Zeitgeist*, which was largely about creating money out of nothing.

His old dad said – far too often – that banking is about dealing with the things you understand and the people you know. He had tried to persuade the old boy that there was money to be made in collateral-ised debt and hedge funds. 'Yes,' he said, 'but what use are they? You can go on calling them derivatives until you're blue in the face, my boy, but show me one.'

He hails a cab. All paper. The City fell in love with the notion of frictionless wealth.

He enters the gold-plated but functional reception of the safe-deposit company – he suspects it has an Arab clientele – in a small and badly converted mews house. There is plenty of that phoney brass that is supposed to evoke gold, but the effect is fly-by-night. He passes through a metal detector, shows his key, and the door to the strongroom, down a short flight of steps, is opened. What he does in there is his business. His key opens the heavy door of a locker, the size of a small cupboard, very smoothly. He sees a neatly bubble-wrapped parcel, picks it up and walks out with it. He wonders what else is hidden in this vault: drugs, krugerrands, piles of dollars, stolen goods. He has the feeling that all these items represent areas of future economic growth – crime, fraud, dishonesty, deception, narcotics, tax evasion, funny money. And he could be going to jail unless Cy comes through. But Cy is allowing him to twist in the wind for a few weeks. He hasn't been able to tell Kim how bad things are and this presses heavily on him too. Back home all is warmth and order – trusting, adoring children, lovely open-faced Kim, with her predict-able but welcome values – and out here all is hellish chaos.

He wonders, a little too late, if he has been followed or photo-graphed. He steps into a pub, clutching his picture under his arm. With one hand he sips a lemonade – ordinary bloke at bar with £30m. Matisse under arm – and then leaves by another door which leads directly into a mews. He's passing, he realises, the front door of the billionaire widow of the first man to invent perforated toilet paper. She's one of their clients and he's dined there once or twice. His father never grasped the idea that great wealth corrupts. Or tends to corruption. His father regarded his wealth as a confirmation of his unique qualities, qualities which selective breeding of the privileged had produced. It is the updated version of the Victorian idea that the English gentleman was the outcome – even Darwin seemed to believe this – of years of evolution, fostered by rugby, cold showers, beating, poor food and study of the classics.

From the mews, standing in a doorway, he calls Kasimir.

'I'm bringing over the picture.'

'Right, we will be ready Mr Trevelyan-Tubal.'

'I'm walking down Dover Street, I'll be there in a few minutes.'

'I can't wait to see it.'

Kasimir is himself a kind of banker. He knows how to read the signs of financial distress and how to maintain decorum. He never utters a single word about his clients, the guilty and shifty sellers and the brash and eager buyers. He knows that their positions can change fast. The art market is inherently unstable because so many of the buyers are megalomaniacs and megalomaniacs believe their own judgements, which don't necessarily apply to art.

Kasimir is waiting. If he is surprised to find that Julian has come on foot, he doesn't comment. He wears a charcoal suit with exceptionally broad pinstripes that hug his elderly but slim shape fondly. His collar is high and cut dramatically away like the wings of a hovering kestrel. It is hovering over a pale-blue silk tie. His hair is slightly orange, thinning at the temples in a Middle Eastern way. Nobody knows precisely where Kasimir's family came from; it is said they were big in the Ottoman Empire until the First World War. And indeed Kasimir retains a grave, Ottoman courtesy. His only weakness is young men. He has a small troupe, an ever-changing cast, which accompanies him to galleries and shows. But even they are tight-lipped, the Trappists of the catamite world.

'Mr Trevelyan-Tubal, how marvellous to see you. Come, come into my office.'

Through the reception – paintings and tapestries on the walls in rich profusion – he shows Julian into his sanctum, which has a reinforced door.

'May I?'

'Of course.'

With a small blade and exquisite delicacy, as if he were slicing a persimmon, he removes the wrapping.

'What a picture,' he says, 'what a wonderful picture.'

They gaze at the deceptively simple view through a window and through the masts of the boats of the fishing harbour.

'My father loved it.'

'We will find a worthy home for it. In honour of your father.'

He smiles a satrap's smile.

'A major private collector, no Russian Mafia, no City boys.'

'No, no, of course not. Am I correct in saying that two years' embargo is required?'

'You are, of course.'

'I know just the person for this magnificent painting.'

'Thirty million net. Is that what you said?'

'Absolutely no doubt about it. Our minimum. I would like to put it away in the vault now.'

'Please do. No, I don't need a receipt from you, Kasimir.'

'Are you still enjoying the Hodgkin, Mr Trevelyan-Tubal?'

'I love it. It's behind my desk in the bank.'

'Wonderful picture. You were absolutely right to commission it when you did. Now . . .'

He shrugs philosophically to indicate that the Hodgkin boom has surprised even him.

'Well, it was you who put me on to him.'

'Ah yes. I think I can secure payment for the Matisse within a few weeks. Is that convenient?'

'Absolutely.'

Close up, Kasimir's skin is pitted, with little black marks in the indentations, and his teeth, when revealed in courteous and dutiful smiles, are very large, almost intimidating, but perfect in shape and colour. Julian remembers him with some prominent gold teeth, but these have all been converted to this dazzling array, like rows of stucco houses in Belgravia. He is a vain old man and probably a tyrant in his private life, but nobody in the art world is more astute or more knowledgeable. He has never been interviewed and he has never written an opinion in any journal. But his private authentication can add millions to the value of a work of art. He will know that something is up, just from the fact that Julian Trevelyan-Tubal, chairman and joint CEO of Tubal's, came himself on foot to deliver the Matisse. He will never breathe a word.

Back at the bank, Julian sends out for some flowers and he writes a short note to be attached.

For Estelle,
   As I said, you are one of us. Deeply grateful,
Julian x

Kim has been trying to reach him. His secretary puts the messages in front of him. She has also sent him a text, her preferred form of communication.

Don't forget, Fleur and Simon dinner tonite @8. lol

How could I forget? I was thinking of you and huskies in Jukkasjarvi (sp?) today. Do you remember? Jx

Hand job? lol

The intimacies between men and women are not for publication, he thinks. They are often innocently obscene or infantile. Nobody, anyway, really knows what goes on between other men and women. Couples who are a delightful and charming double act in public can be shockingly vicious to each other when they think they are not observed. His father was routinely cruel and dismissive to his mother in private, which led to her protracted depression and overdose. Julian was only twelve, and he misses her still.

Simon is in ebullient mood. He doesn't see death as an unhappy event. His wiring has never been quite right. His cheeks, baked to the colour of a Provençal roof tile, become a still deeper tone of raw sienna as he drinks. He likes wine and takes it in gulps. He quaffs.

He has been introduced to the children before they went off to bed, nervously refusing his offer of a bedtime story, based on his own experiences.

'Lovely children. I sometimes wish I had children, but it's not easy when you are doing what I am doing. We all have to make sacrifices, don't we?'

And he's off, around the globe. Kim tries to join in but Julian gives up. Nothing stops Simon's flow. Julian wonders what exactly it is that Simon has sacrificed: he has been paid generously out of the family trust for the twenty-five years since he left Eton, he has had many relationships, most of which ended disastrously and expensively, and for all those years he stayed as far away from the family as he could. Now, however, he thinks it's time to take an active interest in the affairs of the bank: in fact he is prepared to become a director.

'Very good idea, Simon, but these days we ask for a university degree and the Institute of Bankers exam, as well as an MBA or an accounting qualification. And we also need to see some aptitude for maths.'

'I bring a lot of experience of the real world to the table. Wouldn't it be possible to find a role for me?'

'No, the reason we put the need for qualifications in place was precisely because of the family. They all wanted to be directors. And not just the men.'

'Still, now that Dad's shuffled off the mortal coil, I am sure I could make a contribution. Banking has gone global, so everyone says, and I have a worldwide experience of different people and cultures.'

At this moment Fleur arrives.

'Simon darling, how are you? Love the sarong. Isn't it a little chilly around the naughty bits on a night like this?'

'Fleur, my balls are like biltong, they have been sundried and salted. They can take a breeze without flinching.'

Fleur laughs. They all laugh. Fleur seems very relaxed, even a little hysterical. She has a shine as though she's been to the gym. Julian pours her a glass of champagne – she likes a glass of *bubbles* – and Simon thinks he will have a glass too. He alternates between the Berry Bros Good Ordinary Claret and the Krug with impartiality.

Nobody here but Julian knows the trouble they are in. And because he's the brother who didn't go walkabout in a tablecloth, he can't tell them. He's so strung out he feels the cork could blow. He could say, *Here you are, Simon, you peripatetic old card, here's the fucking bank, why don't you take over as chairman and do my time in Wandsworth for me while you are at it?* It's a family bank after all: anybody with a speck of the Tubal gene in him (or her) is welcome.

Fleur and Simon are getting on famously. Fleur is quite coquettish. She has a way of leaning forward and squeezing her breasts together with her upper arms when she is laughing at Simon's anecdotes, most of which involve lovable darkies in many parts of the world. This is presumably going to be the sales pitch when he takes over the bank: we are across all the fuzzy-wuzzy cultures of the world. He says that he has decided not to renounce the baronetcy after all. In fact he's going to a meeting of the Baronets' Society next week. He wonders if he can borrow a dinner jacket; and perhaps Len could drive him in the Bentley to the Reform Club where the dinner is being held.

'We're getting rid of all gas guzzlers. It's hybrids for us from next month. We need to show some corporate responsibility.'

'Aren't you going back to the jungle?' asks Kim.

'No, the commission from the *New York Times* travel pages fell through.'

Unexpectedly, thanks mostly to Kim's limitless empathy, but also, Julian sees, because of his father's death, they settle down into a long and happy evening, although Julian is not able to still the unease which has been haunting him, particularly when he is trying to sleep and which he knows will attack him tonight as he lies down again.

19

THEY ARE SITTING in the editor's old Vauxhall Vectra in the car park of Sainsbury's. Is the editor taking this clandestine stuff too seriously?

'Melissa, I've looked at the printouts. They are designed entirely to disguise the origin of the money, to make it look like genuine deposits. The family trust probably doesn't even know that it has happened. It's been funnelled through what could look like genuine accounts in tax-avoiding countries, back to the bank where it is shown as deposits. Your man has marked all the suspicious ones. If you look at the merry-go-round of money, you can see that nobody would pick it up just by looking at the balance sheets cold. Banks take tens of thousands of deposits every day. What we want now from your man is the paperwork that tells us where this money originated. He's been very clever in taking the money back only so far, to the Turks and Caicos, the Isle of Man and so on, but there is still another trail which, I think, leads right back by a very winding path to the family trusts and to a client trust. But your source hasn't said where. Are you with me?'

'I think so.'

'To me it looks as if the money has come from the Trevelyan-Tubal family trust as he said to you, probably illegally, but at this stage impossible to prove, and also he's marked other entries that probably come from the charitable trusts, some of which have been with the Trevelyan-Tubals for fifty years and longer and they probably leave everything to the trustees, one of whom would have been the late Sir Harry Trevelyan-Tubal.'

'What do we say to our source? And what am I supposed to write, based on this? I mean I am in no position to give the facts. I'm not even sure I understand all of this, Mr Tredizzick.'

'No. Stick to cupcakes and macaroons and Dorothy Wordsworth for the moment. But we will now ask our source to send the second half of his printouts. You should contact him and tell him to speak to me. That's the way he wants it. You must use another phone, a new one.'

'Mr Tredizzick, I really don't want to get too deeply involved. I've been thinking about it and it's not me. It's like I'm being asked to be a sort of, to be the . . .'

She can't say the word.

'Bait. Melissa, remember, you are not doing anything illegal or dishonest. We need to break this story in an innocent and transparent way – in your blog – and then when the excrement hits the air conditioning – when they take the bait – we can stand the whole story up with our documents.'

'Yes, I know, but what if I am questioned?'

'You may be questioned, but what you simply say is that an anonymous source, not the foggiest idea of his name to this day, and don't want to know, contacted you. He read your blog and offered some information anonymously. You passed it on to the editor, and that, Melissa, is exactly what happened.'

'Yes, but what does he want?'

'We don't know. We don't want to know. What we want is to follow a story of legitimate local interest, the shoddy treatment of Mr Artair MacCleod at the hands of one of the richest families in the land.'

'Mr MacCleod is in the money.'

'Oh is he? Where did that come from? I would hazard a guess that it came from someone close to his ex-wife who heard about your blog.'

'It came from his wife herself.'

'You can't get closer than that.'

'Why has she sent him money?'

'The old boy's kicked the bucket would be the sentimental reason, but the more likely reason is somebody's advised her to shut him up. Has he been pestering them?'

'He's asked for information, but they never answer his letters. Mr Gerald Barnecutt of Barnecutt and Barnecutt has tried to get information, but he's like failed miserably.'

'That is what happens, Melissa. These big boys stonewall because they have very deep pockets and, if the little people persist, they set the lawyers on to them and then they bankrupt them with injunctions and libel actions and God knows what all. Barnecutt's your man if you want permission to convert your garden shed into a crack den, but he's completely out of his depth with this one.'

He's enjoying this. But she wonders if he isn't out of his depth too. Particularly, she wonders if there isn't something more sinister behind this that he doesn't understand. When he left Fleet Street, they were still setting the type by hand. She has seen that he is an old leftie, who hates banks and posh people with double-barrelled names and what he calls the aggregation of all power in London, and he hates the cosy relationship between banks, regulators and Parliament, which he says has got us into this mess. The government may be on the warpath now, he says, but they were the ones who were keen to remove the regulations – the policy of the light touch – so that the City could produce even more money. But it's also true that if she sticks to the story and stays clear of the paperwork and all that sort of thing, she can't really be sued or indicted.

She's seen Alan39's face and it's not the face of reason. Something is eating him. Mr Tredizzick is right, she really doesn't want to know any more about Alan39. Now the editor asks her to go and see Mr MacCleod again to find out anything she can about his cash. He wants to know what conditions were attached.

'Can't I phone him?'

'No, you need to see the whites of his eyes.'

'They are kind of yellow.'

'Go and see him. But you can't mention your source or anything.'

'Wouldn't it mean we'd be using him for our own purposes?'

'No, no, it would mean we don't want him shouting his mouth off all over the place before we have the facts. He's got many talents but sadly discretion isn't one of them.'

'Oh, OK.'

'Before you go, get your source to send stage two to me and then we can reasonably break it in your blog, in a very low-key way if it stands up. And then I can write an editorial saying that if there is any truth in this it's a national scandal . . . and so on.'

'I'm off. Can I have some exes? My mother's already complaining that she's subsidising the paper.'

After a little fumbling in his pockets, the editor finds his battered wallet and takes out £100.

'OK, Melissa, see you later.'

'Are you sure this is right, Mr Tredizzick? I hate to ask again, but I'm worried.'

'Do you think it's right for a bank to steal its customers' money, and to pad out its balance sheet fraudulently, whatever the reason?'

'Well, obviously not, if you put it like that, but . . .'

'There's the answer then. The great smokescreen these people have put up is that they are doing something immensely important, way beyond the understanding of mere mortals. It turns out they didn't know what they were doing and that they have been playing fast and loose with other people's money, often only marginally legally. In this case the grand Tubal and Co. seems to have been doing something totally illegal. They have fucked up but their pride doesn't allow them to fail. Too proud to fail, could be their motto. So they steal from their customers. Of course they are proposing to pay it back. So was Leeson. They are not crooks after all. No, no, not at all. But whatever their game is, Melissa, if it goes wrong, pensions, medical research, academic institutions, you name it, all these innocent people and causes supported by the charitable trusts will go down the pan. Do you understand? Do you understand what you have stumbled on, Melissa? Not only is it journalistic gold, it's doing the country a service.'

In his eagerness, he's too close in the small car, his tired old face moist, his thick, nicotine-and-grey hair sticking out now, apparently responding to the static he's generating on the plastic seat covers. His teeth are soiled in the crepuscular light, but his eyes, small though they are – he dabs himself at this moment with a handkerchief from his top pocket – are fervid. He hates these people! It's class war. He hates the upper-class twits who have always had their manicured fingers on the nation's jugular.

'I'll do it,' she says, and gets out.

The windows are fogged and she can just make him out, undulating like an undersea creature caught in a current.

Artair is working on his screenplay – finishing touches, you never know when to stop – and he's happy to take a break. As if in response to his upbeat mood, the weather has become benign and they sit on the slipway outside the boathouse looking across the quiet and unruffled and bucolic estuary. Swans are idling about. Melissa is drinking the viscous, lethal coffee. Artair is wearing a Barcelona match shirt, made for a smaller man. On his back is *ARTAIR* and the number 7. He has a new, jaunty, tweed pork-pie hat, which sits on the sheaves of his hair like a chimney pot.

'Now, Melinda, have you got a boyfriend yet?'

'No time for that, Mr MacCleod. The editor keeps me very busy.'

'What a loss to mankind. Top man, Tredizzick. He was deputy editor of the *Mirror* in London, I think it was. He had a breakdown and decided Cornwall was his spiritual home after all.'

'What caused his breakdown?'

'A fat crook called Maxwell. Beyond parody, a crook on a Homeric scale. You had to admire him for his balls. Balls of brass.'

'How's your screenplay coming?'

'It's brilliant. When you've been in the business as long as I have, you develop an instinct. By the way, is this an interview?'

'No. I was doing a piece on sewage pollution on the beaches. The editor wanted me to look at it.'

'The sewage?'

'No, the underinvestment by local government, the threat to tourism, dead fish, anything, and I thought I would pop in. I hope you don't mind. If I am honest, I want the scoop on Daniel Day-Lewis for my blog. Has he signed up?'

'Signed up? No, no, it doesn't work like that. We are in the phase I call the mating dance. We are circling around one another. My final draft will wing its way to El Camino Drive in a day or two. Whence it will be sent to Daniel in his Irish fastness and he will read it. We are a few months away from consummation.'

'You won't forget me when it's agreed?'

'No, you'll get the news first. I promise. How's the coffee?'

'Strong. I am becoming an addict. By the way, when I phoned, you said some money had come. Did you say it was from your ex-wife?'

'Yes. She wasn't party to the arrangement Sir Harry made, and probably felt, now that her husband was dead, that she should make amends.'

'I hope it is enough to keep you going.'

'Let's just say it's a substantial sum. I'm sure the grant will be resumed now that Sir Harry's gone to bankers' heaven. Can you imagine what that would be like? Verdi at full blast day and night for the tone deaf, grouse season twelve months a year, Krug coming out of the celestial taps, the angels all pole dancers or rent boys, Lucifer dressed as Matron dispensing the cod liver oil, fishcakes served at every meal. Do you know, Melinda, Flann O'Brien wrote a book in which the characters refused to obey the author and took over the story. Does it strike a chord? The bankers took over the lunatic asylum. Flann O'Brien was that rare thing, a seer.'

He stares out across the water, contemplating, she imagines, the qualities of a seer, some of which he, too, possesses.

'Your Mr Barnecutt was suing them, wasn't he?'

'I've called off the dogs of war pro tem. Barnecutt has administered a few whacks, and now we wait to see the outcome. Barnecutt is not as optimistic as I am, but then he doesn't know Fleur. She has the traditional heart of gold. I managed her career for a few years and she won't forget.'

'And your *Thomas the Tank Engine* has been doing well.'

'Yes, the tide is running in my favour at the moment.'

'Right, lovely to see you, Mr MacCleod. And thanks for the coffee: I'm buzzing.'

'What you need is sex and plenty of it, Melinda. Sex is the life force.'

'Oh, OK. I'll see what I can do.'

She drives along the coast to the lighthouse and Smugglers' Cove, where she interviews a local café owner, two landladies and the proprietor of the pitch and putt course. They are all agreed that sewage on the beaches would put off the tourists. *Tourist numbers bound to fall in sewage scandal, say local shopkeepers and hoteliers. Outrage at cuts in spending....*

Is sex the life force? She thinks that older people still see sex as something religious, something extraordinary and precious, definitely more than recreation, which it was at college – most of the time.

From a lay-by, watched by two Friesian cows with curiously innocent faces, like babies trying to get objects into focus, she calls Alan39.

'Yes.'

'Melissa here.'

'Yes?'

'Please send the items.'

'OK.'

He rings off. As she drives back to town she tries to imagine why he is so cautious. Is he a speculator? You can't buy shares in a private, family-owned firm. So how could he make money out of this? It must be revenge. As the editor said, he may have been fired. He wants revenge but he doesn't want to be named at any cost. She wonders if Mr Tredizzick isn't a little obsessed with a kind of revenge too, having suffered at the hands of this Mr Maxwell all those years ago.

Cupcakes and macaroons. It's St Piran's Day soon, and she has found a piece of Chaucer, from 'The Cook's Tale', about pasties, or 'pastees' as Chaucer spelled it in the fourteenth century. *Now telle on, Roger, looke that it be goode/For many a pastee hastow laten blood.* Cornwall will be glad to know that pasties leaked back then, seven centuries ago. Artair's coffee and the blog and the huge events she's somehow, improbably, stumbled across are making her lightheaded. Actually, Alan39 stumbled across her. And that is her best defence.

As she drives through this placid countryside with its mean

bungalows and guileless cows in rounded, infantile fields, she starts to compose the blog:

A psychiatrist recently claimed that women in an adulterous relationship with a married or attached man were likely to leave an item of clothing behind in the marital bed or in the bathroom. Sexy knickers – what he called lingerie, pronounced 'lounger-ay' – are, research has shown, the favourite items. But is this a conscious act or an unconscious act springing from a primitive instinct to oust a rival, asks Dr Reginald S. Katz, celebrity sexologist in Bel Air, California. His speciality is sex addiction, apparently very common in California. Quite popular at my uni too, but that is another matter.

There are two questions I would like to put to Dr Katz: one, how did you do your research? And two, have you considered the women involved here have far less to lose, so they can't be bothered to look for their knickers? I know I can't always keep track of mine.

And so to cupcakes: I have been swamped by recipes (she has had two). I didn't realise that they had become such an obsession in Cornwall. I think there is a connection with the piece about lost knickers: sex. It seems to me, as I said, that cupcakes look like pert breasts. They suggest that the cook, most often a woman, is sending out an unconscious message: come and sample my cupcakes. What do you think of that, Dr Katz? And I don't even have a PhD.

Next Monday is St Piran's Day. You may not know this, but it was first observed by tin miners and the connection between tinners and pasties goes back a long way. And here is a piece I found from Geoffrey Chaucer . . .

This kind of stuff is so easy. She is contributing to global dumbing-down, but the readers seem to like it. Her blog is now the second-most-read site on the newspaper's web page, still some way behind the fate of the Winkles, the town's struggling football team. The Winkles have only won one game all season. There's a tremendous gnashing of NHS teeth in the town. Oblivion beckons for the Winkles.

Later that night, back amongst the knick-knacks and soothed by the distinct aromas of home, as she is typing up her blog, she gets a text from the editor: *dynamite. see you at 8am in car park.*

She is both nervous about what Alan39 might reveal and elated. Unlike the Winkles, she's playing in the Premier League now. *You've got to take it day by day, each game as it comes*, she says out loud, in the voice of a football manager.

Her father knocks and pops his head round the door, ingratiatingly. He carries a cup of Ovaltine. He's taken to wearing an old dressing gown over his clothes after 9 p.m. He's saving on the heating.

'You're working late, sweetie.'

'Blogging, Dad.'

'You were talking to someone, sorry to intrude.'

'Only to myself.'

'You know what they say, you are guaranteed an intelligent listener if you do that? I brought you some Ovaltine.'

'Oh thanks, Dad. That's so-oh kind.'

'Night night, my precious.'

'Night night, Dad.'

After he's gone she wonders if her dad isn't giving her this highly calorific drink each night to prevent her having too much sex, the life force. Unconsciously, of course, because he is in love with her in an innocent, Jungian sort of way, he wants her to grow fat and undesirable. She pours the Ovaltine into the curved avocado basin underneath the bit of mirror inexpertly screwed to the pinkish textured wallpaper, which is coming away where it abuts the basin. She feels guilty: they love her and have cherished her for twenty-two years.

20

KIMBERLY THINKS THAT vegetables are the way forward. Kim has asked Fleur to join her on the board of Urban Veggie. Fleur, who thinks of herself as not quite grown-up, is flattered to be invited to do something so adult. She also knows that half the fun, or more than half, will be the events organised to raise money. Kim takes her to visit a vegetable garden in a bit of unused land beside a canal in Hackney. Here unemployed youths, most of them drug addicts, are supposed to be clearing the ground for planting according to a very detailed plan based on the principles of the Soil Association. Drug addicts, says Kim, need something constructive in their lives. The soil has to be improved first and bags of organic matter have been brought in by one of the bank's delivery drivers, dressed down, in the van that Kim has donated to the project. She and Fleur are wearing green wellingtons and T-shirts – green, of course – which read *URBAN VEGGIE* in large lettering and then *Grow greens and grow greener*, a clever play on words. The volunteers haven't turned up yet for the photo-call – junkies, as is well known, can be unreliable. Three photographers are there, and they dutifully take pictures of Kim and Fleur and the driver digging away, before disappearing. Photographers have a way of being only partially present as though they find it hard to see what's in front of them: they have exhausted their eyes. A reporter from the *Hackney Gazette* asks them how this will affect the lives of disadvantaged youngsters.

'Oh, in many ways. Firstly we need to reconnect with the soil, the land. These kids are alienated' – the reporter looks around to see which kids she is referring to – 'they hardly know that vegetables come from the soil and our project is very involving. But also, none of us should forget that every person on this earth depends ultimately on the food chain and the food chain depends on the health of the planet itself. So the effect is threefold. An inclusive experience for the young, a supply of organically grown vegetables to improve health and immune systems in deprived areas and a sustainable use of our land. But it all begins with the soil, and we must never forget that. The soil must be enriched and improved as a first step towards creating greater biodiversity.'

A lot is riding on this manky piece of wasteland, Fleur sees.

The reporter clicks off his little electronic recorder, mumbles a thank you, and vanishes. Fleur stops digging; it's hard work. She's impressed by Kim's fluency and glowing idealism. She's like Sister Sarah Brown in *Guys and Dolls*, earnestly preaching. Next time she'll bring a tambourine.

'You were great. Very moving, very passionate.'

They stand around looking at the soil, while the driver unloads trays of organic vegetable seedlings and compost from the van. There is no question the soil needs improving: it has a dead, noxious look as though it has forsaken the organic world for something more bohemian. The brambles and dead nettles are infiltrated with all sorts of detritus, little shards of china and glass, fragments of bone, scraps of plastic like butterfly wings, bits of wire, a bag of cement which has set firm, and at least one used condom. The nettles and brambles have already been cut back in a grid, marked with lines of gardening string to guide the young offenders and addicts as they get to work, and the whole plot has been fenced. Fleur wonders if the junkies aren't in some way window dressing; in the van is a small rotovator which could turn over this urban waste in half an hour.

Eventually three young people arrive, two boys and a girl. They are subdued and tattooed; their hair is shaved up the sides and they wear camouflage trousers. At home in her wardrobe, Fleur has a very expensive pair herself, tightly cut around the legs, the newest fashion statement. The large woman who brought the volunteers in a Hackney

Social Services minibus says, 'I could only find these free and then we
'ad trouble with the vehicle.'

'Hello,' says Kim brightly, 'I'm Kim and this is my friend Fleur, and
we're from Urban Veggie.'

She shakes hands with the three young people and they seem mildly
surprised. They are probably more used to people trying to keep some
healthy distance between them. Fleur shakes their hands cautiously.

'Oh, OK, what we supposed to do then?'

'Well, we're going to dig this bit up here and then condition the soil.'

'Oh. Right.'

'That's cool,' says the girl, who seems to be stoned. She has a very
large silver ring in one eyebrow.

'Did anybody read you the instructions?'

'Nuh. You got a drink?'

Kim is prepared.

'Right, good idea, let's all start with a refreshment and then we'll
get going.'

She hands out Lucozade and Ribena and wholewheat buns stuffed
with greenery and the girl rolls three cigarettes which she passes
around. Her skin is very pale, so that it seems to have become trans-
lucent. She doesn't look to Fleur as though she is going to live long.

They work in a desultory fashion pecking at the soil like hens, and
about as effectively, with the shiny new spades. After half an hour
they have made one small trench – you have to dig trenches and back-
fill with the good organic compost – and then they sit down against a
rusting car-body which has at some earlier time in history wound up
here in the brambles. They seem to find comfort in the shadow of this
industrial relic.

'Where did you get them?' Fleur asks Kim.

'They're all on probation. They only do this because it's better than
being in custody on remand.'

'Do they like vegetables?'

'I doubt it. But you gotta start somewhere.'

The driver from the bank takes the rotovator out of the van, starts
it, and ploughs up the rest of the space, watched by the three junkies

on probation. They show a little more interest when the bags of compost – donated by a sponsor – are opened and the time comes to throw it around. But they lack stamina and Fleur and Kim and the driver work hard to get the job done. Fleur enjoys it. The compost is clean and rich and wholesome.

It's ridiculous, she thinks, to have a hired van, two multi-millionaires and the van's driver trying to make a vegetable garden with three junkies who are only here in order to stay out of jail. But she doesn't say it.

'The school kids are great,' says Kim a little desperately. 'Believe me, really motivated. We've got six gardens up and running in schools and they get to eat the vegetables for their lunch.'

'Dinner, Kim, they call it dinner. English kids hate vegetables. They think they are poisonous.'

'You would be surprised. Anyway, this is an educational project. With your acting training you could make a great speaker in schools.'

The junkies believe they have done their stint and go and sit in the minibus with the obese driver, who has been eating Mini Creme Eggs and smoking for the last hour. She starts the van and drives away. The junkies are slumped. Slumping is what they do best, their life's work.

'This is fun,' says Kim.

Fleur wonders if she is joking. It seems not. Between the two of them and the delivery driver they manage to plant a hundred little lettuces, a hundred cabbages, and some mounds of potatoes, which have to be banked up and watered. They leave the watering to the driver. Kim says the canal probably carries Weil's disease.

'Do you do this all the time? All this digging and stuff? I'm totally knackered.'

'No, we have a pretty good band of volunteers – expenses only – who really do the work.'

'So the kids and the junkies and the schools and so on, what are they for?'

'Fleur, we have to work with the community. We can't just say *eat your greens*. We're demonstrating, not farming.'

'Oh, OK. It's very impressive whatever. I really found it rewarding.'

They leave their wellies and T-shirts in the van, say goodbye to the driver and head across the canal over the rat-water to a converted warehouse that contains an organic café – like everything else around here, a little tired and grubby – and order a latte. Kim's Mini is parked safely outside.

'Fleur, what are we going to do about Simon?'

'In what sense?'

'He stayed away for years because he was frightened of Harry, but now he's back to take his place in the family. Julian feels he's carried the load, and he's not happy about Simon.'

'What a mess. I don't know. I'm totally adrift. Simon's got to sort himself out. He'll wander off somewhere, I should think.'

'Yes, maybe, but as the older brother and the Baronet he has the idea that he has come to claim what's his.'

' "Harry of Hereford, Lancaster and Derby am I . . . I lay my claim to my inheritance," ' says Fleur. '*Richard II*. I played a maid at the Young Vic. Is he entitled to anything much?'

'I don't think so. The trust settled a lot of money on him years ago. But I am sure Harry left him some things.'

'It's making me ill. Not the question of who gets what, but the uncertainty. I can't sleep.'

'Yes, Julian can't really sleep. Do you know, when he does fall asleep he dreams he's talking to his pony.'

'That's sweet.'

'You think talking to a horse is sweet?'

'I do. I think it's great. I don't think Harry ever felt stress in his whole life. He just knew exactly what he wanted to do and he did it.'

'Did you love him?'

Fleur pauses.

'I did. But I always liked older men, perhaps because my father left us when I was so young. I needed some sort of reassurance. With Harry, nothing was random or uncertain. You got dragged along in his slipstream. And I loved it. What you are asking, I think, is have I got any plans. The answer is no.'

'Apparently your ex-husband has been writing to the bank.'

'So everyone keeps telling me. They cut a lot of Harry's good causes and my ex was one of them, and he's started complaining. Harry paid him off when we married, but I never knew the details. Anyway, I sent him a small cheque to shut him up.'

'OK. By the way, I've put you on the committee for the Veggie Ball in September at the Dorchester. First committee meeting is on Friday at our place. Is that OK?'

She was planning an outing with Morné, but she can't say no.

'What an honour.'

'Come for supper tomorrow; Julian's off to the States.'

'OK, thanks, let's go somewhere buzzy.'

After they have found their way out of Hackney – a nightmare – and Kim has dropped her back home, Fleur wonders why she was asking her about Artair. Does she think she plans to go back to him? And she wonders just why Julian is so stressed out. Simon is a genial buffoon with a very short attention span and he'll soon be gone on his strangely aimless travels.

Back in the house – lifeless and oppressive – she thinks that maybe there is a connection: Julian wants to sell the house – she's agreed that she can't live here – but Simon possibly thinks he can have it. Something's going on and Julian is the only one who knows what it is. It's a fact that death in a family causes all sorts of tensions among the members, who inflate their entitlement and their closeness to the deceased in the mortal shuffle.

She heads for the gym. As she walks through the car park, a man steps forward from behind a parked car.

'Lady Trevelyan-Tubal, is it true that you are seeing the Saracens rugby player, Morné Nagel?'

'I'm seeing him only in the sense that he is my personal trainer and has been for some months. Are you suggesting something more? If you are I don't think that would be very wise.'

She walks into the gym, feeling drained, her legs about to give way. But she thinks she's done haughty contempt pretty well.

Morné is waiting.

'Have you been blabbing?' she says.

'What? About us?'

'Yes. There was a reporter outside.'

'A reporter?'

'Yes, he asked me if I had been having an affair with you.'

'I never said a word. Honest to God.'

But she knows that he must have said something to somebody, perhaps at the rugby club bar.

'OK, Morné, that's it.'

'What do you mean?'

'You and I will never see each other again. And if you have been spreading rumours, God help you.'

'It wasn't me, I promise.'

'Let's hope not. Now I am going to exercise without your help. I suggest you leave in about an hour and don't talk to anyone.'

He stands silently as she starts stretching. He wants to speak, but he's having difficulty. The great tree of his body is heaving as he struggles to say something, but no words come out.

He's guilty. He turns and leaves.

She goes through her routine doggedly, clinging to the hope that the reporter was just fishing, that somebody at the gym has told a journalist that she and Morné looked a little too cosy. Surely, surely no one knows anything for sure? Unless someone has been bugging the storeroom.

Harry warned her often enough about the press and their eagerness to connect the wealthy and the titled to scandal. He treated them with amused disdain and never answered their questions. Amanda was always ready with an injunction or a suit. She wonders if she can call Amanda or if she should just sit this out. She's longing to see Morné but she has to be strong. She's not a strong woman, but it is plain that her years of cosseting are over.

21

AS THEY LAND at O'Hare, there are still fast-flying flurries of snow over Lake Michigan. The waters of the lake have an icy sheen, a blue-grey that suggests unplumbed glacial depths.

A limousine is waiting and they are taken straight to the hotel through this city of mass – huge blocks of stone, sturdy bridges and great slabs of buildings. Cy's office has scheduled an hour for freshening up before the meeting. Wrapped in a towel, Julian looks down on North Lakeshore Drive. Chicago thinks of itself as a tough, no-nonsense place and maybe this is another reason Cy has fixed the meeting here in a town where once hundreds of millions of cattle were slaughtered and the stockyards ran for miles. Strange how industries change: not far away in Detroit, Ford's defunct River Rouge plant was twelve miles long. Tubal's had helped finance Henry Ford himself. Now River Rouge is largely derelict.

Standing semi-naked, snow driven past his windows horizontally by the high-altitude winds over the Midwestern vastness, he sees an object lesson of how economics works – the cattle and corn hinterland, the huge barges on the lake, the new condos, the ceaseless flow of traffic, the low-rise former immigrant districts, the projects that housed the black arrivals from the Deep South, the solid buildings of downtown, the architectural bravado of the sixties and seventies, the overwhelming sense that, although the buildings are substantial, the beliefs on which they were built are more treacherous than ever. He sees too that London is a little place, a quaint place and a backwater, no match for the elemental vastness of America. And Tubal and Co.,

Bankers at the sign of the Leathern Bottle since 1671, is no different from one of those old-world statues that William Randolph Hearst crated up and sent to California: trophies, nothing more than tributes to a self-invented man. Tubal and Co., the repository of all that make-believe Englishness, is as good as an honorary knighthood for Cy Mannheim from Coney Island.

Cy's penthouse is another ten storeys up. There is nothing above.

'Hi, boys. Welcome to Chicago. What a view. To me it always looks like they never quite finished the place off. Sit down, there's everything you could want in the kitchen, and I figured it would be better if we were alone. Feeling strong?'

Julian thinks that Cy understands him far too well: he likes him, but knows his weakness.

Cy has no files or papers in front of him, just a small hotel pad and a pencil. A waiter pours the coffee and offers pastries or fruit, but Julian and Nigel are in another time zone altogether. They drink coffee, not the hotel stuff in flasks that Cy favours, but proper espresso made by the waiter in the kitchen.

'OK, let's cut to the chase.'

'Let's.'

'You want to sell, I want to buy. I see some synergy and also I just love London. But don't exploit my sentimental nature, OK?'

He laughs, as if to suggest he knows that they know he's kidding. He has a corrugated face, as though the traffic of commerce across it has been heavy, and his hair is curiously barbered so that it sits on his head in little waves, without appearing to be a toupee. It may be the product of hair transplants. He wears an enormous graduation ring on one of his fingers. It's a parochial thing, reminding everybody who cares to ask that he graduated from the school of hard knocks, Coney Island branch. He once told Julian that his family's neighbour was the author of *Catch-22*. And, said Cy, he spoke with a worse accent than me. *Woise. Much woise.*

Cy loves meetings. He loves to negotiate.

'So how much do you want for the old place?'

Julian isn't prepared for this. It's too direct.

'Nigel and I have given you the asset value and freehold value and we have tried to estimate the bank's reputation and history. We would like to retain the freehold, charging you a fair rent. As you know, despite a few set-backs with sub primes and so on, our deposits are healthy.'

'So how much? And by the way, I want the building included.'

'One point two billion pounds, one point four with the building.'

Julian is shocked that it has all, finally, come down to a price.

'We think we can stand that up,' says Nigel calmly.

'OK, sounds like a fair price. I have a few questions for you boys. Ready?'

'Yes, I hope so.'

'Right, the first question relates to some unexplained transfers from various sources in the last few weeks. I don't want any nasty surprises if I buy. I want details of all the deposits over twenty million in the last four weeks. I also want to know exactly the extent of your losses in winding up the hedge fund. It's not clear from what you have sent me. And I would like to know if your family trusts are involved in any way in providing capital for the bank.'

Julian looks at Cy, who is smiling.

'I am not a member of the family, so I don't have much to do with the family trusts. There is a board of trustees,' says Nigel.

'You're one of them.'

'Yes, but only because as the CEO I have to certify the payments from the bank to the trust, but nothing more.'

'Nigel, that's a load of bullshit. You and Julian are practically joined at the hip. Let me put it to you another way to see if you get it. We have some information picked up by my guys that you lost a bundle on the hedge fund and some other stuff and that you don't have the capital. My hunch is that you have been pumping money, let's say £400m., from various sources, and I want to know what the sources are before I buy. It's as easy as that. Do you want to go away and talk about it? I would consider very carefully if I were you.'

He looks at his watch.

'I can give you forty minutes, then I'm back to New York.'

'OK, we will talk and be back,' says Nigel.

In Nigel's room they go through to the bathroom and Nigel runs the shower just in case. After all Cy's people made the reservations.

'Jesus, Nige, where does he get the information?'

Julian feels sick. His head is beginning, ominously, to ache.

'It's inside. It must be.'

'But who knows? Who knows, for God's sake?'

'Maybe he doesn't know, maybe he's just guessing.'

'He knows all right. Do you think it's Liechtenstein?'

'I doubt it. It's just not the way those people think. They have secrecy top of the Ten Commandments.'

'What are we going to say to him?'

'Jules, OK, I think we have two options: one, to walk away insulted and see how he reacts, or two, we tell him the truth. Either way we could be screwed. If we walk he can release the information, if he's got any, and we'll go down. Or he can offer us a low price, taking out all the family and Koopman's money.'

'We've only got a few months. I mean, he could drag this out until we are on our knees.'

'The other way is to deduct the four fifty from the one point four and say that's our asking price. He'll understand.'

'Are you sure?'

'Pretty sure.'

'You think he'll pay a billion so that we can repay the trusts quickly?'

'I think so. But it's a risk.'

'Once we admit to it, he can hang us out to dry.'

'What's the alternative, Nigel? What's our fucking alternative?'

'I don't know. One possibility is for me to talk to him alone and say look, there's family pride here, and you've upset Julian. He wants to walk away. But maybe we can make a deal which saves Julian and the family embarrassment.'

'How would that work?'

'He pays the full amount, let's say a billion two or three and you, not the family, pay him back the four fifty.'

'His board aren't going to buy that. Even his oversight people won't allow that. That's crazy. He doesn't have to do anything. He can sit tight now and drip-feed the market.'

'He won't do that – there would be a run. There would be a fire sale to one of the banks who would cherry-pick our clients.'

Julian feels a surge in the blood.

'OK. This is the deal. I am offering him one option only or I walk. He buys the bank with his private trusts, we sort out the finances, square the trusts and so on, and then he can take it into First Federal and the blinding light of disclosure, or keep it as his little hobby.'

'That sounds like a good idea. Brilliant, actually. But as you said, time is not on our side and if he has the information he can make a call to the FSA or the US regulators and we are dead. So our deal is – am I right? – he buys at a billion plus from his own resources and we use some of the money to sort out the trusts so that they have no recourse. They won't know anyway, but I think we have to do the deal now. Result, he gets the bank, clean as a whistle, and a going concern, working fine, clients happy – all for about a billion.'

'OK, let's give it a try. We have to believe he wants the bank a lot. I am sure that he doesn't want to bring the whole thing down.'

They go back up to the thirty-eighth floor to see Cy who is watching a pre-season baseball game with a drink in hand. The Yankees are playing the Sox.

'Right,' he says taking a lingering glance at the television, 'got your story straight?'

'OK, we will take care of any commitments the bank may have after you have agreed the purchase at one point four billion, and when you make a deposit of five hundred million.'

'So you want me to pay you to clean up your act? Why didn't you do that before you came along with your offer to sell?'

'It's not that simple,' says Julian, 'and you know it, Cy. The old man died in the middle of all kinds of family-trust dealings. There are forty-two interested members. And as for our major client, Koopman's, we have absolute discretion about what we invest in and have done for seventy years. We haven't misappropriated their money at all, but placed it on interest-bearing deposits and warrants with the bank. It's not the way we would have wanted to do things, but we had to avoid a run so they appear on the balance sheet as various deposits, but they have all come via legitimate banks and funds. The accounts for the fund will be published at year end plus a month or two for the Charity Commission to look at them. Our accountants have given interim approval for this. Actually it's way less questionable than Lehman's dodges which were signed off by Ernst and Young or what Northern Rock did. Look, Cy, we had to do something to keep the bank stable. If you destabilise us now, there will be a fire sale and no winners.'

'Are you telling me that all those family members know you have taken – what is it? – two hundred and fifty million from the family trust? And are you saying that Koopman's know you have set up some dummy deposits, via who knows where, in the bank?'

'No Cy, I am not saying that. What I am saying is that strictly in terms of our covenants and statutory obligations, we are clean. I am not saying it's the recommended way of dealing with the matter, but I am telling you that our balance sheet is legitimate. We're one hundred per cent private. As my father said, many times, we should have stuck to what we know. We didn't, and I regret it. I will always regret it. Our hedge funds were a disaster. But we've done what we could. We have done what we had to, to save one of our country's oldest banks. You know that this is a great opportunity for you. You could also sink us in just a few weeks after three hundred years of history by spreading rumours, the rumours you have mentioned. Do you want that? Have you got something against me and my family? Koopman's might lose everything. The family would certainly lose everything. If you choose not to believe me, we are walking. We have had a difficult time, and I am not prepared to play games.'

'Hey, Julian, attaboy. I like that. But I have one condition.'

'What's that?'

'I want you and Nigel to stay on for two years. I don't want all those upper-class Oxford men taking their money out of the bank. It's one billion one on the nose. Including the building.'

'Done.'

They shake hands.

'As a parting shot Cy says, 'How's them alligators doing down in the ole bayou?'

Julian knows Cy won't let them down. They're going to be his alligators soon.

Julian is mortally tired but elated. They order some champagne and watch the barges down below on the lake.

'You were totally great, Julian.'

'I was. I thought, how would the old bastard approach this? I just went on to autopilot, family pride, arrogance, history and God knows what. I thought if I don't convince him we mean business he's going to ride right over us.'

'The way you balanced family, the Charity Commission, history, and skated lightly over the trusts was brilliant. By the end he was actually scared you were going to walk.'

'I turned into my dad. He was so sure of himself that people deferred to him. I have the feeling we could have got more.'

'Maybe. One and a half, even, but he had someone on the inside. He was frightening us, and he got a discount. That's all he was after. He's a total shit, but you haven't done so badly. The alternative is too horrendous to think about. These kinds of guys have to win. The oiks with the dodgy hair from Coney Island who make it big on Wall Street, they have to win. It's all about the deal. And Cy's won. He's secured himself a discount of twenty per cent or more, and bought a piece of banking history.'

'Complete with a couple of genuine toffs.'

'Yup, that's us. But it means he can't blame us for anything he finds.'

'True.'

'The old order changes.'

'It does. You know, Nige, I could have been a real banker.'

They go out to Joe's Seafood Prime Steak and Crab. They are almost hysterical, the tension of the last few days dissipated. They may have been conned, but it could have been a lot worse. Julian has sold the bank and the scandal of malfeasance has been avoided and the trusts will be paid back in good time. Their flight isn't until morning and they are stranded here and it feels like an adventure.

'Do you really think we're out of the woods, Nige?'

'Looks like it.'

'Who was giving him the information?'

'I think it was the hedgies, probably Kevin and Paddy.'

'After they came that close to bankrupting us, that's marvellous. Why would they do it to us?'

'Cy probably paid them, or one of them.'

'Somebody had access, that's sure.'

The restaurant is full of happy, loud, normal people. The men look as if they work in commodities: they are broad with big faces – evoking the stockyards – and the women are consciously sexy, avid, laughing, having a good time. Julian wants to lose himself in this place. He envies these people their carefree lives. A huge plate of stone-crab claws arrives, and the waitress ties the bib around his neck.

'That's one great suit, sir. Let's see if we can keep it that way.'

'Gieves and Hawkes.'

'Real nice.'

Her smile warms him; he's desperate for anything that confirms to him that he is human. The small hairs on the side of her arm brush his face lightly. She brings a large, bright-red crab-claw-cracker. He wants to hold her; he wants to embrace her sturdy, cheerful frame.

'Enjoy. Just call me if you need something, honey. More dipping sauce, or whatever, guys.'

Nigel is already carving away at a huge steak.

'They like you, the ladies,' he says.

'Yes, I was always the good-looking one.'

'They see something in you. They don't see it in me, whatever it is.'

'Nige, before we sell, I'm going to nail Kevin and Paddy.'

'If it's them.'

'I want you to find out.'

'I think we should leave it now, Jules. You've got what you wanted, we've survived the panic. Don't want to prolong the agony or take risks.'

'I'm going to get them. I want to nail their nuts to the floor.'

'Sleep on it, Jules. Really.'

For the first time Julian fully understands his father's vindictiveness. He hated to be thwarted or cheated.

'OK, I'll sleep on it. These crab claws are sensational. You know when they catch them, they just rip the claws off and throw the crabs back. It takes two years for them to grow some more claws. You are thinking, admit it, how do they eat, but their claws are for fighting only. They feed perfectly OK without them.'

'The amazing secret life of the Florida stone crab, revealed for the first time,' says Nigel in a hushed, David Attenborough voice.

'Let's have one of those huge jugs of beer. Let's celebrate Chicago-style.'

Julian hails the waitress, who sails cheerily towards him and takes their order.

'You're being very silly, Jules.'

'About bloody time. I was a human being once, I think.'

Up in his room, Julian, fuddled, looks down on the lake. North Lakeshore Drive has a new aspect; it is now a necklace of light along the outline of the lake, which has turned to a deep impenetrable indigo. Out there, towards Canada, the huge barges and ships move slowly, their bridges ablaze with riding lights all halating in a light fog in blurs of light like spun sugar. England, he thinks, is a Ratty and Mole place by comparison. It's late, but ribbons and shafts and cones of headlights scroll and dip and flare along the lake's margins.

When he turns back, the message light on his phone is flashing and it sends a spasm straight through his body, tight with crab claws and dipping sauce and Goose Island Ale and Key lime pie.

'Hi, darling. Just Kim here. The kids are fine. Sam fell off the new swings and broke his arm, but he's fine. Just a greenstick fracture.

Love you. Oh, and Sam loves his cast. Little boys love an injury. It's more like a brace than a cast, really. Love you.'

Julian lies on his bed; he's shaking. He tries to sleep. He longs – *I am pathetic* – to dream about his pony and hear what she has to say.

22

THE EDITOR OF the *Cornish Globe and Mail* is parked at the top of Bodmin Moor where the road crests before rushing down towards Bodmin. The mists lift from time to time to reveal the Jamaica Inn. Trucks rumble and roar by. Some ponies stand stoically in a huge field, head to tail. It's six o'clock in the morning.

The editor knows that if he seeks permission to publish the documents London will be on the phone very quickly. But he also knows – he's an old Fleet Street hand after all – that a certain momentum can be built that makes it impossible to stop publication. The technique is to release bits of information. His first call is to a friend, retired from the *FT*, but still freelancing on financial matters.

'J.D.,' he says, 'Tredizzick here.'

The voice at the other end sounds a little fractured as though drink and disappointment have lodged permanently in the vocal cords.

'Tredizzick, you old cunt, how are you? And what's the time?'

'It's almost seven.'

'Have you gone mad?'

'I'm fine. I'm fine.'

'Still waving the sword of righteousness?'

'Yes, that sort of thing. But it's mostly polluted beaches and Spanish trawlers stealing our fish. Look, J.D., I have something very big to tell you. And I need your help.'

'OK, but a warning. I am still in my pyjamas. I don't think well in pyjamas.'

'Very big. I have some facts about a certain bank which I want you to leak.'

'Ah, you've become a short seller. Can't help you, old fruit.'

'Don't be fucking ridiculous, J.D. This is big. Wake up. Something huge fell into my lap about the Tubals. To put it very simply, all is not well with Tubal and Co.'

'What, specifically? Dowager aunt choked on *foie gras*, a racehorse had to be put down?'

'They're bust.'

'Are you sure? Jesus, are you absolutely sure? You aren't taking crack before breakfast again, are you?'

'No, I am serious. And I can stand it up. I have a source. We have a source. And documents. If you agree to help I will show them to you, but you can trust me, they demonstrate a massive fraud to prop up the bank's balance sheet.'

'What am I supposed to do?'

'I can't run with this story, cold, on my own down here in the outer reaches of civilisation, but between us we can make this work.'

'Eddie, are you absolutely on the level? This isn't just the last hurrah, Maxwell and your non-existent pension fund or something?'

'No, no. Please J.D., try to listen, I need you to help me with this. Get a train and I will pick you up at Plymouth and you can look at the material with me. It's mind-blowing. Can you come down tonight?'

'OK. Exes?'

'Yes, I'll pay. But not first class. Ad revenue is falling.'

'Do you know the train times off-hand?'

'Yes, I am prepared.'

He tells his old friend the train times and they settle on the 19.45 arriving at 23.27.

'I'll book us into the ultra-luxurious Francis Drake Lodge. Running water in several rooms. Have you got a mobile?'

'Of course. I had to let the carrier pigeons go, they were eating me out of house and home. OF COURSE I'VE GOT A FUCKING MOBILE.'

'OK. Get another pay-as-you-go – yes, we'll pay, with a receipt – then ring me so that I have that number. See you at 23.27.'

Financial journalists come, broadly, in two types, those who admire and suck up to the rich and those who loathe and envy them. J.D. has always been in the second category. He hates their guts.

Melissa finds the editor behind his desk looking at a printout; he waves at her to sit down. He passes her a note. *Ring me in half an hour*.

'Melissa, lovely to see you. Your blog is very good, sparkling. You have overtaken the Winkles as our number one website favourite. Nearly one thousand people in the Duchy read your deconstruction of cupcakes and fifty-two posted comments. Just wanted to say that I am very pleased with your work. By the way, has Mr MacCleod thrown any light on the nature of his windfall?'

'Only that it came from his wife. But you knew that.'

'Is it going to be a regular occurrence?'

'I don't think he knows, but he seems pretty happy. He's got big plans.'

'Good, good. More of the same, please. And keep tabs on Mr MacCleod. He's like a cockroach, indestructible.'

Melissa leaves his fogbound office bemused. Is the cloak-and-dagger stuff really necessary?

She goes to her desk, checks her emails – lots of comment from friends on her blog – and starts work. After a while she sees the editor leaving his office and heading for the stairs, and ten minutes later she calls him. He is in his car somewhere by the sound of it.

'Don't speak, Melissa, just listen. In your blog you should hint that Tubal's is in financial trouble and that, you have heard, is why Artair did not receive his grant. You say unnamed sources have suggested that Tubal and Co. have some financial difficulties and that is the reason the charitable donations have been cut, including Mr Artair MacCleod's. But you rejoice that this dynamo of our local culture will be repeating his renowned production of *The Wind in the Willows* at Easter, and so on.'

'Mr Tredizzick, why exactly do you want me to do this?'

'What we have is dynamite. But it is a fact of journalism that it is far less dangerous to report on what's already in print, in this case on a blog, than to make allegations yourself. I have an old colleague from Fleet Street who is going to help us get the ball rolling. And then there will be utter mayhem. A firestorm.'

'Do we want a firestorm, Mr Tredizzick?'

'Melissa, these people, as we now know for certain, have misappropriated some hundred millions of other people's money and – like my old employer Robert Maxwell – have placed pensions and people's investments in jeopardy. My guess is they are planning to sell the bank and in the meanwhile they are fiddling the figures. And we – thanks to you – have a chance to stop them doing this. We're not talking about some little crook who can't pay his school fees and has dipped into the client account. This is a massive fraud. And behind it is a family so grand that they believe they are untouchable. We'll see. OK, run your blog by me first. I want it by six tomorrow. All right?'

'Yes, fine.'

'Don't be nervous. This is a big moment.'

'I know.'

But she wonders if the editor and his old pal aren't intent on grinding axes. Is it possible that years of disappointment and bitterness have clouded the editor's judgement, that he's after the Tubals as a proxy for this Maxwell? She's Googled Maxwell and his story is almost unbelievable: an absolute fantasist and liar who was once a Member of Parliament and ended his life by jumping off his boat, the *Lady Ghislaine*. She tells herself she must just stick to her story – it has the great advantage of being absolutely true – that an unnamed source picked up on her blog, which was innocently wondering why Artair had lost his grant, and he gave her some information. She's already rehearsing an interrogation: *I met the source – no idea at all who he is – and passed on the information to my editor, who ran with it. It was his decision and his judgement to take it further.* But she can't help thinking that the *Globe and Mail* is pushing its luck taking on Tubal and Co. and the City of London. And she is troubled by the fact that she doesn't know what Alan39 wants. Mr Tredizzick is not interested. He's hell-bent on bringing down capitalism.

Artair is about to send his final version of the script off to El Camino Drive for onward transmission to Daniel Day-Lewis. He has revised one aspect of it substantially: the screenplay is, following O'Brien, going to demonstrate its own artificiality. There will be shots of the filming taking place, and the whole concept of a movie as a contained reality will be exploded; it will be a self-evident sham and the viewer will be offered the opportunity to distance himself, or herself, from the illusion with which most film-goers willingly collaborate. He, Artair, will participate in the movie, although the viewer will know that he is also the writer and director. He will strive to contain his characters. He will demonstrate that there is no such thing as a single objective reality. He's rehearsing a speech in his mind:

> The point it that all art involves illusion; as the great Danish philosopher, Søren Kierkegaard wrote, the striving for truth represents the consciousness of being an existing individual and the constant yearning is the product of the nature of existence. I like to think that it is therefore the artist's single most important duty to show that truth is never at any one moment complete. It is also clear to me that the artist must explore the effects of the oral poetry and the storytelling which have shaped all of our literature and mythology. Every teller of a tale, every translator of a poem, has altered it to his purposes and his understanding of his forebears, so that, as T.S. Eliot said, no poet, no artist of any sort, has his complete meaning alone. His significance, his appreciation, is the appreciation of the dead poets and artists. Probably for this reason, Joyce has Dedalus advocate cutting yourself off from the past.

He's aiming high. The dead poets and artists are not traditional subject matter for Hollywood. But Joyce and Bloomsday have a certain mythical stature that Hollywood will like. He sees a trend towards myth in their animated films that could make the film very popular with the youth of the world who regard so many of the institutions and artifices of society as a kind of tyranny.

And this is the joy of being a creative artist – you might say the responsibility too – that you don't live within the constraints of the conventional and the restrictive: in fact it is your duty to challenge this idea of a single reality.

The phone rings as he's preparing to go out to catch the bus, so that he can send his script, revised, and marked boldly, *FINAL DRAFT*.

'Yuh,' he says, distracted by the enormity of the delusion of the single reality.

'Hello, Artair, it's Fleur.'

'Fleur, good God. How are you, darling girl? I am so sorry about Harry.'

'Thank you. Your note was wonderful, it touched me.'

'Well, that's the least I could do.'

'Artair, I would love to see you again.'

He recognises that little mewling, coquettish note so clearly. Strange – voices, songs, scents – all seem embedded for ever in your brain.

'I would love to see you too, darling Fleur.'

'I wondered if you could come up to London. As you can imagine there are all sorts of things to think about, so I'm a little tied to home at the moment.'

'London. I would love to come up.'

'Could you come tomorrow, perhaps? That's my best day this week. Come for lunch at the house and we can catch up. Come first class.'

'I'm just sending off some rewrites on a screenplay, so I will have a little space in my diary. And my heart, of course.'

'Artair! Now, now. Oh, there's also the question of the grant. I want to make sure that it continues now that Harry has gone. There was a little confusion with the admin at the trust after Harry fell ill, but we can sort it out. The 8.10 gets to Paddington at 12.23. Can you manage that?'

'I think I can, dear girl.'

'I'll send the driver to get you. He'll wait at the barrier with a sign.'

'That sounds fine. Fleur, are you truly all right? These things are not easy.'

'I'm coping, darling, or trying to. The family is closing ranks a little, but still, I'm fine. I'll see you tomorrow. We'll have lunch.'

Artair takes the bus into town. Birds are gathering on the shores of the estuary. He's not good on birds, but in general he thinks they may be small ducks. Perhaps they have come all the way from Africa. That's a very strange thing, the migration of birds. How did the first migrating bird know it had to fly eight thousand miles to get a seasonal meal? He's supposed to have a casting session for the summer season, but he will send his assistant to make a preliminary assessment of the available talent while he goes up to London, first class, to see his dear Fleur.

When he gets to town he registers the script at the post office. The assistant is keen to learn about El Camino Drive.

'It's the middle of Beverly Hills, the place where all the boutiques are,' he says airily. 'Palm trees, shopping, swimming pools; it's a hellhole.'

'Sounds great to me.'

'I prefer Bel Air. Get that off immediately. The world is waiting.'

'Righty-ho, Mr MacCleod.'

Melissa is running her blog by the editor as promised. He likes it. He makes a few small suggestions.

'You don't want to be too definite. It's a rumour at the moment, which you have heard. You're not saying it's true. You are interested in the cultural aspect, not the financial. Just beef that up a little. Otherwise perfect. I like the bit on shoes too. You can work sex into anything. Now it's the shape of shoes, I see.'

'Yes, Mr Tredizzick, shoes are signifiers.'

'Everything is a signifier in your world, it seems.'

'It was linguistics, module 4 at uni. It warped me.'

'Good girl. Keep your nerve.'

She revises her copy and loads it straight on to the system, which is called INSCRIPT. All these systems have fancy names. As she leaves the office at about 6.30 she sees the outline – the ghost – of the editor through the frosted glass of his office, still hunched over his desk and no doubt smoking. He's meeting his old friend tonight. He's sniffing the wind.

Only yesterday she heard from the sports editor that Mr Tredizzick had had two heart attacks but he refused to give up smoking or take exercise. His fingers are permanently stained to a light cinnamon colour, and his skin is deeply furrowed by smoking and poor ventilation. She's not sure why smoking creases the skin like linen, but it does. It seems that in his world it's a matter of pride to be untidy, unhealthy and unillusioned. Not for the first time, she wonders if it's wise for this scruffy old man and this dying newspaper to take on the City of London.

23

FLEUR DOESN'T REALLY know what's going on: she's not privy to the family's closest dealings and fears and plans. She gets news of them, but edited, sometimes by Amanda.

Amanda came to see her again two days ago. She was wearing ridiculous black culottes that reached just below her knees.

'Fleur, we think it would be a good idea if we settled your first husband's claim that Sir Harry agreed to pay him from the Coppélia Charitable Trust. I have discovered that it was twenty-five K a year. Can you talk to Mr MacCleod and arrange it? Not the details, I'll do that, but the general principle, that although you weren't really involved you think it's only right that he should receive what was promised him. Can you manage that?'

'I am not sure. I really don't know any of the details.'

'No, you don't. That's a plus. But it would be helpful going forward to have this settled now. As I said a moment ago, I will handle the paperwork.'

Amanda looked at her coldly for a moment, as if she was trying to recall if she had ever come across anyone this dim before. She quickly cocked her head into an unnaturally reasonable pose, the sort of pose people who don't really like children assume as they listen to a child's ramblings.

'Fleur, let me just say that it would be very helpful to the family and to you – you're part of it, of course – if you would speak to Artair. We really don't want him to talk to the press or claim that he has been robbed.'

'Amanda, sorry, but I can't do it. How's it going to look?'

'All right. I'll speak to Julian. He was particularly keen to get this out of the way when he got back from the States. At the end of the day it's up to him.'

Amanda stood up, leaving her coffee. And later Julian rang.

'Fleur, hello, I hear Amanda rubbed you up the wrong way. Sorry, she's not as scary as she seems. She's got a lot on her plate. She says you wanted details of your first husband's arrangement with my father. That's the problem: we don't really know the nature of it. It may not really have been strictly legal. It was listed as a charitable donation, but the Charity Commission doesn't have any record of it. Amanda's looked. If my father's trust had deeds, we can't find them. Anyway, we are here to make sure Mr MacCleod is paid. But I think it needs to come from you, from one of your trusts. That's all.'

'Julian, what's going on? It all seems so furtive?'

'No, it's not furtive. But we do need to get the estate settled and to separate the personal and business matters. My father was a little lax about these things. The family has always tried to avoid publicity, as you know. Financial markets are very volatile at the moment and your first husband has been talking to a local newspaper. Journalists just love that sort of thing.'

'What sort of thing?'

'Oh, you know, top banking family embroiled in scandal. Rumours fly about. My brother heard one about you and some rugby player . . . all nonsense, obviously, but we need to get everything tidied away. Harry didn't always know the difference between his money and the family's money. Do you think that you can do it?'

Only her actor's training allows her to give the impression of pondering his question seriously.

'Yes, I think I will do it. For you.'

'Wonderful. Thanks so much.'

She imagines a new coldness in Julian, his father's coldness. He tells her that Amanda will set up a one-off payment of £250,000, which will come from her – she will be reimbursed – and for that Artair must promise never to mention the bank again and to call off his lawyer in Cornwall. She must make it clear to Artair that there never was any legally binding agreement between him and the family or with the Coppélia Trust, which has been wound up, and that this offer is made without prejudice, which means, he says, that this is the last word and that it cannot be used in court. She must get Artair to sign a document.

Now she's waiting for Artair. The document is in a drawer in the library. The sun is cascading into the dining room and a large vase of parrot tulips is placed on the gateleg table to make the best of the light. The tulips are pink with a bluish tinge on their ragged edges. She has asked Cook to produce some of her madeleines: Artair once claimed in Brittany that he loved them, perhaps during a Proust phase, and their buttery, eggy, insistent scent is reaching her from some distance along the corridors. She has arranged some serious-looking books casually on a low table, books about music, art and so on, and removed some magazines which Artair would find absurd and trivial. She knows they are banal, but she can see the human drama in stories of Botox and divorces and the adoption of orphans by celebrities. It's just snobbism to pretend no interest in this freak show; it is, after all, entertainment – fiction with photographs.

She sees that she's on the spot. The mention of Morné has frightened her. How much do they know? She wonders if the family were keeping tabs on her, in order to have some cards to play in any settlement. Do they know about Bryce? What did old Simon actually say about a rugby player? And what did Julian mean by saying that Harry didn't always know the difference between his own money and the bank's? She's never had anything to do with the bank, apart from going to dinners and events with Harry, but the implication is that there has been some abuse, which they are trying to sort out, and she has been given the task of putting Artair back in his box, or else.

She goes into the kitchen. Cook is transferring the madeleines from a wire rack where they have been cooling, on to a large plate; now she starts to dust them with icing sugar. She's not the comfortable, bow-fronted, cheery kind of cook, but a businesslike, thin contemporary cook. She has made a lobster salad and – under mute protest – a chocolate pudding, Artair's favourite. With it, he liked tinned cream and she has found some in a Greek supermarket.

'It looks lovely, Fadila.'

'Thank you, lady.'

'Will you tell Luis to get a bottle of Krug up from Sir Harry's cellar . . . My guest likes champagne.'

'Yes, lady. It is already in the ice. You said before.'

Fadila's English, like her cooking, is low in calories. Harry lured her away from a Portuguese family restaurant in Pimlico. He did a lot of luring in his time. Fleur doubts if she will stay now that the house has gone quiet. She sees with painful clarity that Harry's friends and dependants – not clearly separated in his mind – are not very interested in her. They have made the right noises since his death of course, elegant notes arrived, but the elderly wives are frightened of her.

When the front-door bell rings, Luis is there in his short white jacket to greet the visitor.

He shows Artair into the drawing room. Artair is wearing a smallish checked hat on top of his hair, which is now almost white. He is covered from head to toe in a dense green overcoat which he hands magisterially to Luis after a brief struggle to get it off. Underneath he wears worn corduroy and a spangled waistcoat over a green T-shirt. He appears to have been rummaging in the props cupboard.

'Fleur, my darling, you look wonderful.'

He kisses her on her cheeks three times and then takes her hand and kisses that. His teeth are grey and chipped. She hasn't seen bad teeth for a while.

'How are you, dear Artair?'

'Marvellous. But I've missed you for every one of the eighteen years.'

'We weren't right, really, were we?'

'Who's to say? You were too young, of course.'

'Not any more. I feel I am ageing fast.'

'You really don't look a day older.'

She's wearing black leggings under a small and youthful pleated skirt; she spent some time deciding on this look. She feels more like Emma Bovary than ever. Artair looks terrible: his nose and cheeks are a mass of blood vessels just under the skin, and melanin spots are on triumphal march across his brow.

Luis pours the champagne into two long flutes. Artair gulps his. He accepts another.

'How's the theatre company, Artair?'

'Well, thanks to your cheque, it's fine for the moment. But big news, completely confidential, yes?'

'Yes, of course.'

'The news is that I am in negotiation with Daniel Day-Lewis about a film – could possibly be theatre – based on the life and works of Flann O'Brien.'

'You always loved Flann O'Brien. Is Day-Lewis up for it?'

'So far, so good. I'm not allowed to say more. You know the business.'

She remembers these wild swings of optimism and expectation. Then, she thought they were inspiring, his naïve belief in the inevitable triumph of art over bourgeois values and his confidence in the effect that the old Celtic legends – presented by himself – would have on the ancient but forgotten cultures when he reconnects them with their melting, misty past. As she remembers it, his belief was that we are all the products of our history and our race memories; even memories we are not aware of are buried within us and need exhuming. Absolutely mad nonsense, but even now she understands the yearning that lies behind it.

Artair is staring past her.

'Jesus, Fleur, that looks like a Cézanne.'

'It is. Harry has – Harry had – three Cézannes. Two are on loan, and then there's this one, Mont Sainte-Victoire, of course.'

'My God, it is so beautiful.'

He has another draught of champagne.

'So, so beautiful.'

He stands in front of the picture, transfixed. From behind he seems to be trembling. His little hat is oscillating in sympathy.

'Artair, are you ready for lunch? You must be hungry.'

He turns.

'Until your cheque arrived, I had been living on pasties. I am not complaining, but the life of a serious artist is not easy. No, it's not easy.'

And it has obviously not been easy for him, that's for sure. But she saw, even in her short time in the theatre, that most actors and directors thrive on the ups and downs and the many false hopes and the occasional successes. It's a sort of addiction, the high of an unexpected job instantly banishing the low of unemployment. The steady and the predictable are a kind of hell for actors.

She and Artair walk through the library to the morning room. In his presence she sees this house, this huge house where no children have lived for years, for what it is, a mausoleum. Artair must be asking himself how one woman can live here alone, surrounded by wonderful paintings and cosseted by servants. Even now, as they pass the French windows, she can hear a lawnmower at work outside. She suddenly thinks it makes a noise like the flamingos on Lake Natron. Her mind is prone to odd leaps at the moment, brought on by isolation. So strange that she should think of Kenya at this moment: she was there on her honeymoon with Harry. They slept in a huge safari tent under storm lanterns and their guide tried to kiss her when Harry went on a bird walk. The vanity of young men. There was always something about her that made men think it was fine to try it on: she's not the kind of girl who will take offence, they thought.

'Fleur, this house is astonishing.'

'I'm moving out soon. The family trust owns it. You never quite know what belongs to the family.'

'Aren't you family?'

'Yes and no. Mostly, I'm just the bit of fluff the old boy took a fancy to. And we never had children, so I don't quite qualify.'

'Did you want children?'

'Harry didn't. He persuaded me that I didn't. Now I think I regret it. Come, here we are, Cornish lobster, followed by chocolate pudding with tinned cream. And madeleines with the coffee. Do you get the theme?'

'I'm overcome, Fleur. You always were such a kind girl.'

Luis, his face as adamantine as a picador's waiting for the bull to enter, serves them. Artair's table manners were never good, but now they are explosive. He ignores the silverware and picks up a large piece of lobster tail, dips it into the lustrous mayonnaise and pushes it into his mouth, where his ancient, world-weary teeth cut surprisingly cleanly through it.

'Artair, tell me all about your project. It sounds so exciting.'

He wipes his mouth on the sleeve of his T-shirt, where his rather skinny old arms poke through. His torso is massive as though the pasty diet has reached his chest to the neglect of his arms and legs. Waving a lobster claw, he describes the challenge of demonstrating that art is an illusion, that truth, as Kierkegaard said (he pronounces the philosopher as *Kierkegourd* with many glottal acrobatics), is never at one moment complete.

And he explains his master plan: using Flann O'Brien's appearance at the first Bloomsday as a framework, he will make a film which will challenge all the conventions of art and society. He's tearing at the lobster now, biting through the shell on the legs – she can see why his teeth are worn – bits of shell fly on to the floor, mayonnaise glistens on his lips and further afield; his eyes are wild with the beauty of art, the prospect of transcendence. He catches his fingers in the lobster tweezers.

'Ow, fuck. Fleur darling, this house reminds me of a poem by Baudelaire. It's called 'L'invitation au Voyage'. It recalls a place in the south and a house.

'There everything is order and beauty
Luxe, calme et volupté
Furniture gleaming
Burnished by the years
We would grace our bedroom
With the most exotic of flowers …'

'I forget the next few lines, it goes on, oh yes . . .

> 'The oriental splendour,
> All of it would speak
> To the soul, secretly
> In its gentle, native tongue
> There, everything is order and beauty
> Luxe, calme et volupté.'

He looks around.

'"*Luxe, calme et volupté*". I took the stony road, but I could grow used to this. The poem rhymes in French, by the way.'

Fleur is weeping. She seems to be doing a lot of that these days. Artair stands clumsily and then kneels beside her and holds both her hands.

'I'm sorry. Maybe it was too much.'

'No, Artair, no. Thank you. I remembered so clearly how you used to recite to me and how we used to talk until dawn after a show.'

Show, her mother's word.

When she's back in control of her fragmenting self, she rings the bell and Luis picks up the wreckage of the Cornish lobsters and wipes away the mayonnaise pointillism impassively. While he is busy, Fleur sits, eyes downcast at the gleaming table, burnished by the years, and she remembers how young she was and how hopeful and she sees that Artair has done something heroic: he has kept faith with art and its power. She sees that Harry and the family, for all their taste and sophistication, never speak to their souls. They have taste, but cannot make art. They have style, but they don't have love. They have wealth, but wealth has isolated them. They make polite, inherited conversation, but deep down they are disdainful and contemptuous. They have exquisite manners, but these are designed to hide their lack of interest.

Luis brings the pudding, a large slab of baked chocolate, exactly how Artair likes it; she doesn't tell him that the Bournville Cocoa has been replaced with Paul A. Young's finest, 70% cocoa solids, at

£20 a bar. She has asked Luis to bring the open tin of Nestlé Extra Thick Cream. He has placed it on a silver tray, with a silver spoon next to it.

Artair is elated and touched. He pours the cream in a wave on to his huge slice of pudding.

'This is magic. Absolute bloody magic. You always were a wonderful girl. "*Luxe, calme et volupté*". Roy Campbell translated it as "There will be nothing but beauty, wealth, pleasure/With all things in order and measure." Ridiculous but it rhymed. Yes, I will have some more.'

Artair is in full flow. It's magnificent, grand and crazy. He talks about Olivier and Peter Sellers and Peter Brook and the giant Jim MacCool, Dickens, the Celtic bards, and he even speaks about the Israeli writers he has met in Jerusalem who were originally from Iraq.

Finally he pauses, upending the tin to get the last drippings of the cream, and Fleur says, 'Artair, can I tell you about my proposal for your theatre?'

'Oh, yes. Yes. Please do.'

'I am proposing to give you £250,000 as an endowment for your company. It's not from Harry's funds or the family trusts, but my money, from my own trust.'

'Don't be ridiculous.' He is frozen, with a silver teaspoon dripping Nestlé Cream on to the table. 'I can't accept that.'

'Artair, you must. It seems Harry's grant was stopped after he became ill. No one knew about it or what it was, and from what I have been able to gather, it was never even set up properly. I'm trying to be a bit more responsible, so you will have to promise not to talk about it to anyone. I don't want the publicity and nobody in the family wants this mentioned again. I will have to ask you to sign something, but it's for the best. You can have the money as soon as you want it and all you have to do is tell me where to send it.'

Artair is still wearing his small hat. He takes it off in a reflex gesture of gratitude. The space between his two parallel side-panels of hair is like a parterre, very precisely delineated.

'I can't take it, Fleur.'

'Artair, my darling, the family has everything, beauty, luxury, ease, but no one speaks secretly to their souls. Artair, take the money, take this money and do something wonderful with it.'

She's overwrought by Artair's grandeur and innocence and she can't bear the idea that he won't take her money.

'Please, Artair.'

'On one condition.'

'What's that?'

'That you become the patron of my company.'

'Does that mean I get free seats?'

'And free pasties. A choice of cheese and onion or meat and potato. And maybe one day you will act for me again.'

'I don't think so. OK, as I'm officially your patron, can I ask you to sign some papers? We'll do it over coffee and madeleines in the library.'

She can't tell him that Amanda put the tabs in the legal folder herself and that Amanda reminded her firmly, twice, that he must sign all three copies of the deed.

Artair looks up from signing. His mouth is whitened with icing sugar.

'Do you miss Harry?'

'I'm afraid.'

'Don't be afraid. You were made to fall in love. And remember, you're one of us again. Don't worry.'

And she takes some comfort from this, absurd though it is to accept comfort from Artair, who now imagines himself in *Dombey and Son*, despite the fact that he is wielding her Mont Blanc rather than a quill. She suspects he would like blotting paper and a wax seal.

24

THE EDITOR AND J.D. plotted in a small bedroom of the
Francis Drake Lodge. It had stained carpets: the physical and spiritual
detritus of loneliness and furtive sex and cigarettes and fatal takeaway
meals had left their mark on this dog kennel. The two elderly men
were planning the downfall of the House of Tubal.

By four in the morning, the plan was agreed: J.D. would leak, casually, to a colleague at the *FT*, a rumour that Tubal's was in serious
trouble: there are unconfirmed reports that the balance sheet has been
padded. J.D. will follow this up on Monday in an occasional column
he writes for the *Evening Standard*, saying that rumours were flying
around the City that Tubal's is virtually bankrupt, like Northern
Rock, and for much the same reasons. There are even unconfirmed
reports of inflation of the balance sheet. By Tuesday a tip-off will lead
to the editor of the *Cornish Globe and Mail*, who is the recipient of
some anonymous documents. The editor will adopt a high-minded
attitude, saying that an innocent blog by a very junior reporter has
led to an anonymous tip-off, followed by the documents, which
appeared to him – he was once on the financial pages of a national
newspaper – to be genuine. Other experts agree with his judgement.
The papers suggest a major misuse of trust funds in order to bolster
the asset ratio. He, the editor, will be sending copies to the FSA or the
Charity Commission as soon as he has heard from them. It is his duty,
he believes, to hand over these documents if the authorities wish to
see them. The newspaper will anyway publish extracts shortly.

By the time the plan was agreed, they were exhausted. The editor wondered for a moment if they weren't too old for this sort of thing, which was once the whole purpose of their careers – the exposing of crooks. They are both left over from an era of smoke-filled rooms and powerful trade-union bosses, bowler hats in the City, comfortless childhoods, the promise of socialism to come: jam tomorrow. It was the creed – the religion – people professed, but in reality didn't really believe. But both J.D. and the editor knew that the four sheets from Tubal's computers revealed something very important in their close script and that was the traditional arrogance and contempt of the high-altitude financial classes for ordinary people. What they were forgetting, perhaps, is that the people as a coherent and decent group with shared values has never been anything more than a convenient myth, and now it has, anyway, gone for ever, lost in a world of compulsive gratification and trivialisation, where culture and art and learning are no longer the goals of this once decent class – if it ever existed. Now the whole country longs for celebrity and easy money and exemption from all forms of restraint. Money dominates every life.

All this the editor knows. The truth is, he has known it for more than two decades but his bitterness obliges him to ignore the facts as they present themselves to him daily.

It's Monday. The editor is at his desk. The *FT* has run a few lines in the 'Mammon' column, enough to allow J.D. to add a little weight to the rumours in his Monday column. He has emailed the copy to the editor at home:

> *Tubal and Co., blue-blooded bankers to the wealthy and titled since 1671, have run into serious problems with the collapse of its Lion Fortress Hedge Fund. Now losses are said to have been far more extensive than reported and may place the bank's independence in question. The rating agency has declined to comment on any possible downgrade of the bank's rating. Troubled waters may lie ahead for the Tubal family after three hundred years of plain sailing.*

In truth, rating agencies never comment. The editor loves this hoary old ploy: you call someone who won't answer and make the refusal sound ominous. The editor knows what will happen soon: his number will be leaked and his phone will ring wildly. But for the moment there is a deathly silence. The *Standard* only hits the streets at midday since it was sold to a Russian for one pound. He sits in his office, idly scanning the latest news about the Winkles – bad – and the fact that a hundred-foot retarded whale creature has washed up on a beach, probably drowned by a trawler's three-mile-long nets, undoubtedly the Spanish bastards' illegal nets. Porthilly Ices reports that ice-cream sales are up with the arrival of warm weather; the new clotted-cream-and-toffee line is particularly popular. And the EU has finally rejected the Cornish pasty as a protected mark. It seems they didn't see anything special in Cornish gristle and suet and the meaty bits left over on the abattoir floor. To hell with them, he thinks, he's got bigger things on his mind. He wants to call J.D., but he knows that would be a bad idea: the story will gather its own momentum.

Artair's money has arrived in his account. It's put him in a very strong position in relation to the manager. He has decided not to move his account just yet: the bank is on probation. They have offered him a personal banker. He phones Melissa to tell her that his money has arrived and he is fully funded for ten years, which, he says, may well be long enough. As he thought, it was just an administrative mistake. Nothing sinister. She seems pleased for him. He tells her he is almost into pre-production.

'Oh, I love *The Wind in the Willows*.'

'No, Melinda, I am talking about my project with Daniel.'

'Great, wonderful, any news we can print on that?'

'Not yet, but you will be the first to know.'

Julian and Nigel have early printouts of the *Evening Standard* piece, sent on by Nigel's contact at the newspaper. They are in Julian's garden, which opens into the shared gardens behind, seven private acres of trembling spring.

Two people are out exercising their dogs. As they pass Julian and Nigel, sitting wrapped against the early chill at a table under the mulberry tree – just coming into leaf – they wave cheerily. Dog people, Julian thinks, have an idealised vision of a world in which everybody is matey and loves animals and likes a chat. Julian pours the coffee. It's a blend that Kimberly favours, because it's produced under the Fair Trade scheme. Of course, economists think the Fair Trade scheme is about as useful as a window tax, but it's actually pretty good coffee grown at high altitude in Central America, perhaps Belize or Honduras. He can't remember: they are possibly the same place. Julian is trying to calm himself with these harmless thoughts. He sips his coffee and picks up the printout. It's only a paragraph in a column in the not-too-serious business pages of a free-sheet, but he feels his insides lurch and a migraine beginning to form. It always starts in the same way, with a bubbling somewhere to the back of his head that gives birth to the headache proper. Then it feels as though the inside of his head is being rasped by gravel and the whole thing forms into a compact mass of dark pressure waiting to be born. It's a form of parturition.

'Oh, just fishing,' says Nigel, swallowing his coffee carelessly.

'Can we stop it?'

'We will issue a statement. We mustn't look as though we take it too seriously. I've got Eric on the case. He's way ahead. Apparently the information was leaked by someone to this Cornish newspaper, and, so Eric thinks, they have leaked it to the *FT* and now that dickhead at the *Standard* has picked up on it. As I said, just fishing.'

'This looks organised. Do you think it's organised, Nige?'

'I don't think so. Let's see what evidence they can produce. It's easy enough for a source to make allegations but you know for the FSA or the Charity Commission it's very different. You've got to tough it out. You are the eleventh generation of Tubals and the people out there know the bank's history. This isn't Northern Rock or any bank with a lot of footballers for clients. This is old money.

Nobody wants to see a scandal, except a few muckrakers in the press. I'll put Amanda on alert.'

'Eric must find the source. It has to be one of the hedgies. We've got to get to him.'

'Julian, look, they haven't got anything firm yet as far as we can tell. I've ordered some software to scan all the systems. Until we know anything, we have to play a very straight bat, stall for a few weeks, come up with as many delays as we can, and also you must go and see the Secretary of State. Once Cy has paid over the money and we've straightened everything out, the whole thing should go away. An enquiry, the FSA faffing about, perhaps a reprimand in a year's time. That's it. Look, they don't even want to go after Lehman's, who hid $50bn. That's ten times the GDP of Montenegro.'

'Nige, even this government, desperate as they are to get re-elected on their wonderful financial policy, is not going to be able to resist if the press demands some heads on a plate. You can just see how they will frame it.'

'OK, so go and square Koopman's. Speak to Kronwinkel. Tell him that the hedgies placed some money in a dodgy fund and that you are sorting it out. Business as usual, Charity Commission's accounts in order. Kronwinkel likes a quiet life. Tell him our auditors are on side. They will be – I have spoken to Derek this morning – and they'll give an interim approval. And we must talk to Cy. He is way too big for the government to ignore. Just make sure when he's actually going to pay, then that gives the Business Minister the opportunity to say look, we've been involved in encouraging First Federal to buy Tubal and Co., and I'm glad to be able to announce that it's all agreed. It's all for the best and in the national interest – blah-blah. If it emerges that an enquiry is required, we will institute one . . . all that sort of guff. Cy may even get a grant or some tax breaks.'

'Do you want to speak to Cy?'

'No, I think you should do it. He's back in Florida so you can call him at about noon. He likes you: you've got class.' (He tries a Bronx accent, unsuccessfully.) 'And I think you should get on to Goldstone. Actually it's probably better to wait a day or so until you've squared

Koopman's. Explain to them how dangerous these rumours are and say they must refute them if called on. But Cy must also be in the loop.'

'If he isn't already.'

'What do you mean?'

'I think he may have been pulling the strings. I think he's bought one of the hedgies. And by the way, you seem to have forgotten that you said it was just fishing.'

Kimberly comes out into the garden. She's wearing that morning look – pale, still a little bemused, a child who has woken from a profound sleep, surprised to find that the world is still there. She's in her long silk dressing gown with the Chinese embroidery.

'Kim,' says Nigel, standing up. 'How lovely you look.'

'No make-up, this is the real me. Sorry. Not too disappointed?'

'No, you look fabulous.'

And she does.

'Julian, Len's outside,' she says. 'Apparently you wanted him here at 6.30 and he's been waiting.'

'Yes, I did ask him to be here. We won't be long. Can you tell him to wait, half an hour max. What do you reckon, Nige, half an hour?'

'Max.'

'Can I bring you anything? Some muffins or juice? More coffee?'

'Ask Daniela to bring them out. That would be lovely, darling. And get Len in for a pee, his prostate is not good.'

Silently they watch her go back up the brick path, through the little avenues of red tulips and yellow irises, through the box parterre and up the steps to the back of the house. Julian feels his head filling dangerously.

'Nige, if anyone asks about the hedge fund, we need to bring up Professor Kuhn's name: his model, his bloody Nobel-prize brain's model, for which we paid him $7m., proved faulty. Kuhn and many people believed that risk could largely be taken out of investing and I have already held my hand up, and said yes, we were taken in. But we are on top of it and the bank is properly capitalised as will become apparent as soon as the accounts are published. That's our story. Right?'

'Yes, that's it. You sound just like your father.'

'Oh shit, not really?'

'To the life.'

The Slovakian comes out with a plate of muffins, a jug of freshly squeezed orange juice and a new pot of coffee. Julian asks her to get his Migraleve from the bathroom cabinet. She smiles complicitly. They share a little conspiracy on domestic matters.

The editor receives his first call just before lunchtime. It's the assistant to the deputy financial editor of *The Times*. She says her boss would like to speak to him.

'Fine, put him on.'

'David de la Selle is on the line for you.'

'Thank you.'

'Hello, is that Mr Tredizzick?'

'It is. To what do I owe the honour of a call from the Thunderer?'

'Don't piss about. I think you know. We are obviously interested in your story and your sources. Have you actually seen the documents mentioned?'

'We have never mentioned documents. We have never said anything, as it happens.'

'No, not in print, but somebody's leaking.'

'Mr de la Selle, we do have a big story. And we will handle it in our own way. Why would I give it to you?'

'If it's true, it's a matter of public interest. Are you saying a famous City bank is involved in fraud? It's obviously very sensitive at this time. Politically.'

'Thanks for explaining. It's still the Dark Ages down here. I'm not saying anything yet, beyond the fact that we have received information which we believe is at least credible, and we will pass it on to the FSA if they wish to see it. We will be publishing our story in three parts, starting on Thursday.'

'What are you waiting for?'

'Just checking our facts.'

'That would be a very good idea.'

The phone rings again and the editor gives the same information: *We will publish on Thursday, and we will pass on our information to the authorities if they request it.*

Nigel calls Julian.

'Eric just called. His man spoke to this little weasel in Cornwall, the editor of a local rag, the *Globe and Mail*. He's going to publish on Thursday. He's happy to let the FSA see what he has.'

'Thursday. Shit, what does he know?'

'He wouldn't say.'

'OK, I'll speak to Cy and then I'll get on to Goldstone, depending on what Cy says. If he's got details of the deposits, they will take months to trace. And I've checked with Amanda, the power of attorney covers us on the family trust.'

Massive doses of migraine pills – nearly twice the recommended dose – have kept the migraine in check just below the level of incapacity, but his vision is beginning to blur.

'Cy, morning. Lovely day here, sun shining, birds singing, all that sort of stuff. How are you?'

'It better be important. I'm on my spring break. Just done twenty lengths of the pool. What's your problem?'

He's panting still.

'Who says there's a problem?'

'What you think I am, an idiot? There's always problems.'

'OK. There's some press report about the bank. A newspaper in Cornwall received, they say, some information about asset manipulations.'

'Have they published?'

'Not yet.'

'What's the name of this newspaper?'

'The *Cornish Globe and Mail*.'

'And who owns it?'

'I don't know.'

'Jesus H. Christ. Find out, and get back to me. Anything else?'

'OK, what I want to know is if I can tell the Minister privately that you are buying the bank, all agreed, and that you will stand it up if the Minister wants to speak to you.'

'No problem. He owes me big time. We put a bundle into his scheme to save National Expressways. Now we have to avoid a shit storm. You know what happens with regulators if they get boxed in by the fucking media? They think they have to act tough. Suddenly they remember the public interest. Speak to Goldstone and tell him to call me any time. I'll explain to him that we are guaranteeing Tubal's liabilities, if there are any – when are the final accounts due? – OK, that won't be a problem. I'll get somebody to work on it at the same time. Keep close. If anything comes up, announce a thorough internal investigation. Are your accountants on side? Good. Can you handle it?'

'No problem.'

'And the deposit is on its way.'

He feels reassured after speaking to Cy. Cy can move mountains. He swallows some cold water: his eyesight is not good and his throat is strangely constricted. His secretary tells him that Estelle would like a word.

'OK, ask her to come over in about an hour. We'll call to let her know. What's it about?'

'I don't know. She speaks only to God.'

'And God is me?'

'Looks like it.'

'OK! Promotion at last.'

He calls the Minister's private number and leaves a message. Goldstone will know it's urgent. Within five minutes he calls back. He is in his car being driven somewhere.

'Julian, hello, how are you?'

'Fine, Olly, and you?'

'Phh, you know, chasing my tail. I take it this is not about tennis?'

'No. I just wanted to tell you first that Cy Mannheim has made us a very good offer for the bank and we have accepted.'

'That's a shame. But still, why are you telling me this now, Julian?'

'Well, you may have seen that there are some reports out there that we are in financial difficulties.'

'Are you?'

'No more than anybody else. Our interim accounts show that we are doing pretty well this quarter. Obviously we don't want a panic at this stage.'

'No, I can imagine you don't. What am I supposed to do?'

'It's not for me to tell a secretary of state what to do.'

'It never inhibited your old man. Tell me.'

'OK, the hedge fund left us exposed, thanks to a certain Nobel laureate, but we have pumped in capital, our own mostly, to keep everything on an even keel, and we have agreed a price with Cy, which takes the situation fully into account, so if you can simply help keep a lid on it for a few months, everything will be tidily squared away. There are some rumours in the press too.'

'Look, I'll need the detail. Come and see me this evening, obviously not in my office, and brief me. Better, I'll come to your house if that's convenient. And I'll speak to Mannheim. It's probably a good idea to get the paperwork flowing.'

'He says you can call him any time. Come for supper.'

'Thanks, that would be good. I'm just off to address a meeting of the small-business folks. Shits as they are formally called in this office. They are in a very bad mood. See you at about eight?'

'Fine. Don't come in your official car.'

'I'll come on my bike.'

The Minister is an advocate of cycling and a bachelor. Although they didn't really know each other then, they were contemporaries at Cambridge and it provides a bond. Of course Goldstone is only interested in making financial policy look good until the election. They both understand the deal. But he also has a more than sneaking reverence for the very rich.

He calls Kimberly.

'Hello, darling. All well?'

'I'm fine. How about you? You were developing a migraine,

weren't you? I can always tell by that look when your eyes begin to cross.'

'No, I'm on the mend. Look, Kim, Olly Goldstone's coming for supper at eight. He'll be late. Can we have something ready in my study upstairs?'

'What's he want?'

'Oh, it's probably the usual, cash for the Party, or some committee or something he would like me on.'

'Is everything all right?'

'What do you mean?'

'Well, you and Nigel skulking in the garden at dawn and Olly in your study secretly at night?'

'There is something going on, but it's all good. Trust me. Can we leave it at that for the moment?'

'Yup, I guess so. We don't want me to worry my pretty little head unnecessarily, do we?'

'No, we don't.'

'OK, honey. I've got to go, and you've got to save the nation.'

'I'm trying. Love you.'

He hates this dissimulation. It's eating away at what's left of his innocence. He feels as if he is being hollowed out.

He asks his secretary to get Estelle. She arrives with piles of paper, enveloped in by her old-lady microclimate. She wants to discuss the provisional list for the memorial service. He begs a few days' grace.

'By the way, what's going to happen with the villa?' she asks.

'I think Kim and I would like to use it more. But no hurry. Why do you ask?'

'Well, your brother wants to move in. In fact he's there now looking the place over. He has some suggestions for improvement.'

'Oh, shit. Can't he go back to Africa or somewhere?'

'And also, Lady Trevelyan-Tubal was asking what the plans are.'

'It's complicated, as you know. We need to settle my father's estate. Amanda's across that, but probate is going to take a few months, maybe as many as eight. In theory, Simon's probably got as much right as anyone. And we need to know what Fleur wants. You have use of your cottage, as you know.'

'A friend rang to say she had seen some reports in the *Standard* about us.'

'Yes. There has been something pretty silly. But it's under control. The less said the better at the moment. Thanks, Estelle.'

Estelle stands up. She knows when she is being dismissed. His father was a master of the art of cutting a conversation he didn't want to pursue. He had even been known to stand up and shake someone's hand while propelling him towards the door and, at the same time, showering him with farewells. She leaves, trailing that distinctive scent. It's Yardley English Lavender. His mother wore it.

'Estelle,' he calls after her. She pauses, turns expectantly and dramatically like an actress in an old film.

'It's wonderful to have you here in Bread Street again. I feel strangely reassured.'

'Oh, thank you.'

He thinks that under stress he's instinctively taking on his father's habits. His secretary gives him the name of the group that owns the Cornish newspaper and the name of the CEO in London and some briefing notes. Like most newspaper groups, the note reports, it is making substantial losses. He phones Cy and gives him the information. He's using an encrypted phone. He can't email Cy or ask his secretary to send anything to him.

'Great. I'll get someone on to them. Keep your nerve, my boy.'

'I am. Don't worry. I'm seeing Olly tonight.'

Keep your noive, keep your noive.

Julian thinks he exaggerates his accent. His migraine is beginning to recede. Kim has left him a message about the school play tomorrow. He says to tell her he will go straight to the school. It's a performance of *Thomas the Tank Engine* with Sam in a big role. As what, a train?

Melissa and the editor meet in the early evening in the car park behind the jobcentre. The car is becoming increasingly cluttered with the evidence of the editor's late-night habits – greasy papers lying on the floor alongside cans of Diet Coke. His cigarette butts fill the ashtrays and overflow.

'OK, Melissa. I wanted to talk to you, to keep you in the loop. We are going to publish on Thursday, but I don't want to pull you in any deeper. You have done a fine job, terrific, but it would be unfair to involve you in what's going to happen over the next few days. Forget about Artair in your next blog. I've had lots of questions about your blog and the informant, and I have stuck to the facts. Just to repeat: you received an anonymous tip-off, met the person in question and he promised to send documents to your editor and I have seen them. But you are not part of anything that has happened or will happen. Later we can tell the full story, but there's a way to go.'

She sees that he is trying to protect her from something.

'Is everything all right, Mr Tredizzick?'

'Everything's fine. I've had a few veiled threats. The usual bluster. But stay away from the office and I will call you from time to time. If they get rid of me, I've made sure the documents go to the right place.'

'What do you mean, "get rid of me", Mr Tredizzick?'

'Oh, some snooty lawyer rang. She said her clients were taking this libel very seriously. And our HQ in London is not happy. A man I have never spoken to before told me that they were in no position to fight any legal actions. They want us to drop it. Injunctions are flying. My job is probably on the line. All the usual, as I said. So stay safely away.'

Was he aware that this business would entail threats to his job and some London bank suing him and the company? She suspects that he was. Yes, this is his last stand. He looks a little distracted and blinks a few times in the crepuscular car as though his eyes are failing him.

'Mr Tredizzick, are you all right?'

'You're a sweet girl. I'm fine. OK, I have to go now, but I'll keep in touch. Here's a cheque for your expenses for the week.'

He hands her an envelope.

'Look after yourself, Mr Tredizzick,' she says as she gets out of the car. He gives her a jaunty President-Obama-entering-his-helicopter salute.

When she gets home she sees that the cheque is not from the news-paper but from a joint account in the name of Mr and Mrs Edward Tredizzick.

Julian arrives home just before eight. Olly Goldstone is already there, sitting with Kim in the dining room. He's not in a suit, but a pair of jeans and a tight, shiny cycling jacket. His good, dark, straight Jewish hair is a little damp and sticks to his head in a boyish way.

'Secretary of State,' says Julian, 'what a privilege.'

'For me too, to talk to your wife alone for a minute.'

Kim says that supper is ready and whenever they want to they can go up to the study.

'Must we?' says Goldstone.

There is a suspicion that he is gay, but there has never been any scandal, no Brazilian rent boys or lovers, the sort of thing that the newspapers – always on the lookout – would have discovered. His success is due, Julian thinks, to his relentless and impenetrable charm.

When they are sitting in the study, after Kim has made sure they have everything they need, Goldstone wants to talk about Julian's pictures. He particularly likes the new picture which Kim gave him for his birthday and which now hangs to one side of the fireplace.

'Interesting work. Right, Julian. Tell me what's happened. This is entirely between us and will go no further. The background, of course, is that our financial policies are working and we don't want any flies in the ointment at this stage. Altruism is not an issue.'

'I understand. Look, to go back a bit, I fell for Professor Kuhn's theory and I advocated the bell curve model. We lost a lot of money when our main hedge fund went down. In the meanwhile, I had been having talks with Cy Mannheim. I had to decide if we could still really compete as an investment bank, or whether it would be better to go back to commercial banking. But my judgement was that even that would be slow death.'

'I've talked to Cy, by the way. He called.'

'Fine. Well, as I said, we pumped in a lot of money to keep the bank's rating high. We obviously didn't want a run.'

'The question is, Julian, and you must forgive me for asking, has the bank been in breach of regulations?'

'No. Our family trust has put in money.'

'How much?'

'Two hundred and fifty million, sterling.'

'As a loan?'

'As an investment. We have made deposits in various funds and deposit accounts. And the Koopman Charitable Foundation have also put in some money. A hundred and fifty, to be precise.'

'Do the trustees know?'

'To be brutally honest, they don't need to know until we present the accounts. I have a meeting anyway to talk to them about it. But you can see that it's doubly important we avoid a run.'

Goldstone is smiling as if to confirm that they are men of the world.

'OK. Before I get the department involved, Julian, this is our plan. You must announce the sale to First Federal. We will say we favour it. And later we will, if there's any more trouble, announce an enquiry into certain deposits over which some doubts have been raised. The FSA and the BOE will also want a look-in, but I will speak to them. They understand the national interest and the risk to the banking system. If required, our enquiry will anyway take precedence. With any luck you can get the sale away in a few weeks, you can sort out your accounts and we will enquire away for months if we have to. Kicked into touch, is the phrase the commentators like to use. Easy for them. Are we – broadly speaking – on the same page?'

For two hours they go over the plan. Which ultimately has only one aim, to keep the lid on this until the election is over. Nobody wants to see, as Goldstone says – almost without irony – an English bank, small but iconic, going down at this particular time. Of course the sale will be going through the department, but he will make sure the Permanent Undersecretary understands what's at stake. The government may even be able to offer First Federal some special conditions.

Goldstone prides himself on a sharp understanding of the City, but also on having a very clear idea of how to confront political problems.

'Julian, we don't want any surprises. Ring me urgently if anything comes out of the cupboard.'

Strange phrase, Julian thinks. It's almost as if Goldstone likes to flirt with danger.

'What if you lose the election? Then where do we stand?'

'I don't think the other lot will want you to sink. Anyway, you were at school with them. Have a chat if the time comes.'

'You and I were at Cambridge together.'

'There's Cambridge and Cambridge.'

'True.'

'Now, on with the bicycle clips and off into the night.'

'Where's your security?'

'I gave them the night off.'

'On what excuse?'

'I am having ballroom dancing lessons. Everyone's doing it. But keep it under your hat: it's a little frivolous for a minister of the Crown. Love to Kimberly. You're a lucky chappie.'

Goldstone places his cycle helmet on his head, dons some yellow cycling glasses, zips up his jacket, and he's off, out through the side entrance which leads to the garages around the corner.

Lucky chappie. Does he mean lucky to have Kim, or does he mean to have the Rt. Hon. Oliver Goldstone, QC, MP on his side, pro tem, as these legal chappies say?

Julian goes up to see the children sleeping in the gently revolving light, which is said to be soothing, but may be inducing narcolepsy. He blesses them silently. Their faces appear to be underwater.

25

FLEUR FINDS A letter from Morné. He asks if she could consider being a patron of a charity called the Disabled Rugby Footballers' Trust. She wants desperately to see him but at the same time she can't have anything to do with him after what Julian said. She has felt alone and diminished since Harry's death. Only Kim has really been kind. With Morné she felt her spirits released, but now forces are gathering to confine her. Am I paranoid? she wonders. She writes Morné a brief and formal note.

After a few months, when my life is more settled and I feel stronger, I would like to hear more about your charity.

When I feel stronger. It's a Jane Austenish sentiment. What she means is, when the will is settled and along with it the dust, she will seize any opportunity to have sex with him again, even if it involves visiting brain-dead rugby players in hospices. But she is in a Byzantine world now. Great wealth and privilege are settling themselves into new shapes and forms, now that the emperor is dead. If Harry was the emperor, she was more concubine than empress.

She and Kim are due to address a school on behalf of the Veggies and she's been reading the pamphlets and preparing her talk. It seems like an appropriately responsible thing to be doing. Organic vegetables are, she thinks, a sort of moral crusade rather than a health issue. The vegetables – cropping well, says Kim – are not vegetables so much as a substitute for the Communion host. Partake of this and you will undergo spiritual transformation. You will become not only outwardly healthy, but inwardly enlightened. She's wondering what to wear. She's going to give information on composting and she thinks she should look sort of earthy herself.

Kimberly sees the sodden clay soil of London enriched with organic material, breathing freely again and providing a home for earthworms – which she calls night crawlers – and good bacteria. It's a dream of heaven, an essential element of all religions: the day when all will be reconciled.

Artair sees a world where art and Mammon are reconciled. In truth it's probably more a world where the artist is in charge. There always seem to be elites. No man can serve two masters. When she was trying to act, Fleur believed that artists really did hold the keys of the kingdom, but she came to see that the bankers are in fact in command of our world. Harry, for all his love of paintings and the ballet, believed that bankers are the glue that holds society together. They are part of a higher elite, who really understand how the world works. Their understanding of money has given them something incomprehensible to politicians and ordinary people. Without their capital, directed to where it is needed, the whole system would collapse. Who is more important to stability, a Rothschild or a prime minister? Harry asked. He seemed to think that there was only one answer. But now, now that the system has come so close to collapse, thanks to the bankers, would he have changed his mind?

She has narrowed the choice of dress suitable for her talk down to three: one looks a little extravagant, with large flowers on white, the second is perhaps too severe, and the third is too short for a serious topic like compost. She calls Kim for advice.

The editor is preparing his bombshell. It's going to be trailed on the front page in a banner: *The Cornish Globe and Mail's exclusive evidence points to blue-blood banking scandal.*

Inside pages run pictures of the façade of Tubal and Co. in Bread Street, under the sign of the Leathern Bottle, and some society photographs of the family are spread about. The editor writes that he has seen evidence, and financial experts have confirmed the authenticity of this evidence, which points to a massive misuse of funds by Tubal and Co. He explains the Cornish connection, and how the paper came to be in possession of these documents. A rather smudgy scan of one of the documents runs beside his op-ed. These documents will be made available to the Financial Services Authority and the Serious Fraud Office if asked. The editor speculates on what the effect of this scandal will be on Whitehall.

He is working on the layout for tomorrow's first run. He has ordered ten thousand more copies printed, raising circulation to twenty-two thousand. Sales have fallen nearly seven per cent in the last four months alone. He's planning to spin this story out, explaining the central role of the paper in bringing this arrogant bunch of bankers to book; this brave little regional newspaper is serving the national interest. There's a portrait of reporter and blogger Melissa Tregarthen, twenty-two, who first got wind of the scandal.

At four o'clock he calls the editorial staff together in the canteen. He stands with his back to the high windows that look out over a few neglected warehouses and a canal. The windows are all broken or crazed. He explains to the staff what is happening and apologises for the secrecy. He mentions Robert Maxwell and says that, like the Maxwell case, this one demonstrates arrogance on a Homeric scale and contempt for the little people who don't live in London and don't make a habit of stealing other people's money. Melissa is standing by the huge tea urn. A few people clap when the editor pays tribute to her. She is embarrassed as her colleagues – there are eleven of them – applaud her.

Back in his office the editor receives a call from South West Distributors.

'Mr Tredizzick, I am sorry to say we cannot distribute tomorrow's paper.'

'Why not?'

'We had a call from the managing director.'

'What managing director?'

'From Twelvetrees Media. A Mr Lionel Beck.'

'Nonsense. Just distribute. I will take the blame.'

'Can't do it, Mr Tredizzick. They said your newspaper has been sold. It may even close. We won't be paid for the last six months if we distribute. I'm very sorry, Mr Tredizzick.'

The editor speaks to his managing editor, who doubles as chief accountant. He's in the dark; he's been told nothing, but the editor can see that he fears the worst already. The superior logic of money always dominates these people's thinking.

'We've got to get the paper out.'

He probably sees a heroic action, papers smuggled out, samizdat plastering the walls of the town. He calls Melissa into his office. He tells her that there is an attempt to suppress the story: she must stay in the building and blog and upload the story so that it gets out regardless. One of the techies will help her. She thinks: he cannot win this battle. But she sits at a workstation and Gavin, the techie, comes through to help her upload the editor's op-ed on to her blog.

At five, just as she sees the material integrated into her blog, there is a stamp of feet on the stairs and four security guards in blue uniforms and bulky body armour enter the room. With them is a lawyer who asks for the editor. He enters the editor's cubicle and the security men stand at the exit to the stairs. They fold their arms in a passive-aggressive gesture. It's unmistakably a signifier. Melissa asks them what they are doing, and they say they are protecting the property of the new owner: you wouldn't believe what people run off with.

After about twenty minutes the editor emerges from his office. He's holding a piece of paper. Melissa has never seen such a thing, but she knows it's a letter of resignation, demanded by the lawyer. She feels a desperate poignancy as she sees his haggard, defeated face. Her tears rise uncontrollably.

'My friends, my colleagues, this is a terrible day for this newspaper and for journalism. The newspaper and the building have been sold and the new owners are closing us down. Twelvetrees Media Company assures us that there will be redundancy payments along union guidelines. I have been dismissed. Now everyone must quit the buildings, taking only personal possessions, and on no account removing any items of the company's property. Cardboard boxes are being provided and they will be inspected by the security guards on the way out. I will be trying to speak to London and the union and we will announce on local radio the location of a mass meeting to protest the decision and to secure your rights.

'I am very, very sorry about what has happened, but I can't apologise for trying to run a story worthy of the name of journalism. Can I remind you of what Tom Paine said? "Those who expect to reap the blessings of freedom must, like men, undergo the fatigue of supporting it." Keep up the good fight, my friends and colleagues.'

As he says it the editor looks mortally fatigued. His high-flown rhetoric seems to make the lawyer uneasy: he gestures and one of the security guards steps forward and leads the editor to the door. To a casual observer it might look as if he has been arrested. The rest of them place their tragically inadequate personal possessions into the cardboard boxes provided. Melissa thinks that the boxes are similar to those Lehman Brothers' staff took out of their front door, before the television cameras, on the day that capitalism almost went down in September 2008.

Two days later Julian and Nigel take a suite at the Connaught. They don't want to be at the bank. The bank itself, like the Parthenon, must float unruffled above this sordid business. Business as usual, keeping clients happy. Their suite is dominated by a huge vase of lilies and other overbred flowers, which give off a powerful aroma. The bathroom is scented by sachets of bath additives, soaps and gels.

Nigel is impressed with Cy's people.

'They've bought out the newspaper group, the whole thing. The company can't believe their luck. All that lay ahead for them was bankruptcy.'

The board of Twelvetrees Media has made a statement saying there is absolutely no credible evidence as far as they know of any malpractice by Tubal and Co. and, in off-the-record briefings, the editor has been described as a fantasist with a drink problem, who had a grudge against the City that flawed his judgement. Twelvetrees Media regrets that this was allowed to go as far as it did and confirms that Mr Tredizzick has been dismissed for breach of trust.

'Amanda has issued six injunctions and threatened libel to all and sundry,' says Julian.

'She is terrifying.'

'Guess why she's so keen to shut this up.'

'I think it might have something to do with the family trust.'

'Exactly. Now what we need is for Goldstone to issue a statement. But I think he'll wait a few days. He's going to want to see how this plays. I know he's got the Bank and the FSA on side. It's wonderful how an election focuses the mind.'

'You sound – sorry, Jules – more like your old dad every day. He saw the workings of democracy as pure opportunism.'

'Short-termism is hurting this country,' Julian says, in his father's voice. God help me if I am becoming like my father, he thinks.

'OK, Nige. Koopman's. Do I tell them what has happened or leave them?'

'I think you have to update them right away. Just say that their deposits are underwritten by Cy and that, although you are selling, you and I will be staying on. Do it before we issue a press release to that effect.'

'Yes, I think that's right.'

'Do we tell them we are sending the money back after the sale, or do we gradually move it off the balance sheet?'

'I am sure we can think up a good tax reason for leaving it. Let's sleep on it. But we need them to say they understand and are fully apprised of the situation.'

'I agree. Speak to Kronwinkel tomorrow. They wouldn't have noticed until the Charity Commission's accounts were published, of course. Rip Van Winkle syndrome.'

They go through a long checklist, prepared by Nigel, of meetings with the lawyers who are handling the sale of the building, the merchant bankers who are dealing with Cy's people, the arrangements for the directors' meeting to inform them and, later, the staff of the sale, the electronic reporting to the FSA, their latest fad, and a hundred other matters, including the memorial service for Sir Harry.

At midnight, the Secretary of State for Business, Innovation and Skills, Oliver Goldstone, calls.

'OK, it's under control. The PM believes that there should be a small price to pay, an acknowledgement by you of his personal intervention and the government's prompt action to ensure the smooth transition into the ownership of First Federal, which will ensure the survival of this iconic British institution and avoid uncertainty. Yes, Julian, I know what you are thinking. Further down the line there may have to be an enquiry, but of course announcing one will be a last resort to hold off the media. I didn't say that. Anyway, the thinking around here is that we won't be in power by the end of the year, and so you will be dealing with your chums. I didn't say that either.'

'What's the remit of the enquiry likely to be, if there is one?'

'Well, as you intimated, there seems to have been some administrative problem, perhaps negligence, with various trusts. We have been sent the papers by this Cornish editor, and they aren't all good, but the FSA has looked at them and they don't think there are grounds for prosecution. Get the bank sold, get the money in, and then we can see if there has been any breach of the rules. Sound reasonable?'

'Not especially. Olly, you know, it turns out that what my father always said, that government is mostly about opportunism, is true.'

'How right he was on so many matters. Including sticking to what you are good at. But you must know that when you ask a favour from government, there's a price to pay.'

'I did know that. Yes. I just hoped that it wasn't going to be the same this time.'

'Well, I think I am the bearer of more good news than bad, don't you? Just think where this could have gone. Got to rush.'

'What did he say?' asks Nigel.

'He wants me to talk up the government and the Prime Minister in return for his intervention.'

'What did you expect?'

'The fact is buggers can't be choosers. And we've been buggered. He's not in politics for the good of anybody, he's in it to demonstrate what a clever little shit he is.'

His phone rings. It's Goldstone again.

'Oh sorry, one more thing, the PM would like you to run your statement by me before you release it. OK? I know it's the oldest cliché in the book, but we must be reading off the same hymn sheet.'

'What hymn sheet would that be, Olly?'

THE END

There are beginnings and there are ends, and there are also many ways of telling the same story.

Melissa Tregarthen is on a train reading *At Swim-Two-Birds*, Artair MacCleod's favourite. She's seen him once, on one of her increasingly rare visits to her parents. She lives in London now, at London Fields. She's making notes. She likes to be prepared.

> *One beginning and one ending for a book is a thing I did not agree with. A good book may have three openings entirely dissimilar and interrelated only in the prescience of the author or for that matter one hundred times as many endings.*
>
> *People talk about true stories. As if there could possibly be true stories; events take place one way and we recount them the opposite way.*
>
> *I mean to say, said Lamont, whether a yarn is tall or small, I like to hear it well told. I like to meet a man who can take a hand to tell a story and not make a balls of it while he's at it. I like to know where I am, do you know. Everything has a beginning and an end.*

Melissa wonders: can a story really have many beginnings and a hundred endings? The beginning and the end, she sees, are arbitrary. If the new government hadn't come in, determined to prove that it would not show special favour to the City, the ending to this story would have been different. If the editor hadn't died in

St Stephen's Hall of the House of Commons, waiting to give his evidence, things would have been different again. And if the editor had not taken the precaution of sending all his documents to every Member of Parliament, the Financial Services Agency, the Bank of England and the financial editors of the major newspapers, the Financial Services Agency would not have mounted an exemplary dawn raid on insider traders and stock manipulators in three banks and two stockbroking houses. These raids demonstrated what everybody knew, that many City people had not learned the lessons of the past few years.

The train is following, for the moment, the course of the Thames. The countryside looks untroubled, unaware, eternally indifferent.

Melissa works for a free newspaper, writing mostly about lifestyle matters. She has lost seven kilos and she has appeared a few times in television discussions about City corruption, but has been careful to limit her contribution to her own experience and anyway the recession is fading in the memory, both of the people and of the television companies.

When she was called to give evidence, Melissa stuck faithfully to her story, which was, of course, true: Alan39 had approached her as a result of a piece she wrote on local theatre. She took it to Mr Tredizzick, her editor, who has since sadly died, on the day he was to make an appearance before the committee. She didn't understand the paperwork her source sent on to Mr Tredizzick. Mr Tredizzick told her that it demonstrated that misconduct was taking place. She also testified that she had no idea who Alan39 was when she met him, but she had been able to identify him when he was arrested by the Serious Organised Crime Agency on a charge of data theft. The chairman of the committee, a jowly man in a confidently striped shirt, described her as a good witness and a breath of fresh air, and thanked her warmly on behalf of the committee.

*   *   *

Julian Trevelyan-Tubal and Nigel Stafford were reprimanded by the parliamentary committee for failing to meet the required standards of accounting, and banned from holding a senior position in banking or finance for five years. By implication, the previous Prime Minister and his Secretary of State were equally guilty, perhaps more so. The committee was hampered by the fact that no one, no members of the Trevelyan-Tubal family, none of the trusts the bank handled, nor any single member of staff, testified against Mr Trevelyan-Tubal.

Ms Estelle Welz was particularly clear that, when she witnessed the signing of documents shortly before the death of Sir Harry Trevelyan-Tubal, there was no pressure on her to sign anything and she confirmed that she had accepted, after seeing the medical certificate, that Sir Harry was no longer capable of making rational decisions. She was family. There was a sense that even the members of the committee understood that this was a political drama, staged after the main event. Everyone was entitled to write his or her own script.

Mr Cy Mannheim was not called to the enquiry. Some journalists said that the new government was kowtowing to him because of his enormous wealth; others said that a few years ago he had been given special exemption because of his help in saving National Expressways. The chairman of the committee issued a statement saying that even if the committee had wanted to interview Mr Mannheim, it was not within their powers to demand his attendance at a British parliamentary enquiry.

People talk about true stories. As if there could possibly be true stories; events take place one way and we recount them the opposite way.

Melissa often thinks of Artair MacCleod.

Her mother and father miss her but they are proud of her, although they still don't understand exactly what happened at the *Globe and Mail*. But then, as she said, who really does?

The newspaper building stands empty; opportunist pigeons have taken up residence. The ground floor is now enclosed by a colourful hoarding which is decorated with pictures of young people working out in the proposed gym and enjoying cappuccinos in the coffee shop and relaxing in their stylish apartments and lofts, as they experience the exciting contemporary lifestyle which the development presages. The building has been renamed the Duke's Quarter, a sly reference to Prince Charles, Duke of Cornwall. No development has taken place yet, apart from the vivid hoarding. Melissa remembers Mr Tredizzick's speech, which mentioned Tom Paine and the rights of man: 'Those who expect to reap the blessings of freedom must, like men, undergo the fatigue of supporting it.' Poor Mr Tredizzick. He was fighting a different battle for a different England, an England that no longer exists – if it ever had. Nobody now thinks about reaping the blessings of freedom; instead they hope to win the Lottery or become celebrities.

There are, anyway, different kinds of freedom. (Isaiah Berlin, philosophy, module 12.)

There are beginnings and there are ends, and there are also many ways of telling the same story.

The Hon. Charlotte Stammers, the CEO of Tubal and Co., issued a statement after Mr Trevelyan-Tubal and Mr Stafford were fined a quarter of a million pounds each by the Financial Services Agency for misreporting; she said that there was never any intention to defraud, but Mr Trevelyan-Tubal and Mr Stafford had resigned as soon as the error was spotted. She regretted their loss but nonetheless, under her leadership, she was determined that the bank should return to its core values, so successfully articulated by her uncle, the late Sir Harry Trevelyan-Tubal. She is privileged, and a little humbled, to find herself in this position, the first woman to head up the bank.

After his censure and fine, Julian Trevelyan-Tubal took a few months out to explore the land of Israel. His wife Kimberly and the two children were living in a rented house on Martha's Vineyard where Kim was working, with her architect, the award-winning Thomas

Soderling, on the renovation of the Smalley House, a thirties mansion in sight of Gay Head Lighthouse. It has two hundred yards of private beachfront.

Julian worked unpaid for a while at a horse ranch in the hills above Galilee, not far from where Christ delivered the Sermon on the Mount. The owner of this improbable Jewish ranch, Uri Peley, told Julian that he had travelled in South America and decided that he wanted to have his own *estancia*. The Rancho Eldorado was the result. Barbecued steaks and giant earthen platters of hummus were served outside the log cabins every evening. Down below the Sea of Galilee gleamed, coruscated, in the setting biblical sun.

Julian rode out with Uri for three days, spending one night at a Bedouin encampment, the second in an authentic Sioux tepee in the mountains and the last lying in a sleeping bag out on a hillside under the beckoning stars near Tiberias. And then he stayed on for a few weeks as an unpaid helper. He wasn't used to western saddles, but he quickly got the hang of them. The clients were mostly tourists. He saddled their horses, helped the riders adjust their stirrup leathers and gave them advice if they asked. He sometimes accompanied them on day rides. He bought a pair of chaps. In this way he explored the land of his ancestors from on top of a horse. Uri Peley never asked what he was doing here on his own; Peley had adopted a minimalist cowboy personality. They mostly talked horses and Julian found these conversations absorbing and calming. There have always been horses in human lives: they have a gentle, innocent quality.

Julian spoke to Kim every day. The children are already losing their British accents. Once she asked him, *Are you exploring your roots?* And he said, *In a way*, but even that was not strictly true. In Jerusalem he had visited the holy sites. He was not moved by the overexcited religions themselves, so much as by the inescapable realisation that no one on this earth can cope with their own mortality. For two thousand years Jerusalem has been the world capital of yearning, a yearning for something other. This yearning is an essential quality of being human, and it was that which moved him, although the quest is doomed.

During the parliamentary enquiry and the FSA's questioning, he had weighed the idea of killing himself. But he had done it theoretically, without any real intent. Also, he remembered that when his mother had killed herself he and Simon were utterly bereft. At first they were told that she had died of an illness in hospital, but other children knew the truth and it soon came out. A blanket of shame covered them, as if they had been responsible. He and Simon had never been able to discuss it. They had felt betrayed and utterly abandoned. In London after the memorial service, at which he read his loopy poem and a whimsical travel piece, Simon told Julian for the first time that their mother's suicide had produced in him a sense of loneliness which had never left him. He had come to hate their father. And perhaps that is why Julian is travelling and living among strangers, to get over his loneliness and shame.

But now the time has come for him to go home to his children who are his flesh. That's the only miracle he believes in, the miraculous transubstantiation of his flesh to his children's. It's his last day and he has to muck out three stables before he takes the ramshackle bus to Ben Gurion, Tel Aviv Airport, in time for the night flight to Boston. Strangely, although he has lived amongst horses for five weeks, he hasn't dreamt of his pony once. He may have lost the ability to converse with horses.

There are beginnings and there are ends, and there are also many ways of telling the same story.

Fleur is living in her house in Tuscany for the time being. She remembers Artair reciting: 'There, everything is order and beauty'. Here, the order and beauty are her creation, all hers. She feels properly at home for the first time in her life.

Bryce comes to visit her often. They are lovers. And, more unusual, they are in love. She has given money to Morné's charity, which supports disabled rugby players, but she hasn't seen him since the memorial service and then it was only to shake his hand formally. Bryce is her world now. They travel when he is not required on the boat. Boris Vladykin very rarely takes *Niobe* out; he thinks, on reflection, that it's a little too old-fashioned. His fellow oligarchs are not impressed by the brass push-and-pull plumbing and the narrow mahogany deck. Bryce says they don't realise that a boat like this is a never-to-be-repeated classic, pure class. Fleur has asked him to investigate the cost of buying it back: there has not been much of a market for classic boats since the credit crisis.

Fleur is pregnant and Bryce is very happy about it. It seems he always wanted to have a child. They can't get married because of the stipulation in Harry's will, and she hasn't the strength to challenge this Old Testament provision. Instead they are going to have a small, improvised blessing in the unused chapel that stands amongst cypresses on a hill behind her Tuscan house, with a few friends as witnesses. It will be followed by what Bryce calls a *bounce-up* at the trattoria.

Kim has invited her to Martha's Vineyard for the house-warming in July, but she is dreading telling her that she is living with Bryce. Also she wonders how Julian will take the news. It's not dignified: Bryce was Julian's employee. She loves Bryce and she won't go to Martha's Vineyard without him. Bryce has a quality she has never encountered: he is completely content – *bien dans sa peau*. He makes few demands and he says that having an ankle-biter will be totally awesome. He foresees no difficulties. In fact he seems to have no idea of futurity. She has only been to Antibes once, just before the memorial service, and it was then that she met up with Bryce again. Simon has been living in the villa temporarily: he is off to Bhutan soon, at the invitation of the King, to look for the yeti. The King has a personal yeti-finder; this man searches assiduously. He has made a photographic record of unexplained footprints, and collected some fur.

Fleur marvels at the way things turn out. What Artair said to her has, improbably, proved to be right: she has found someone to love whole-heartedly and without reservation.

There are beginnings and there are ends, and there are also many ways of telling the same story.

Alan39 was given an eight-month sentence, half of it suspended. It turned out that he was indeed one of the hedge-fund managers, as Julian guessed; he had learned, months before he was fired, how to hack into the system. He was bitterly angry because he believed he was cheated of a bonus owed to him by the bank. He claimed in court that he had sold the information to First Federal Bank to help them in their bid for Tubal and Co., but no credible evidence of this claim was produced by his barrister. The barrister also said that his client had had contact with an unnamed person acting for First Federal Bank of New York and he had given this unnamed person the printouts in return for $150,000. He was paid in cash. It was this individual's idea that he should leak the information to the press. The Serious Organised Crime Agency's counsel said that the defendant, Mr Patrick Carpenter – Alan39 – had been unable to produce evidence of this transaction. The agency had seized his computer in a raid and obtained all his phone records without finding any connection to First Federal. Nor was there evidence of any bank deposits that could have related to the supposed $150,000. He appeared to have been motivated entirely by a desire for revenge.

The former joint CEO of Tubal and Co., Nigel Stafford, said in the course of his evidence that the bank had put in place a new and sophisticated program which scanned and analysed every attempt to access the system and grouped the results automatically. Surprisingly quickly, patterns emerged which pointed to Mr Carpenter, who had been let go after the collapse of the Lion Fortress Hedge Fund.

I like to know where I am, do you know. Everything has a beginning and an end.

Estelle has spent the last few months at her cottage in the grounds of the villa. She finds ministering to Sir Simon Trevelyan-Tubal fulfilling. He seems to have taken over Harry's role in her life. He makes demands, but they are the demands of an innocent child. For instance, he likes Ovaltine beside his bed at night, and he has a very complex regime relating to his bowels. Sometimes, if his bowel function has been poor, he asks for muesli in the middle of the afternoon. He attributes this problem to his travels and the strange things he has eaten. He has sacrificed his bowels to his curiosity.

Estelle misses the Matisse that hung in the hall. Although Harry gave it to her, she is happy to have exchanged it for membership of the family. She is slowing down and she finds that some days she confuses Sir Simon with Sir Harry. Simon looks very much as Harry did when she first worked for him. For his turtle-dove-serenaded and rosemary-scented passeggiata around the garden, he has taken to wearing Harry's plum-coloured trousers and his Lock's panama. When his trip to Bhutan is postponed – the yeti hunter has died of pneumonia after too many arduous nights in the service of his king in remote and freezing high-altitude mountain valleys – she finds that she is pleased. They have settled down into a domestic routine: she is his lost mother.

There are beginnings and there are ends, and there are also many ways of telling the same story.

Melissa is on the train on the way down to see her parents. As she reads, Flann O'Brien becomes a mantra, in time with the regular, repetitive music of the wheels on the track.

The train is approaching the Tamar. She has told her parents that her blog has won a prize of £5,000, the free-sheet is doing well, and she has been commissioned to write a children's book. But she has not yet told them that her new boyfriend – it is not a coincidence – is also the editor who has commissioned her to write the book. She doesn't go straight home to see her parents, although she knows they are waiting eagerly, the fatted calf lowing apprehensively, but takes a taxi to see Mr MacCleod. The estuary is calm today and avocets are fussing on the shoreline.

Artair comes out of the lifeboat station to greet her. His ravaged face is alight.

'Melinda, Melinda, you look pale and interesting. Perhaps a little too thin, but I am not complaining. Come in. I want to introduce you to a friend.'

She follows him into the main room, and there is Daniel Day-Lewis, sitting on the broken-backed sofa, wearing black cowboy boots.

He looks up from a script and says, 'Hello.'

People talk about true stories. As if there could possibly be true stories; events take place one way and we recount them the opposite way.

ACKNOWLEDGEMENTS

I owe everybody at Bloomsbury who has been involved with the production of this book a great debt. It is, of course, their job, but somehow publishing is not an ordinary job, involving as it does delicate judgements of all sorts and the tender egos of writers. I am deeply grateful to all, including – among many – Michael Fishwick, Alexandra Pringle, Katie Bond, Alexa von Hirschberg, Anna Simpson, Trâm-Anh Doan and Mary Tomlinson.

I have taken advice on banking and how it works, but I have decided not to name any of those I consulted.

Also, I would like to acknowledge the friendship with, and frankly, my dependency upon, my agent James Gill.

A NOTE ON THE AUTHOR

Justin Cartwright's novels include the Booker-shortlisted *In Every Face I Meet*, the Whitbread Novel Award-winner *Leading the Cheers*, *White Lightning*, shortlisted for the 2002 Whitbread Novel Award, *The Promise of Happiness*, winner of the 2005 Hawthornden Prize, the acclaimed *The Song Before It Is Sung*, and, most recently, *To Heaven by Water*. Justin Cartwright was born in South Africa and lives in London.

A NOTE ON THE TYPE

The text of this book is set in Adobe Garamond. It is one of several versions of Garamond based on the designs of Claude Garamond. It is thought that Garamond based his font on Bembo, cut in 1495 by Francesco Griffo in collaboration with the Italian printer Aldus Manutius. Garamond types were first used in books printed in Paris around 1532. Many of the present-day versions of this type are based on the *Typi Academiae* of Jean Jannon cut in Sedan in 1615.

Claude Garamond was born in Paris in 1480. He learned how to cut type from his father and by the age of fifteen he was able to fashion steel punches the size of a pica with great precision. At the age of sixty he was commissioned by King Francis I to design a Greek alphabet, for this he was given the honourable title of royal type founder. He died in 1561.